Praise for *New York Times* Bestselling Author Kody Keplinger

The DUFF

"[A] well-written, irreverent, and heartfelt debut." — *Publishers Weekly*

"Sharp, hot, thoughtful, and searingly honest, *The DUFF* is one of the best young adult novels to come along in ages." — Elizabeth Scott, author of *Living Dead Girl* and *The Unwritten Rule*

"A complex, enemies-with-benefits relationship that the YA market has never seen before. . . . Her snarky teen speak, true-to-life characterizations, and rollicking sense of humor never cease in her debut." — *Kirkus Reviews*

"What's best here is Bianca's brazen voice. Even when confused, she is truer to herself than most." — *Booklist*

"Edgy and compelling. I couldn't put it down!" — Simone Elkeles, author of *Rules of Attraction*

Lying Out Loud

"Just like the recipients of Sonny's fibs, readers will find themselves duped by her creativity, unabashed courage, and hilarious snark. Until it all blows up. Fierce, fresh, total fun." — *Kirkus Reviews*

"Readers will cringe as [Sonny] digs herself deeper and deeper into trouble, then app   w to develop trust in her relationships wit   se, a hot romantic interest." — *VOY*

"Sonny is a realistic and very num   d even though she is a liar, her motivations are all too believable." — *School Library Journal*

LYING OUT LOUD

KODY KEPLINGER

SCHOLASTIC INC.

Copyright © 2015 by Kody Keplinger

This book was originally published in hardcover by Scholastic Press in 2015.

ISBN 978-0-545-83110-9

10 9 8 7 6 5 4 3 2 1   16 17 18 19 20

Printed in the U.S.A.   40
First printing 2016

Book design by Yaffa Jaskoll

For Amy L.
My Online BFF.
My Mean Sheep.
You always have faith in me.
Even when I don't have
faith in myself.
Thank you.

1

I, Sonny Elizabeth Ardmore, do hereby confess that I am an excellent liar.

It was never something I aspired to be, but rather a talent that I couldn't avoid. It started with lies about my homework — I could *actually* convince teachers that my dog ate it, with fake tears and everything if needed — and then I told lies about my family — my father was an international businessman, not a deadbeat thief who'd been tossed in jail when I was seven — and, eventually, I was lying about everything else, too.

But as excellent a liar as I may be, lying hasn't led me to much excellence lately. So let the record show that this time I am telling the truth. All of it. The whole shebang. Even if it kills me.

I tell the most lies on bad days, and the Friday my cell phone — one of those old, clunky, pay-as-you-go bricks that only played polyphonic ringtones — decided to stop working after six long years of use, was a particularly *bad day*.

It had flatlined sometime in the night, a peaceful, quiet sort of death, and left me without my usual five a.m. alarm. Instead, I awoke when Amy's phone (the newest, most expensive model of smartphone, naturally) began blaring an all-too-realistic fire truck–style siren.

I bolted upright, my heart jackhammering, while next to me, on her side of the bed, my best friend snoozed on.

"Amy." I shoved her arm. "Amy, shut that thing off."

She groaned and rolled over. The siren kept wailing as she fumbled with the phone. Finally, it went silent.

"Why in God's name would you want to wake up to that sound?" I asked her as she stretched her long, thin arms over her head.

"It's the only alarm loud enough to wake me up."

"And it barely accomplishes that."

It wasn't until then that I realized what Amy's horrible wake-up call meant. I was supposed to be up before her. I was supposed to get ready and sneak out of her house before her parents woke up at six. But my phone wasn't working and it was six-fifteen and I, to put it bluntly, was fucking screwed.

"Why don't you just tell my parents you fell asleep here last night?" Amy asked as I scrambled around the room, dragging out the duffel bag of wrinkled clothes I kept hidden under her bed. "They won't care."

"Because then they'll want to go reassuring my mom about where I was," I said, pulling a green T-shirt on over my incredibly impressive bedhead. "And that'll open up a whole new set of questions, and just no."

"I still don't see why you can't just tell them she kicked you out." Amy stood up and started combing her dark curls, which, despite all the laws of physics, still looked perfect after a night's sleep. Amy was one of those rare people who looked gorgeous first thing in the morning. It brought a whole new meaning to "beauty rest." I would have hated her for it if I didn't love her so much.

"It's just too complicated, okay?"

I took the comb from her and began to work out the knots in my hair. That was the only thing Amy and I had in common — we both had insanely curly hair. Like corkscrew curls. The kind that everyone thinks they want but, in reality, you can't do a damn thing with. But where Amy's were long, dark brown, and perfect, mine were shoulder length, blond, and slowly destroying my sanity. It took *forever* to pick out the tangles each morning, and today, I didn't have forever.

"Well, I hope you and your mom get it worked out soon," she said, "because I love having you stay here, but this is getting a little too complicated."

"You're telling me." She wasn't the one who was about to make a two-story drop out of a window.

In the hall, I could hear Mr. Rush moving around, getting ready for work. Now, with my teeth unbrushed and without a speck of deodorant to cover up my glorious natural odor, was the time to make my escape.

I ran over to Amy's window and shoved it open. "If I die doing this, please deliver a somewhat humorous but overall heartbreaking eulogy at my funeral, okay?"

"Sonny!" Amy grabbed my arm and dragged me away from the window. "No way. You're not doing that."

"Why not?"

3

"For starters, it's not safe," she said. When she realized that wasn't enough to deter me, she added, "And also you'd be dropping right past the kitchen window. If Mom's down there eating breakfast and sees a girl falling from the sky . . ."

"Good point. Damn it. What do I do?"

"Just wait until everyone leaves," she said. "You can sneak out and lock the door with the spare key. It's under the —"

"Flowerpot next to the door. Yeah. I know."

And while this was a more practical plan, to be sure, it wasn't the most suited for punctuality. Amy's parents didn't leave until seven-thirty, only fifteen minutes before I had to be at school. The minute the front door slammed, I scrambled down the hall and into the bathroom to finish my necessary hygiene rituals before bolting downstairs and out the door myself.

I locked up, then cut across their backyard and down Milton Street to the Grayson's Groceries parking lot, where I had left my car the night before.

"Hello, Gert," I said, tapping the hood of the old silver station wagon. She was one ugly beast of a car. But she was mine. I climbed into the front seat. "Hope you slept well, but I'm in a hurry, so please don't be in a shitty mood today."

I turned the key in the ignition. It revved, but the engine wouldn't turn over. I groaned.

"Not today, Gert. Have some mercy."

I tried again and, as if she'd heard me, Gert's motor finally started to hum. And, just like that, we were off.

The bell had already rung by the time I pulled into the senior parking lot, which meant the main door had locked and Mrs. Garrison, the perpetually grumpy front desk lady, had to buzz me in.

"Sonya," she said, greeting me when I got to the main office.

I cringed. I hated — *hated* — my full first name.

"You're late," she announced, as if I somehow wasn't aware.

"I know. I'm sorry, I just . . ."

Showtime.

My lip started to quiver and, on cue, my eyes began to well up with tears. I looked down at my shoes and took a dramatic, raspy breath.

"My hamster, Lancelot, died this morning. I woke up and he was just . . . in his wheel . . . lying so still. . . ." I covered my face with my hands and began to sob. "I'm sorry. You probably think it's stupid, but I loved him so much."

"Oh, sweetheart."

"I know it's not an excuse, but . . . I just . . . I'm sorry, Lancelot."

I was worried I might be playing it up *too* much, but then she shoved a tissue into my hand and patted my arm sympathetically.

"Let it out," she said. "I know it can be hard. When I lost Whiskers last year . . . Listen, I'll write you a note for first block. I'll say you had a family emergency. Don't worry about it. I'll make sure this is excused."

"Thank you," I sniffed.

The tears had dried up by the time I reached my AP European history class. Mr. Buckley was in the middle of his lecture when I slipped into the room. Unfortunately, he never missed anything, so there was no chance of me sneaking back to my chair without him noticing.

"Ms. Ardmore," he said. "You finally decided to join us."

"Sorry to interrupt," I said. "I have a note."

I handed him the slip of paper I'd been given at the front desk. He read it quickly and nodded. "Fine. Take your seat. I suggest you borrow notes on the first part of the lecture from one of your classmates."

"That's it?" Ryder Cross asked as I slid into the seat behind his. "She comes in half an hour late and there are no consequences?"

"She has a note from the office, Mr. Cross," Mr. Buckley said. "What consequences would you suggest?"

"I don't know," Ryder admitted. "But she disrupted the class by coming in late, and it's not as if this is the first time. Back at my school in DC, the teachers were much more strict. Excuses were rarely accepted. And the students cared much more about their education, too. Here, it seems like just about anything can get excused."

I rolled my eyes so hard it hurt. "Then go back," I suggested. "Don't worry about us simple folk here in Hamilton. We'll make do without you. I assure you, you won't even be missed."

There was an appreciative murmur from the rest of the class. Even Mr. Buckley gave the tiniest of nods.

Ryder turned in his seat so that he could look me in the eye. The sad thing was, if he hadn't been such a tool, he probably would have been popular around here. He had smooth brown skin and shockingly bright green eyes. His black hair was kept short and neat, but he was always dressed as if he was on his way to

6

a concert for a band no one had ever heard of. Slightly disheveled, but in a very deliberate way. His clothes, though, always looked like they'd been tailored to fit his lean, muscular frame. On occasion I'd even seen him wear thick-rimmed glasses that I *knew* he didn't need.

In other words, he was hot, but in an annoying, hipstery sort of way.

Since he'd arrived at Hamilton High at the beginning of the semester, he'd done nothing but dis everything about the school and its student body. The lunches at his school in DC were so much better, the kids at his school in DC walked faster in the hallways, the teachers at his school in DC were more qualified, the football team at his school in DC won more games, et cetera, et cetera.

Now, I wasn't exactly bursting with school spirit, but even I couldn't stand his attitude. Which became even more repulsive when he started posting snarky Facebook statuses about how lame our small town was. You'd think our lack of five-star fine dining was putting him in physical agony.

The long and short of it was, Ryder came from money. Political money. His father was a congressman from Maryland — a fact he never failed to share at any opportunity — and in his not-so-humble opinion, Hamilton and everyone who lived here sucked.

Everyone, that is, except Amy. Because Ryder had developed a disgustingly obvious and totally unrequited crush. I couldn't fault him for that, though. Amy was gorgeous and rich, just like him. Amy, however, was the kind of girl who gave personalized Christmas cards to all of the lunch ladies, and he was a dick.

He was still staring at me, and I suddenly became all too aware of the jeans I'd been wearing for almost a week without washing them and the torn hem on the sleeve of my T-shirt. I straightened up and stared him down, daring him to compare me to the girls at his school in DC, but before he could say anything, Mr. Buckley cleared his throat.

"Okay, class. Enough's enough. History is long, but we only have a year to get through this material. Now, let's get back to the Great Schism, which, I know, sounds vaguely like toilet humor, but we're going to press on, regardless."

Ryder turned back around in his seat, and I went about my business taking notes on that unfortunately named moment in history.

Things were looking up until third block, when I realized I'd left my chemistry book at Amy's. I had to convince Mrs. Taylor, who was a total hard-ass and known to give detention for lesser things, that I'd been tutoring at the local children's hospital in Oak Hill and had accidentally left it with one of the kids.

"I'll get it back from her tomorrow," I said. "I'm going to see her before she starts her next round of chemo. I promise to get it back then."

And she bought it. Hook, line, and sinker.

I was aware of my status as a terrible person. But I liked to think of my lying abilities as gifts. And why else would I have them if not to be used? Especially on days like this, where everything just seemed to be going wrong.

I didn't have enough money in my wallet for lunch, so rather than admitting that things were shitty at home and I was broke, I

8

told the much-too-soft-hearted cashier that I'd given my last dollar to the homeless man who occupied the corner a few blocks from school.

She covered it for me.

Then the strap on my crappy two-dollar flip-flop broke, a volleyball slammed right into my face in gym class, and, to top it off, I started my period.

Amy would call it karma. She'd say this was the universe's punishment for all the lies. But, the truth was, the lying helped. When everything felt out of control, it put me back *in* control.

I was sure the day couldn't get worse, which was, perhaps, my fatal flaw. When you let yourself think that things can't get worse, they inevitably will.

"So I'll see you tonight?" Amy asked as we headed out into the senior parking lot.

"Yep. I can't text you, though, so you'll have to watch for me. I'll be outside around the usual time."

"Okay." She gave me a quick hug. "Have fun at work."

I waved as she hurried off to her Lexus. I tried to tell myself I wasn't horribly jealous of her and her rich parents and her fancy car. I had Gert, after all. Who wouldn't want Gert?

I might have been good at lying, but even I didn't buy that one for a minute.

I climbed into the car and tossed my backpack into the passenger's seat. "All right, Gert," I said, sticking the key in the ignition. "Time for work."

But while I was a reliable employee (most of the time), Gert had decided she wasn't in the mood today. The engine revved and

9

revved, but nothing happened. The battery was dead, and I had to be at the movie theater for my shift in twenty minutes.

I grabbed my cell, planning to call Amy to ask for a ride, only to then remember that my ancient phone had recently breathed its last breath. I hopped out of the car, hoping to flag her down before she left the parking lot, but I was too late. I could already see the Lexus speeding off into the distance.

There was no way around it. I was stuck. I'd have to find someone to jump-start my car, and who knew how long that would take.

And just then, because it's possible that all Amy's theories about the universe's revenge were true, the sky opened up and it began pouring rain. Leaving me with only one thing to say:

"Motherfucker."

2

The senior parking lot was already close to empty when the rain started. I sat inside Gert, watching the exit and hoping someone would come out soon. Unfortunately, the first person to appear, my would-be savior, was a tall boy in the T-shirt of an obscure band, a distressed but still clearly expensive hoodie, and two-hundred-dollar jeans.

"You've got to be kidding me," I said as I reached for the door handle. I wanted to just wait for the next person to come out, but who knew how long that would be. Chances were, the rest of these cars belonged to the overachieving types who stayed after school for chess club and student government. Those nerds and their resume-building activities were no good to me right now. So Ryder Cross was my only choice.

I hopped out of the car, holding my history textbook over my head to protect my curls from the downpour of doom.

"Ryder!" I shouted. He was already halfway across the parking lot. "Hey, Ryder!"

He stopped and turned to look at me. He didn't have an umbrella, and the rain was making his clothes cling to him. The view wasn't half bad. Unfortunately, however, my next question would require him to speak.

"My car's dead," I said. "Do you have jumper cables or something?"

He started walking in my direction, but he was shaking his head. "I don't."

I sighed. "Of course not. Let me guess, the cars in DC don't die? Or need repairs?"

"Can't you call someone?"

"My phone doesn't work."

"Seems like everything around you is faulty."

"Well, not everyone has politician parents to pay for our things. Some of us actually have to work for what we own. Your concern is appreciated, though."

He rolled his eyes. "If you're going to be like that, then forget it. I was going to let you use my phone."

"Really?"

"Yeah. I'm not an asshole."

"Debatable."

"You'd be calling Amy, right?"

And there it was. The ulterior motive I'd been expecting. He was right, though. Who else would I call? I knew she wouldn't have jumper cables, but she'd at least be able to give me a ride to the theater.

We climbed into Gert, both of us soaked. The carpeted seats would be brilliantly moldy the next day — something to look forward to. He handed me his phone, the same model as Amy's, and I quickly dialed her number. It was the only one I had memorized.

"Hello?"

"Hey, Amy."

"Sonny? Where are you calling from? I don't recognize the number."

"Our favorite human being was kind enough to bestow the honor of telephone usage on me."

Silence.

"I'm borrowing Ryder's phone."

"Oh."

I didn't have to see her face to know her tiny button nose had wrinkled.

"My car's dead and my phone is broken. And my shift is in . . . oh, seven minutes. Please help."

"On my way."

I returned the phone to Ryder. "She's coming back to get me. So you can go now." And then, with every ounce of willpower I had, I forced myself to add, "And thanks. For the phone."

He shrugged, but he didn't move to get out of the car.

"Do you need something?" I asked.

"No. I just figured I'd stick around until Amy gets here . . . just to see you off safely."

I snorted. "Oh, yes. I'm sure my safety is a priority of yours. Stop wasting your time with this crush on Amy. It's annoying and pathetic and, if you want the truth, she's not into you. At all."

"Sorry. I didn't realize you spoke for Amy now."

"I'm her best friend. I know how she feels about pretty much everything. I'm just trying to save you the heartbreak."

"You care about my heartbreak about as much as I care about

13

your safety." He shook his head. "I'd rather hear Amy's feelings from Amy, if you don't mind."

"You won't. As much as she can't stand you, she wouldn't tell you that. She's too nice."

"Clearly it hasn't rubbed off on you."

A second later, Amy's Lexus turned the corner into the parking lot. I grabbed my bag and climbed out of the station wagon, Ryder not too far behind me. Amy slid into a parking space, and I heard the click of the passenger-side door being unlocked.

"Later," I said, hopping into the Lexus, but Ryder grabbed the door, sticking his head into the cab before I could close it.

"Hello, Amy," he said.

"Oh. Hi, Ryder."

"How are you?"

"I'm fine."

"Which is code for 'annoyed,'" I said.

She elbowed me.

"Sorry for the inconvenience," he said. "It was really nice of you to come back and get Sonny."

"Of course. Thank you for letting Sonny use your phone to call."

"*Sonny* is right here," I said. "And I already thanked him."

"So, Amy, are you doing anything this weekend?" Ryder asked.

Amy glanced at me, her eyes widening in a way that clearly meant, *Oh, dear God, help me get away from him.*

"Um . . . I don't know," she said.

"Well, we should —"

"Go," I interjected. "I can see you're trying to court my lovely friend here —"

Ryder flustered.

"— but it's raining and you're holding the door open and getting my right side soaked in the process."

"And she's late for work," Amy added.

"That, too."

"Right. Sorry about that. I guess I'll see you at school Monday?"

"Probably," Amy said.

"Excellent. See you around."

Ryder stepped back, but he held the door open for just a second longer, ensuring the right leg of my jeans was thoroughly drenched before he closed the door. I glared at him out the window. Somehow, he didn't seem to mind that he was sopping wet. And from a purely aesthetic perspective, I didn't mind that he was either.

"Why must someone so handsome be such an ass?" I asked as Amy pulled out of the parking lot.

"All of the handsome ones are," she said.

"Not your brother."

"He used to be."

Amy's brother, Wesley, was a few years older than us. He'd been blessed with the same godlike DNA as the rest of the Rush family. He had the same dark, curly hair as Amy, the same tall frame, only where she was slender, he was broad and toned.

It would be fair to say I'd had a slight crush on Wesley growing up. It would be more accurate, however, to say I was madly, deeply, head over heels in love with him up until a couple of years ago.

Throughout most of high school, Wesley had been what you might call a "player." He hooked up with every girl who showed interest.

Every girl but me. To him, I was little Sonny Ardmore, his sister's troublemaking but undeniably adorable best friend. Flirt as I might, Wesley never seemed to see me as anything other than the nine-year-old who had once broken her arm attempting to ride the banister in his house.

Not that it mattered much now. His senior year, Wesley had actually started dating someone seriously. Her name was Bianca, and now they were both off at college in New York City, still together.

It was several minutes later when we pulled into the movie theater's parking lot. I worked at a tiny movie theater in Oak Hill, the next town over from Hamilton, where all the big box stores, restaurants, and alcohol could be found. Hamilton was a dry, one-stoplight town with a minuscule population. Oak Hill was the closest thing to a "city" we had until you reached Chicago, which was a couple of hours away.

The oh-so-cleverly named Cindependent Theater only showed foreign and indie flicks. And I had the honor of handing our pretentious customers their extra-buttery, fat-loaded popcorn. Not exactly my dream job, but hey, it paid.

"Thanks," I told Amy. "I'll get a ride back to your place."

"With who? None of your coworkers live in Hamilton."

"I can hitchhike. There are some really cute truck drivers who come through here."

Amy swatted my arm, and I laughed.

16

"I'll figure something out."

"Or I could just pick you up and drive you back to my place."

"But your parents —"

"It's Friday night. It's normal for you to stay over. They won't mind, and they won't even think to check in with your mom. And tomorrow my mom can go jump your car." She smiled. "It doesn't always have to be complicated, you know?"

I nodded. "Fine." I leaned across the seat and hugged her. "You're the best. I don't know what I'd do without you."

If anyone had said that to me, I would have made a funny quip or replied with something snarky — purely out of habit. But not Amy. She just hugged me back and said, "I don't know what I'd do without you either."

I climbed out of the Lexus and hurried through the nearly empty parking lot, toward the theater.

"You're late!" a voice yelled the second I walked through the door.

"Sorry, Glenda."

"Not gonna cut it this time, Sonny."

My boss, a tall, broad-shouldered woman with a chin-length black bob and cat-eye glasses, stepped out from behind the popcorn machine. Judging by the scowl on her face and the veins bulging in her thin neck, I had a theory — an inkling, really — that she *might* be pissed.

"We just started screening that new sea turtle documentary and you missed the rush. You left us short staffed."

I glanced out the window. There were, at max, six cars in the parking lot. "Rush? Really?"

"It's Friday."

"It's three-thirty."

"No. Three-thirty is when you're supposed to be here. It's almost four."

"Glenda —"

"I'm sick of this, Sonny. This happens all the time. I told you last time you were late that if it happened again, you'd be fired."

She had, that was true. But I'd kind of figured she was blowing smoke. She'd threatened to fire Grady, one of my coworkers, a thousand times, but he was still here. I'd honestly thought it was impossible to get fired from Cindependent.

"On top of that, you come in here looking like crap. Look at you, Sonny. You're soaking wet. No one wants you handling their food like that."

"I'm sorry, Glenda. My car broke down and my phone isn't working. I was trying to get help, but then it started raining —"

"Stop. Your lies don't even sound believable anymore."

"But I'm not lying!" Not this time, anyway.

"Why should I believe you?" Glenda asked.

I couldn't think of an answer. In the year I'd been working at Cindependent, I'd lied to her countless times. *Yes, I did clean the gum off the bottom of the seats in theater two. . . . No, I didn't spit in that asshole's soda. . . . I'm late because my grandfather had a heart attack — don't worry, he's fine now!* She really had no reason to believe a word I said.

"I'm done, Sonny," she said. "You're fired."

"But I . . ." And again, I actually told the truth. "I really need the money. Right now more than ever."

Her face softened, but only a little. "Then maybe you'll be more responsible at your next job." And with that, she turned and headed to her office.

I had to borrow Grady's phone to call Amy. It had a thin coat of butter on the keypad, and I kept it about an inch from my face to avoid cross contamination. Amy hadn't even gotten to Hamilton yet, so she just turned around and headed back to the theater to pick me up.

I waited outside, in the rain. I knew if I waited inside, I'd just end up punching the popcorn machine. Not because I'd gotten fired. Who needed some shitty job at a movie theater? I mean, *I* did, but that was beside the point. No, it wasn't getting fired — it was everything. Everything with my mom and my phone and my car and my awful day and my awful life.

Yes, I was a whining, teenage cliché. And, according to Amy, I had a flair for the dramatic, so there was a slight chance that, had I stayed in the theater, I may have made matters worse by pouring a Cherry Slushie on Glenda's head. It was, after all, something I'd fantasized about doing since I'd been hired.

But I still had my dignity — dented though it may have been — and I refused to give in to my wrathful adolescent urges.

"You okay?" Amy asked when I climbed into the Lexus a few minutes later.

It was a testament to how much she loved me that she let me get into her fancy car — twice now — while I was sopping wet. She hadn't even cringed.

"Swell," I said. "Just swell. Let's get out of here. Please."

"Good night, girls," Mrs. Rush said, poking her head into Amy's bedroom later that night. "We're headed to bed."

"Night, Mom," Amy said.

"Good night, Mrs. Rush."

She smiled at us, then slipped back out of the room.

It was just past eleven, and despite being dry once again, snug in some frog-patterned pajamas Amy had lent me, I was still in an awful mood. Amy was doing her best to comfort me, seemingly unaware that I was a lost cause.

"What about Giovanni's? That Italian restaurant in Oak Hill? You could get a job there," she suggested once her mother had gone.

"Brenna Steward works there. She says the owner makes passes at all the young waitresses."

"Ew. Do you think that's true?"

"I don't know, but I'd rather not find out." I flopped backward onto her bed. "Besides, my dry wit — charming as I know you find it — isn't always appreciated by the general public. Which does not bode well for me when it comes to tips."

"That's true."

I glared at her. "You were supposed to disagree with me."

"Oh, I mean . . . people love you, Sonny. I'm sure your sense of humor —"

"Too late now," I said. "Jump ship while you can."

"You'll find another job," she assured me. "My mom will go

help you with your car in the morning, and you can use my phone until yours is fixed. No one but Wesley ever calls me anyway. Besides you, but you're always here, so . . ."

"Thanks," I said. "You're being very sweet, and it's appreciated. But right now, I think I'd rather just wallow."

Amy sighed. "All right."

I buried my face in her pillow and listened as she stood up and walked across the room. I heard her laptop booting up at her desk. I figured she was doing homework until . . .

"Um, Sonny? I know you're busy wallowing, but you're not going to believe this."

I kept my face in the pillow. "I've told you before — if it's a Nigerian prince offering to wire you millions of dollars, don't send him your bank account information."

"It's not that. Ryder Cross e-mailed me."

Now I sat up. "What did he say?"

I was across the room, peering over her shoulder, before she could answer.

Hey, Amy —
It was really nice talking to you this afternoon in the
parking lot. I'm just sorry the awful weather and your
friend's schedule cut our conversation short.

I snorted. " 'Your friend'? Like he doesn't know my name. And what conversation? You were barely talking to him."

"Keep reading," she said.

But I'd really like to keep talking to you. Maybe we
could get dinner sometime? I know there aren't any
nice places to eat in Hamilton, but Oak Hill has a few
decent restaurants. I was thinking maybe next Friday
night?

"Oh my God," I said, unable to even read the last little bit of
the e-mail. "He asked you out."

"I know. I don't even know why he would."

"Because you're gorgeous? That part is obvious."

She blushed.

"Less obvious," I said, "is why he thinks he has a chance. Amy,
you have to reply to him. You have to say you'll do it."

"What? I don't want to go out with Ryder."

"You won't. You'll just say you will. Just to tease him a bit."

"I can't do that," Amy said. "It's too mean."

"Then I'll do it. Move over."

"Sonny, you can't."

"Please," I begged. "I've had an awful day and fucking with
Ryder's head will make me feel so much better."

"I thought you were wallowing?"

"Being mean is so much more fun than wallowing. And he's
such an asshole. You know it, too. He deserves some torture after
the way he's talked about Hamilton and everyone who lives here.
Let me pick on him a little bit. Please?"

She chewed on her bottom lip. Amy was anything but mean.
Even to people she hated, she was always incredibly polite and
respectful. It was unnerving, really.

But if anyone could convince her, it was me. Sonny Ardmore — a bad influence for thirteen years and counting.

"Fine," she said, scooting over so we could squeeze together on the chair. "But only because I know it will cheer you up . . . and because he really is awful. Maybe this will get him to leave me alone."

"That's my girl."

I hit the REPLY button and started to compose my masterpiece, reading it aloud as I typed each sentence.

"Hello, hottie."

"Oh God," Amy squeaked. "I'm already feeling weird about this."

"I'd love to keep talking to you." I read it to her in a slow, sexy voice. "But not at a restaurant. My room is much more comfortable. And the only thing I want to be eating is whipped cream off your chest, lover boy."

"Sonny!" Amy cried. "You can't say that!"

"Why not?"

"He'll think I'm some sort of freak."

"That's the point. He'll be creeped out — and perhaps slightly turned on, though he'd never admit it — by your over-the-top e-mail and too embarrassed to ever speak to you again."

"But what if he tells other people about this e-mail?"

"Who would he tell? No one can stand him. He doesn't have friends."

She sighed, which I took as permission to continue.

"You mentioned my friend in your e-mail. Sonny would also like to be present for this 'conversation.' She loves to watch me fool around with guys. Though recently, I found some creepy voo-doo dolls of the guys I've been hooking up with in her drawer. And, come to think of it, a few of them have had some serious accidents. I hope the possibility of a few broken bones doesn't scare you off."

This time, she giggled. Just a little.

"I have to say, Ryder, I'm so glad you e-mailed me. I've had my eye on you since you got here. I tried to play it cool, but secretly, I've been building a shrine to you in my closet for months. It's nothing special — just a few pictures I took of you on my phone while you weren't looking and a life-size sculpture I made of you using garbage and gum I scraped out from under your desk."

"Oh, that's so gross!" Amy gasped. "Ew."

I continued, "I can't wait to show you my work of art. I know you'll appreciate it. So it's a date. Friday night. I'm going to blow your mind, Ryder. You have no idea. Love (because that's what I am, in love with you), Amy."

I sat back and admired my brilliant prose. Beside me, Amy was giggling, but she also looked a bit nervous.

"You can't really send that, you know," she said.

"Yeah," I agreed. "That's cool. I got it out of my system. But you've got to admit — it's a pretty epic love letter."

"Sure," Amy said.

"I'm saving it," I told her. "You're going to want to look back on this one day when I'm some sort of famous poet . . . or crimi-nal mastermind being hunted by the authorities. Whichever comes first. It'll be worth something."

I leaned forward and moved to click the SAVE button, but Amy's elbow bumped mine by accident, and my hand slipped. Instead of SAVE, I clicked SEND.

"Uh-oh."

Amy saw it at the same time I did. Her eyes went wide and she slapped a hand over her mouth. "What just happened?"

I clicked over to drafts, hoping to see the e-mail there, safe and sound. But no. "It sent," I said.

"No, no, no!" Amy looked horrified. "Oh my God."

"Well . . . he'll never ask you out again?" I offered. "Ugh. I'm sorry. That really wasn't on purpose. I swear."

"I know. I bumped you." She bit at her pinkie nail. "This is awful. I can't believe we sent that. It's so mean and . . . There's no way of, like, getting it back, right?"

"That's not exactly how the Internet works."

"Ugh." She buried her face in her hands. "I hope he doesn't read it."

"He might not," I said. "He might realize too late that asking you out was a mistake and he doesn't have a chance in hell, so he won't read the e-mail. He'll save himself from the heartache. There's actually a good chance of that."

Amy looked skeptical.

"I'm serious," I said.

But I was just saying that to make Amy feel better. I knew he'd read it. He'd be an idiot not to. I just hoped he didn't forward it to anyone. If someone teased Amy about this, I'd never forgive myself.

I wasn't convincing her, though. I could tell she felt awful, and I wished that I'd just wallowed earlier.

"I should send him an apology e-mail," she said.

"No," I said. "I'll do it. I'm the one who wrote the stupid thing. I'll e-mail the apology."

"Are you sure?"

"Yep." I would hate every second of it, but I'd do it for her.

"Thank you," she said. "Now let's go to bed. I'm exhausted."

"Yeah," I said. "I'm tired, too. Practically falling asleep as we speak."

It wasn't the last lie I'd tell that night.

3

I pretended to sleep until Amy started snoring. It really was astonishing that someone so adorable could make such a horrific noise. It was about ten times louder than her speaking voice, and it came from deep in her throat. Amy wasn't usually a mouth-breather, but at night? Jesus.

It used to keep me up when we were little. We'd have sleepovers, and I'd stay up all night, staring at the ceiling. Eventually, I got so used to the demon that possessed Amy's body at night that it became a sort of rhythmic, guttural lullaby.

Not tonight, though. Tonight I was wide-awake.

Slowly, I crawled across the huge bed and climbed over Amy. She kept snoring. Once she started, there was no stopping her until someone shook her awake the next morning. She took being a heavy sleeper to a whole new level.

Even so, I found myself tiptoeing across the carpet toward her desk. I picked up her laptop and slipped out the door and down the hall.

The Rushes' house was ridiculous. Three floors, giant bathrooms, ginormous walk-in closets — Wesley's room even had a freaking balcony. But my favorite, favorite room in the Rush house was the recreation room. It was just down the hall from Amy's room, and it was every teenager's dream. There was a pool table; huge, comfy couches; and, as of Amy's seventeenth birthday, an old-fashioned pinball machine. But the best part was, hardly anyone knew it was here.

I'd been to a few parties at the Rush house — usually thrown by Wesley when he was home from college — and no one ever seemed to find this room. With the door shut, it was easy to mistake it for just another bedroom. Which made it the perfect little hideaway when you wanted a break from the rowdy youths. Or, you know, when you wanted to make out.

The only time I'd ever found the rec room occupied during a party was this year, on the Fourth of July, when I caught Casey Blythe, a former Hamilton High cheerleader, sucking face with her boyfriend, this nerdy kid named Toby Tucker. But Casey was best friends with Wesley's girlfriend, so she had inside intel on where all the best places to fool around in the Rush house were.

Other than that little incident, no one ever seemed to come into the rec room besides me and Amy. We hung out in here sometimes, when we didn't have homework to do. I'd play a game of pool against myself while Amy utterly destroyed on the pinball machine.

Tonight, though, it was just me. I wasn't in the mood for a solo game of pool, so instead I got cozy on one of the couches and propped open Amy's laptop. I had a paper due in English, and I figured I might as well get started on it while the productivity booster known as insomnia stuck around.

I'd just opened a new Word document when I heard a small *ping* and frowned. Then there was a second *ping*. The same sound, but somehow more insistent.

I hadn't realized an Internet window was even open, but when I clicked around for a second, I discovered I had an instant message on my e-mail server.

From Ryder Cross.

RYDER: I know I'm not the most well-liked guy right now, but that e-mail really wasn't necessary.

RYDER: I was putting myself out there, and I don't appreciate you and your friend (I know you didn't work alone) mocking me.

I shrank back into the cushions, shame writhing in my gut. I didn't give a shit if I was a jerk to Ryder, but I hated that he thought Amy had been part of it. I mean, she had, but not willingly. Neither of us had actually wanted to send that e-mail.

I sighed and, since I promised Amy I'd apologize to him, started to write back.

ME: I know. I'm sorry. We got carried away. It's not an excuse, but I had a shitty day and I took it out on you. We really never meant to hit send. I'm sorry.

A second later, he responded.

RYDER: I accept and appreciate your apology.

RYDER: I'm sorry about your bad day.

ME: Thanks.

I opened my Word doc again, thinking that was the end of it, but barely two minutes later, there was another *ping* and I groaned.

"Damn it, Ryder. I already apologized. What more do you want from me?"

But when I saw his instant message, I couldn't help but smile a little.

RYDER: I know this is random, particularly since we're not in the same class, but you have Mrs. Perkins for English, right? Have you written the paper on *Julius Caesar* yet?

ME: Funny. I was literally about to start on that. I know. I've procrastinated.

And then, because I couldn't help myself:

ME: I bet the kids back at your school in DC weren't so irresponsible.

RYDER: Ha-ha. I know. I bring up my old school too much. Is it that annoying?

ME: Yes.

ME: Incredibly.

RYDER: Sorry.

RYDER: But, if it helps, whether the kids in my old school procrastinate or not, I do. At least with English.

RYDER: Especially with Shakespeare.

ME: Not a fan of the bard?

RYDER: I wouldn't say I'm not a fan. But I am not the best with iambic pentameter. Every word of dialogue goes right over my head.

ME: Alert the press! Ryder Cross just admitted he's not perfect at something. Quick, has hell frozen over?

RYDER: Never mind. Forget I said anything.

ME: I suck with Shakespeare, too.

RYDER: Yeah?

ME: Yeah.

It was true. I was the most miserable translator to have ever touched the work of Sir William. Last year, when we were studying *Macbeth*, I got so lost trying to understand it that at one point I threw my book across Amy's bedroom and swore I'd never go to school again. "Who needs English?" I'd asked her. "I'll be a mime. I'll join the circus. Screw my education!"

Lucky for me, Amy is excellent at deciphering Shakespeare's long monologues, and she taught me a trick — it all starts making sense if you *hear* it. Seeing the words on the page is too much, too difficult to find the rhythm, but if you hear it, it becomes clearer. And lucky for me, Amy, who would make a brilliant thespian if she weren't so painfully shy, was willing to read to me.

I'd gotten an A on my *Macbeth* paper because of her, and now I was about to have an encore performance with my *Julius Caesar* paper. Amy had read me the play two nights ago, and she hadn't had to do nearly as much explaining this time.

ME: It helps to hear it.

RYDER: What?

ME: If you can get someone to read it to you —
someone who understands it — it starts making a lot
more sense.

RYDER: Oh. I don't really have anyone who could
read it to me.

RYDER: My mom could, but I'm not asking her.

ME: What about a study buddy? Someone else from
English class?

RYDER: Again, I'm not the most well-liked guy at
school right now. Even the teachers can't stand me.

I didn't know why, but somehow his honesty about this surprised me. Not that it was a secret. No one really tried too hard to
hide their disdain for Ryder, but he was so arrogant, so conceited,
that I just assumed he thought the world was as fond of him as he
was of himself.

But just then, he didn't seem too conceited. Actually, he was
almost tolerable.

RYDER: Which, if you ask me, is entirely unprofessional.
Not that I'm surprised. Most of these people are hardly
qualified to call themselves educators.

Scratch that part about tolerable.

ME: I'm going to ignore that.

ME: Maybe you could watch a staged play? I bet you could find a video online. Or at the library?

RYDER: That's not a bad idea, actually.

When he didn't type anything else, I assumed the conversation was over. I went back to my paper, but after writing, deleting, rewriting, and deleting the first paragraph, I realized there was no way I could focus right now. Something Ryder said had lingered in my head, and perhaps I am nosy, but I just had to ask.

ME: Why won't you ask your mom for help?

RYDER: It's . . . complicated.

A minute later:

RYDER: Do you really want to know?

ME: Sure. It's not like I'm doing anything else right now.

RYDER: What about your paper?

ME: I already told you I'm a procrastinator. I'm sure your parental drama is far more interesting than Brutus's betrayal of Caesar.

ME: Though hopefully less bloody?

RYDER: LOL. Yes, less bloody.

ME: My, my, Ryder Cross. I never took you for the chat-speak type. LOL indeed.

RYDER: That's my dirty little secret. I sometimes write like an actual teenager. Don't tell anyone.

ME: Too late. I now have dirt on you. Mission accomplished.

He wrote back with an emoticon of a face sticking its tongue out at me. I laughed.

ME: More dirt! This is my lucky night!
RYDER: Damn it. I'm playing right into your hands, aren't I?
ME: That you are, sir. That you are.

Whoa, wait. Was I bantering with Ryder Cross? My archnemesis? The Lex Luthor to my Superman? The Loki to my Thor? The peanut butter to my jelly? Okay, I know most of the world thinks those last two go together, but I personally find the combination rather abhorrent and just ew.

But I totally was. Ryder Cross and I were teasing each other in a surprisingly nonhostile way. I suppose this was the power of the Internet.

ME: So . . . your mom?

It took Ryder a little while to type out his response.

RYDER: My mom left my dad. But instead of just divorcing him and moving to a new house and letting me continue at the school I've been attending since I was five, she insisted on packing up everything, moving hundreds of miles away, and dragging me with her. It's like she didn't care what I wanted. I had friends in DC. I had a girlfriend. I was at one of the top schools in the country. But that didn't matter. She had gotten a new job and I had to come with her to this tiny town in the middle of nowhere. I freaking hate it here.

RYDER: Sorry. I know my saying that is why everyone here hates me. I guess to be fair, it's not so much the town as the situation. I don't want to be here.

ME: No . . . I get it, actually.

And I did. I knew Ryder didn't like Hamilton — everyone knew that — but I'd never really thought about it from his perspective. Being pulled out of a place where you were happy, where you had friends, couldn't be easy. I couldn't imagine how miserable I'd be if I'd been forced to move somewhere hundreds of miles from Hamilton. From Amy.

I'd probably be kind of an asshole, too.

RYDER: So, yes. That's why I'm not asking my mom for help. I've barely spoken to her since we got here in August. Petty, I know.

ME: You're seventeen. I think you're allowed to be petty. Especially about something like this.

ME: But why can't you go back? Live with your dad?

Again, Ryder took a while to write his answer.

RYDER: I asked. Before we left, I asked to stay. But my mom wouldn't let me.

ME: Why?

RYDER: I have no idea. Because she's selfish? Because she wants to punish my dad by keeping me away? Not that she has any right to punish him. She's the one who left. She's the one who asked for the divorce. Dad doesn't want it. He still hasn't signed the papers.

ME: Do you think they might get back together?

RYDER: That would be difficult with her being a few states away and all.

RYDER: I don't know. And lately, I can never get ahold of my dad. His secretary always says he's busy, and he doesn't answer his cell. I know he's got a lot going on in Washington, but . . .

RYDER: Okay, I know this isn't the cool thing to say, but I miss him.

ME: I'm sorry, Ryder.

RYDER: I don't want you to be sorry. I don't want anyone to be sorry. Except maybe my mom.

I pulled up Google and tried to find a picture of Ryder and his family. I figured it wouldn't be hard since his dad was in Congress. They probably had plenty of photos from the campaign trail.

Within a minute, I'd found one. In the picture, Ryder was standing between his parents. His dad was older than I expected. Or maybe he just looked old because of stress. I knew politicians supposedly aged quickly. His hair was gray but well kept. He had

Ryder's bright green eyes and a charismatic smile that could definitely win a vote or two. On Ryder's other side was his mom,
a very pretty black woman in a perfectly tailored suit. She was
tall — taller than her husband — and while her eyes were darker
than Ryder's, they had the same shape, large and striking.

And in the middle was Ryder, dressed in a suit very similar to
his dad's. His hair was a little longer then, but not too much. What
I couldn't help noticing, though, was his smile. It was huge and
genuine and . . . so happy. I'd never seen the boy from my class
smile like that before. I didn't know he could.

ME: I could help you Parent Trap them if you like?

RYDER: What?

ME: *The Parent Trap?*

RYDER: Sorry. Still lost.

ME: Oh. My. God.

ME: You're kidding, right?

ME: THE PARENT TRAP? Twin girls meet for the first
time at summer camp and scheme to reunite their
parents? The remake starred pre-train-wreck Lindsay
Lohan?

ME: YOU HAVE NEVER SEEN THE FREAKING PARENT
TRAP????

RYDER: I have not, but does this really warrant
cyber-shouting?

ME: YES!!!!!!

RYDER: Okay.

ME: I weep for your childhood.

I spent the next twenty minutes explaining the plot of *The Parent Trap* to him, complete with YouTube clips from both the original film and the remake. When I was done, Ryder informed me that it didn't sound like that great of a movie, and I told him to, with all due respect, shove it.

But we kept IMing after that. About other movies (he was totally into indie art-house flicks, the more subtitles the better, which is, frankly, disgusting) and books (we both struggled with Shakespeare and *hated* Nathaniel Hawthorne with equal passion) and just . . . random stuff.

ME: Okay, deep dark secret time. I am a wannabe grunge rocker.
RYDER: Seriously?
ME: Seriously. I don't play any instruments. I can't sing to save my life. But I guess that didn't stop Courtney Love. And I have a lot of secret angst.
ME: If I could pull off flannel, I'd wear it every day.
RYDER: I think you'd look cute in flannel.

I blushed, then realized I was blushing and immediately felt disgusted with myself.

RYDER: So what are you secretly angsty about?
RYDER: If I can ask.
ME: Mostly my mom.
RYDER: This seems to be a running theme this evening.
ME: She is . . . flaky. To say the least. Unreliable.

Truthfully, sometimes I think she wishes she never had
me. Sometimes I think she pretends she didn't.

The second I sent that message, I regretted it. It was way more
than I'd planned to share. It was too honest. Too much. Too close.

I didn't talk about my mom. Not in detail. Not even with Amy.
I was the queen of glossing over things. Of turning small truths
into big lies.

But now Ryder Cross, of all people, knew one of my darkest
secrets. Or, at least, a tiny piece of it. I felt uncomfortable, suddenly, and I was eternally grateful that he couldn't see me. That
even though I'd shared too much, I could at least hide behind this
computer screen.

RYDER: Wow. That does sound like inspiration for a
grunge album.
RYDER: I won't push you to talk about it, but obviously
I understand complicated family situations, so if you
ever want to share, I'm here to listen.
ME: Thank you.

We chatted for a little while longer, mostly about his favorite
band — Goats Vote for Melons, which I'd never heard of, despite
his fears that they were becoming too "mainstream."

ME: God, you are such a hipster.
RYDER: Ugh. I'm NOT a hipster.
ME: Exactly what a hipster would say.

He sent me the smiley face with its tongue sticking out. Very mature and all. Then he wrote:

RYDER: I should probably go. It's late.
RYDER: Whoa — look out your window.
ME: Both creepy and cryptic, but all right.

I glanced up and gasped, startled. Outside the window, the sun was just beginning to peek over the trees. I looked at the clock and was stunned to see that it was nearly six in the morning.

I'd been IMing with Ryder all night.

ME: Wow.
RYDER: I know.
ME: I had no idea we were on here this long.
RYDER: Me either.
ME: I should get to bed.
RYDER: Me, too. But I really liked "talking" to you.
ME: I liked "talking" to you, too.

And, weirdly, I had.

ME: Let's do this again sometime.
RYDER: I'd like that.
ME: Okay, well . . . good night. Or, good morning?
RYDER: LOL. Good morning, Amy.

I frowned, reading his message again.

Amy?

I was about to write back, to correct him, but he'd already logged off. I figured maybe it was just a typo, a mistake. We were both sleep deprived, after all. But as I was about to log out, a terrible realization hit me.

Amy had never logged out earlier. Why would she? It was her computer, after all.

I'd been instant messaging with Ryder for hours, and this whole time — this whole damn time — he thought I was Amy Rush.

And that's how this whole stupid thing began — with a lie that I, for once, hadn't even meant to tell.

4

"Wait . . . so he thinks he was talking to me?" Amy turned to face me, stopping our Saturday morning trek through the hub of commercialism and public massage chairs known as Oak Hill Mall.

I gave her a sheepish grin, one I had perfected a long time ago. Amy didn't look so much angry as . . . horrified.

"I know. I'm sorry. I didn't realize you were logged in. On the plus side, he's not mad about the e-mail."

I expected her to point out that it was her laptop and Ryder had e-mailed her so *of course* she was logged in and how could I be so stupid? But this was Amy. Ever-sweet, ever-forgiving Amy.

"It's an honest mistake," she said. We kept walking, dodging around a group of middle school girls who were emerging from Hot Topic. "But what does this mean? What did you two even talk about all night?"

"Nothing," I said. "And . . . everything? It was bizarre. He's obnoxious, but . . . maybe he's not quite as awful as I thought?"

"Well, I guess that's nice to know."

We stepped into the food court and headed toward the closest counter. A bored-looking guy stood behind the cash register, re-adjusting his navy-blue hat that was, by far, the worst part of his work uniform. It made me wish I didn't have to ask him my next question, but alas, a girl's gotta make a living.

Or at least make enough money to buy a new cell phone.

"Hey," I said to the bored guy. "This place hiring?"

"Yeah."

That was seriously all he said. Then he stared at me, his eyes nearly as dead as his monotone voice. Dear God, I hoped something besides this job had been responsible for sucking out his soul.

"Can I get an application?" I asked.

"I guess."

He turned around and went in search of an application, moving slow and stiff, like a zombie. A zombie that smelled like deli meat.

I turned to Amy and raised an eyebrow. She shrugged.

"So, anyway," she said. "About Ryder —"

"Amy!"

Amy jumped and we both turned to see a thin, blond girl waving. She was probably a few years older than us, and she was sitting alone, eating a burrito. She kept waving, then signaled Amy to come over and join her.

I looked at Amy. The smile she gave in return was fake, but only I would've known that. She raised her hand in a small, embarrassed wave and then turned away, ducking her head as if she hadn't realized the girl wanted us — well, not us, Amy — to join her.

I glanced between the disappointed-looking blond and my anxious-looking friend. Before I could say anything, though, Zombie Cashier returned with my application.

43

"Here."

Amy snatched it from him, said a quick, "Thanks," then tugged me out of the food court.

"I was gonna apply at some other places," I said.

"You can do it later." She handed me the application. "You wanted to apply to the bookstore, too, right?"

"Yeah." I frowned at her. "So who was that girl?"

"Madison," Amy said.

"Who?"

"She used to date my brother. Before Bianca."

"Huh." I glanced back as we walked away from the food court. The girl, Madison, was still eating alone. And she looked rather annoyed about it. "For some reason I don't remember her."

"Weird." She shrugged. "Anyway, about Ryder . . ."

"Right." We walked into the bookstore and made our way toward the front counter. "I still can't believe I chatted with him *all night*."

"Do you think you like him?" she asked.

"Of course not," I said. "I just . . . maybe don't despise him? Plus, it's weird now that I know he thought he was talking to you. But maybe it's not a big deal."

We reached the counter and I asked the woman behind the register for an application. Once I had it in hand, Amy and I decided to browse the shelves for a while.

"So, what are you going to do?" Amy asked, picking up a copy of *Cyrano de Bergerac*. She was supposed to read and analyze a play for her drama class.

And then I said possibly the most ironic thing that has ever come out of my mouth. "I'll just tell him the truth."

Amy glanced up at me, and the surprise on her face did not go unnoticed. "That's it? That simple?"

"I mean, it'll be weird," I admitted. " 'Hey, Ryder. So I know you thought you were talking to a smoking hot, boobalicious lady the other night, but actually it was me, her moderately attractive but still utterly charming best friend. Sorry about that.' "

Amy balked. "Sonny, don't say that."

"What? That you're boobalicious?"

"Well, that, too," she said. "But that you're only moderately attractive. You're beautiful."

I laughed. "I love that you're trying to boost my ego right after I refer to myself as utterly charming. But let's be serious. Next to you, *anyone* looks only moderately attractive."

She ducked her head and picked up another play in order to hide her face.

"Anyway, it'll be fine. I'll tell Ryder what happened. It doesn't have to be dramatic."

And the funny thing is, at the time, I really believed that.

When Amy and I returned from the mall that afternoon, Mrs. Rush drove me out to the high school. Luckily, it appeared that the battery had died because I'd accidentally left the lights on, not because it needed to be replaced — that would have been a nightmare. But with a little effort and a pair of jumper cables, Mrs.

45

Rush managed to get Gert purring again. Or wheezing, which was a more accurate description. Either way, I was mobile once again.

Which meant I was able to park Gert in the grocery store parking lot, where she waited for me on Monday morning.

Amy had set her own phone alarm to my schedule, and while the shrill siren noise sent me bolting upright, Amy hadn't even stirred. I'd reset the alarm to her schedule (and turned the volume up a little) before sneaking out of the house.

Most days, I got up early, got ready at Amy's, then sat in the parking lot until it was time to head to school. Usually, I dozed off in Gert's front seat, then had to rush to avoid being late for class. Not today, though. Today I forced myself to stay awake.

I knew Ryder always arrived to class early, and I wanted a chance to talk to him before Mr. Buckley started lecturing about the Crusades or the Inquisition or whatever tragic religious conflict we were learning about now. I was hoping to explain what had happened in our IMs, make it known that I no longer thought of him a complete tool bag (only a partial tool bag) and maybe, just maybe, invite him to sit with me at lunch.

Ryder had other plans, however.

As expected, he was already in the classroom when I walked through the door. He was flipping through the pages of our textbook and jotting down notes on a yellow legal pad as he went. He was wearing a dark green T-shirt with some strange logo on it that, even across the room, made his eyes pop more than usual. Once again, I was struck by how attractive he was. And now that I knew he wasn't 100 percent awful . . . well, let's just say there was an uptick in his hotness factor.

All of a sudden, I was nervous. I took a deep breath and tried to shake it off before walking over to him.

"Hey," I said, sliding into my seat.

He didn't look up, and I thought maybe he hadn't heard me. So I cleared my throat and said again, "Hey."

"Hey." His voice was flat and he kept on working, not even glancing back at me.

Okay, so maybe this would be harder than I'd thought.

"So, uh . . . I need to talk to you about something. The other night —"

Suddenly, Ryder spun around in his seat, facing me. But the look on his face was less than kind. His eyes were narrowed and cold. Even in all our bickering, he'd never looked this pissed. I was so surprised that I sat up straight.

"The other night," he said. "You mean that e-mail I received?"

"Um . . ."

"Because I know that wasn't all Amy," he said.

"No, it wasn't. But, Ryder —"

"For the life of me, I can't understand why she'd be friends with someone like you, Sonny."

No, this definitely wasn't going as planned. I gritted my teeth. "Will you just shut up and listen to me for a second?"

"I'm done listening to you," he snapped. "Despite everything you've said, Amy and I have a connection. We chatted online all night after that ridiculous e-mail."

"I'm aware," I muttered.

"She's funny and smart and beautiful . . ."

I rolled my eyes. Because of course. Of course he mentioned how beautiful she is.

"And you," he said, glaring at me. "You're just a . . ."

I waited, knowing what he was going to say. A bitch. Amy was funny and smart and beautiful, and I, Sonny, was just a bitch.

But he didn't say it. He just shook his head, turned back around in his seat, and mumbled something. I don't think he meant me to hear it, but I did.

"And you're not good enough for her."

My fists clenched beneath my desk. "Yeah?" I said. "Well, neither are you."

Just then, Mr. Buckley walked in the room, putting a stop to any snappy retort Ryder might have thrown at me next.

Fuck it, I thought. I'd been wrong. Ryder was an asshole. That all-night chat had clearly been a fluke, and there was no point telling him the truth about it. Even if he let me get a word out, he wouldn't believe me. Or it would just piss him off even more.

So I got my textbook and went right back to hating Ryder Cross.

5

I don't know how I met Amy Rush. I'd love to tell you this charming story about how we bonded over a shared box of crayons in preschool or something — and who knows, maybe we did — but I can't remember. That's how long ago it was.

I know we were young, three or four, maybe. It was before my dad was arrested for the first time. He used to drive me to her house for playdates on the weekends. Dad told me I could invite Amy over, too, if I wanted, but I never did.

Because even as a little kid, I was embarrassed. At that point, my parents and I were living in a trailer out on the edge of Hamilton. And Amy lived in a mansion. Plus, there was my mom, who, I was convinced, would forget to make us dinner or something. I didn't want Amy to see where I lived. I guess there have always been parts of my life I kept hidden, even from her.

But that didn't stop us from becoming insanely, maybe unhealthily close. We were two halves of a whole. We needed each other for balance.

She kept me calm, put me at ease when I was freaking out.

Like when we were seven and I accidentally broke the arm off my favorite doll. My dad had just been arrested, and Ramona was the last gift he'd given me. As I sat there, on the verge of an all-out tantrum, Amy gently removed Ramona from my arms, retrieved some glue from her dad's desk, and put the doll back together. Sure, her arm was a little crooked after that, but that was okay. Amy had, for the most part, solved the problem.

Meanwhile, I spoke up for her, got angry for her, when she was too scared or embarrassed to. Like when we were freshmen and this gross upperclassman named Randy smacked her ass in the hallway.

Amy was so upset and humiliated, and I was pissed on her behalf. So the next time I saw Randy, I threw him up against the wall and gave him a swift knee to the groin. Who cared if I was half his size? Hell hath no fury like a girl defending her bestie. I got two weeks in detention for that, but he never bothered Amy again, so it was worth it.

Amy and I needed each other. Neither of us really had other close friends. We were the type who were friendly with everyone — excluding Ryder Cross, of course — but I think most people felt sort of left out when they spent time with Amy and me. There was too much history, too many inside jokes, and, yeah, maybe our closeness was a little bit weird to some.

But we were okay with that. It was just us. Sonny and Amy. Amy and Sonny. Where she went, I went.

Which was why I got a little panicked when I saw the stack of college applications sitting on her desk.

"Is it already time for these?" I asked, picking up a Cornell application.

"Yep. I got those from the guidance office today." She'd just let me into the house after her parents had gone off to bed, so we had to keep our voices low.

"Wow." I flipped through the stack. "Dartmouth, Stanford, Columbia . . . Very ambitious, Ms. Rush."

"There are a few safety schools in there," she said as she changed into her pajamas. "Have you thought about where you're applying?"

"Not really," I admitted. "I figured I'd follow you wherever you were accepted and live under your bed in your dorm room."

She laughed.

But I hadn't exactly been kidding.

"You better start thinking about it," she said. "These next few months are going to go fast. I know you get overwhelmed with paperwork —"

"False."

She rolled her eyes. "You take three days to fill out a one-page job application."

"I . . . like to be thorough."

"Anyway," she said. "I'd be glad to help you fill them out."

"Thanks," I said. "We'll see."

The truth was, I was sort of deliberately avoiding thoughts of college. Sure, I had decent grades (I was an AP student, after all), but I wasn't going to be able to afford tuition. Especially not to the schools Amy was applying to. In just a few months, we'd be separated.

She'd be off at some Ivy League university, and I'd be stuck here.

And that terrified me.

I'd been avoiding it, pretending college was a long way away and I had no reason to worry about it yet, but we were seniors now, which meant it was time to start figuring my shit out.

I wasn't ready to deal with it yet, though.

Maybe that's why I got so enraged when Ryder hated on Hamilton, because I knew this place was going to be my home for a very, very long time. Whether I liked it or not.

Amy finished running a comb through her hair. "Okay. You ready for bed?"

I shook my head. All the college talk had gotten me too worked up to sleep. "I need to work on a paper. Mind if I use your computer?"

"Of course not. It's all yours."

"Thanks." I picked up the laptop and stepped out into the hall-way. "Sleep tight."

"See you in the morning."

I'd barely gotten the laptop set up in the rec room when I heard a *ping* from the e-mail tab. I rolled my eyes, knowing before I even looked who was messaging me. Or Amy, rather.

"Not now, Ryder," I mumbled. "Not in the mood."

A minute later, there was another *ping*.

RYDER: How was your day?

RYDER: Are you done with that English paper yet?

I was determined to ignore him. After the way he'd talked to me in class that morning, he didn't deserve my time. But five

52

minutes later, there was another *ping*, and this time, I couldn't ignore his message.

RYDER: So Pearl Jam is going to have a concert in Oak Hill.
ME: WHAT?!?! When? Where? Link????
RYDER: Ha. I knew that would get your attention.

I sighed, disappointed.

ME: Not cool.
RYDER: Sorry. I had to try.
ME: How did you know I like Pearl Jam?
RYDER: You love grunge, so I just thought of the most cliché grunge band I could. Other than Nirvana, of course.
ME: Wow. So now you're calling me a cliché. Nice.
RYDER: You call me a hipster. It only seems fair.

He signed that one off with a smiley face.

ME: I'm a cliché, but you are the King of the Emoticons. Tell me, Ryder, how many selfies have you taken today?
RYDER: None. I don't even have an Instagram.
ME: Hipster.
RYDER: I can't win with you.
ME: This is probably true.
RYDER: That's not going to stop me from trying.

Despite my better judgment, this made me smile.

And that was how I ended up chatting with Ryder — again — for most of the night.

RYDER: My mom is driving me insane.

ME: Welcome to adolescence. You'll fit in well here.

RYDER: She won't even let me watch the coverage of Dad's campaign. It's hard enough to find it anyway since he doesn't represent this district, but if she hears one of his ads on my computer, she shouts at me to turn it off.

ME: Wow. Harsh.

RYDER: Hopefully I can get to DC for Thanksgiving next month. I'm desperate to get out of this stupid boring town.

ME: Again. Harsh.

RYDER: Sorry. I'm working on it.

ME: But I hope you are able to go back to DC. I'm sure your dad and your friends will be glad to see you.

I hated myself for keeping up the conversation. But as much as I wanted to despise him, Ryder was kind of being tolerable.

ME: So, you had a girlfriend in DC?

RYDER: Yeah. Eugenia.

ME: Whoa. Terrible name.

RYDER: It really, really is.

ME: So what happened?

RYDER: Nothing. We broke up when I moved and she's already dating someone else. My best friend, actually.

ME: Oh. Ouch.

RYDER: I'm honestly not that upset about it. We dated for over a year, but it never really felt serious. More convenient than anything.

ME: So romantic.

RYDER: I don't care that she started dating Aaron (my friend). That's fine. I'm more upset that she and Aaron and everyone seem to have moved on without me so fast. They were the reasons I was upset to leave DC. They've been my friends since elementary school. And now, just a few months after leaving, I hardly hear from them. I get the occasional comment on my Facebook posts, but that's it.

ME: Well, if you don't mind me saying so, they suck.

RYDER: Ha.

RYDER: They don't, really. That's the worst part. I get it. It's easy to drift apart. It probably wouldn't be so bad if I'd actually managed to make friends here. If I'd moved on, too.

ME: Not to harp on this, but if you'd just ease up on the constant Hamilton bashing, you might be surprised how many friends you'd make.

RYDER: I know. I really am trying.

RYDER: But even if I stopped, I don't know how simple it would be to make friends. Hamilton's a small school. You all have known each other forever. I'm an outsider here.

ME: Maybe, but it wouldn't be too difficult for you. If you'd be cool, people at Hamilton would love you. Especially the girls. You're fresh meat, a boy we've never seen throw up on the school bus or go through the worst parts of puberty. Plus, you're not a bad-looking guy, you know.

I could not believe I'd just typed that. *Mortified* doesn't even begin to cover it. It was true, of course. He was hot, and if he wasn't such a dick about our hometown, girls probably would have thrown themselves at him. No, not probably. Most definitely.

But I didn't have to *tell* him that.

Ryder sent back a smiley face emoji. I sent back one rolling its eyes. And eventually this devolved into an oh-so-sophisticated emoji war. The battle was long and there were many casualties, but eventually, with the peace offering of emoji sushi, a cease-fire was called.

If only it were so easy in real life.

The next day, though, Ryder was back to being unbearable.

"Mr. Buckley," he said, raising his hand. "When are we going to start practicing DBQs?"

"Excuse me?"

"DBQs," Ryder repeated. "It stands for data-based questions. They'll be on the AP test in the spring."

56

"I'm aware what a DBQ is, Mr. Cross. I am the teacher here, after all."

I expected Ryder to make a snide comment about this, but he managed to restrain himself and instead asked, "So when will we start practicing them?"

"After Thanksgiving."

"Don't you think that's awfully late?"

"Oh dear," I said. I was less able to restrain myself. "That's *far* too late. Did you know that in DC, students start preparing for AP tests just out of utero?"

Ryder turned to face me, mid-eye-roll. "While your hyperbole is ridiculous, we do start preparing way in advance. And our AP test results reflect it."

"If only you'd spent as much time working on your social skills."

"*You* are going to lecture *me* on social skills?"

"I'm sorry. Do us ignorant country folk here in Hamilton not communicate to your liking?"

"It's not a problem with *everyone* in Hamilton."

"Enough," Mr. Buckley said. I was actually amazed at how long he'd let this go on. I suspected he got as much entertainment out of the sparring as the rest of the class did.

And . . . I think I kind of enjoyed it, too.

Honestly, though, it was amazing how funny and pleasant Ryder could be over IM, only to turn around and be a pompous jerk in real life. I was getting some serious whiplash.

Which was why I couldn't respond to his IMs anymore. *No más.* I was done. It was already weird enough since, both times, I'd been on Amy's account. She didn't know about the second conversation, and I'd had to lie when she asked me if I knew why Ryder had given her a mixtape (seriously? Who has tapes anymore?) of some weird, poorly recorded band and asked if she'd sit with him at lunch.

"No idea," I'd said. "I mean, we know he likes you. . . . What did you say?"

"Thank you, but that I always sit with you," she'd replied.

Well, that was easy enough. Ryder would never sit at a lunch table with me. So I just shrugged.

Lying was easy. What was worse was that these conversations had totally confused my once unwavering disdain for Ryder Cross.

It had been easier when I hated him.

6

I would. Not. Respond.

Once again, insomnia had me sitting in the Rushes' rec room well after midnight, only this time I didn't have any homework left to do. Instead, I was torturing myself by looking up how far all of the colleges Amy was applying to were from Hamilton.

Answer: Really freaking far.

What the hell was I going to do? I hadn't heard back from any of the jobs I'd applied for, I had no money, and when Amy left for college, I'd essentially be homeless. It wasn't as if I could keep sneaking into her parents' house.

Needless to say, I was already feeling a bit depressed and a little lonely when I heard the *ping*.

"Not falling for it this time, Ryder," I mumbled.

Ping.

Nope.

Ping.

"Damn it."

I told myself I was just going to log out of Amy's e-mail. I told myself I wasn't going to look at the message. But, as we've established, I am a liar, even when I'm talking to myself.

59

RYDER: Hey, Amy, are you there?

RYDER: I'm sorry. It's late, and you're probably not even near your computer. But I just found something out and I need to talk to someone. You were the only person I could think of.

RYDER: Sorry. Never mind.

As much as I wanted to ignore him, I couldn't. There was something sort of desperate in those messages that I couldn't just walk away from.

To my surprise, I was . . . concerned. About Ryder Cross.

ME: Hey, I'm here. What's going on? Are you okay?

RYDER: Not really.

RYDER: Do you have a few minutes?

I should've said no. I should've logged off.

But my own loneliness — mixed with my concern and curiosity — got the better of me.

ME: I've got all night.

I closed out the other Internet tabs, almost glad for the distraction. I couldn't keep thinking about Amy leaving me for college. I wanted to go back to covering my ears and pretending it wasn't happening. And if my only distraction was Ryder, so be it.

RYDER: My friend Aaron called me tonight. I knew
something was up when I saw his name on my phone.
He hasn't called me in over a month.

ME: This is the one who's dating your ex-girlfriend,
right? The girl with the terrible name?

RYDER: Right, but it wasn't about that.

RYDER: He was calling because he saw my dad, and
he wanted to warn me.

ME: Warn you about what?

RYDER: He saw my dad leaving our house (Aaron
lives next door) with this woman.

RYDER: This model.

He sent a link to a Google Images page, and I clicked it. My
screen filled with dozens of shots of a beautiful brunette —
Annalise Stone. She was a runway model from New York and only
a few years older than Ryder and me.

ME: Wow. She's pretty.

ME: Wait. Do you think he's seeing her?

RYDER: Why else would she be leaving our house?

I wanted to make some sort of joke in response to this question, but I got the sense that this wasn't the appropriate time.

ME: I don't understand. I thought he didn't want to
divorce your mom.

RYDER: That's what I thought, too. So I asked her.

RYDER: She didn't want to tell me, but apparently that's why she left. Because he's been seeing this woman for a while.

ME: He's been cheating?

RYDER: Yeah.

RYDER: But he refuses to give Mom a divorce because he thinks it'll hurt his chances in the election in a couple of weeks.

ME: Well, so will sneaking around with a model half his age.

RYDER: I'm guessing he's trying to keep that secret. But if Aaron could find out, the other candidates could, too.

ME: I'm sorry, Ryder.

And I was. I knew just how fraught with disappointment parental relationships could be. And how fucking much it could hurt when the people who raised you let you down.

RYDER: I feel like an idiot.

ME: Why???

RYDER: This whole time I've been blaming my mom. I've thought of her as selfish and cold. In reality, she was trying to keep me from hating Dad. No matter how much he hurt her.

ME: That doesn't make you an idiot.

RYDER: Maybe not, but worshipping Dad does. I've

been thinking he was this saint. Even when I couldn't
get him on the phone, I made excuses for him.

ME: He's your dad. No one blames you for loving him.

RYDER: Maybe they should.

I didn't know how to respond to that. I hadn't spoken to my
own father in years, and my mom . . . well, I was hardly the person
to give advice on the subject.

Luckily, Ryder saved me from having to come up with a reply.

RYDER: Sorry. This conversation got incredibly emo
incredibly fast. Quick, say something funny.

ME: Something funny.

RYDER: Ha.

RYDER: You're such a riot.

ME: I know. I should really do stand-up.

RYDER: I'd pay to see that.

ME: I bet you would. Getting tickets to my shows will
be nearly impossible. The critics will love me. I'll be
known as the funniest comedian to ever come out of
Hamilton.

RYDER: Do you really have any competition in that
regard?

ME: Probably not.

RYDER: I didn't think so.

ME: . . . You're not an idiot, Ryder. You don't have
anything to feel bad about. Your dad does.

RYDER: Thank you.

RYDER: For listening, I mean. Or reading? Anyway, I mean it. When I found out, you were the only person I actually wanted to talk to.

RYDER: That probably sounds ridiculous.

ME: No, it doesn't. I'm flattered, actually.

ME: And the feeling's mutual.

I hated admitting it, but I'd been thinking about our other IM conversations a lot, too. When I noticed *The Parent Trap* was on TV, I'd wanted to message him. When I got an old Nirvana song stuck in my head, I'd wanted to send him the link to the video.

It was absurd, especially considering the fact that I'd wanted little more than to strangle him less than a week ago. But I couldn't deny it. Something about Ryder Cross had gotten to me, and as much as I tried, I couldn't shake the feeling of not hating him.

Of maybe sort of liking him.

RYDER: I'm glad to hear that, Amy.

Amy.

Damn it. I'd done it again. I'd actually let myself forget. He thought I was Amy. He wasn't opening up to *me* but to her. Because while I maybe sort of liked Ryder, he maybe sort of hated me.

I should have told him the truth right then. I know I should have. I should've typed out something like, *Yeah, about that. This is actually Sonny. Sorry for the confusion.* But I didn't want to make him feel weird or embarrassed after opening up about his parents.

So I decided to wait.

RYDER: By the way, I watched *The Parent Trap*.

ME: YOU DID?!?!

RYDER: Don't start with the shouting again. Ha-ha.

RYDER: It was on TV on Saturday, and since I have yet to develop a social life here . . .

ME: And?

ME: AND???

RYDER: It was okay.

ME: Just okay?

RYDER: Just okay.

ME: Our friendship is over. Done. Kaput. I can't associate with anyone who doesn't love *The Parent Trap*.

RYDER: So we're friends, then?

I chewed on my lower lip, my fingers hovering over the keyboard. Were we friends? No. No, we couldn't be. Not when we'd only really had two pleasant conversations before tonight. Not when he thought I was someone else.

But it felt like we were.

ME: Well, we were until you expressed your incorrect opinion of a film classic.

RYDER: It was the Lindsay Lohan version.

ME: Still a classic!

RYDER: I take it back, then. The film was brilliant.

RYDER: So we can be friends now?

I hesitated before replying. Because what I was about to say wasn't the right answer.

ME: Yes.

RYDER: Good.

ME: Good.

But the closer Ryder and I got online, the more we seemed to argue in real life. Every day, he said something entirely asshole-ish, which, of course, I had to call him out on. It was so commonplace now that Mr. Buckley seemed resigned to letting us fight it out.

But whenever anyone else said something rude to or about Ryder, I felt a little defensive on his behalf. Like, it was okay for me to mock him, but no one else. Because unlike them, I knew the other side of Ryder.

Even if he didn't realize it.

Not that I hadn't tried to tell the truth. Twice I'd attempted to IM him from my account to explain, and both times he'd logged off immediately. So that was a bust.

But pretty much any time I was on Amy's account, he'd message me. And a couple of times, I was the one who started the conversation.

ME: Do you watch the local news?

RYDER: Huh??

ME: The six o'clock news. Do you watch it?

RYDER: Um, no. No one under the age of fifty watches the local news.

ME: Well, give me a walker and call me Granny. Because I do. Every night.

RYDER: I can't decide if that's pathetic or adorable.

ME: So one of the anchors, Greg Johnson, lives in Hamilton.

RYDER: And?

ME: And I ran into him today. I was pumping gas when he and his stepdaughter pulled up. She goes to school with us, but she's a few years younger. A sophomore, I think.

RYDER: Uh-huh.

ME: Anyway, I told him what a fan of his I was, and when we went in to pay for our gas, he was like, "Don't worry, I got this. Anything for a fan."

RYDER: That's nice of him.

ME: HE PAID FOR MY GAS!

RYDER: WHY ARE YOU SHOUTING?

ME: BECAUSE IT'S A BIG DEAL!

RYDER: Is it, though?

ME: Excuse me, Mr. Big City, but around here Greg Johnson is practically famous. He's the closest thing we have to a celebrity in Hamilton.

RYDER: Again, not sure if this is sad or adorable.

ME: He's also very handsome, so there's that, too.

RYDER: Is it weird that I'm a little jealous of this guy now?

I felt a smile spread across my face. I knew it was wrong. I knew he thought he was flirting with my best friend, not me. But I couldn't help it.

ME: If you pay for my gas, I'll call you handsome, too.

RYDER: Duly noted.

7

By the end of October, there was no way around it. Somehow, I'd developed a big, stinking crush on Ryder Cross.

And he had one on my best friend.

But somehow, I thought I could fix that. I could turn this around and make Ryder see that I, not Amy, was the girl he should be with. It would just take some planning, a lot of lying . . .

And a little help from my best friend.

"You want me to do what?" Amy's eyes were wide and totally freaked out.

I glanced around our table to make sure no one was listening. It was Monday, and I'd spent the weekend piecing together my plan before springing it on her over lunch.

Satisfied that we weren't being spied on — and that Ryder was nowhere near us — I explained.

"Not just *you*. I'm in on this, too."

"That's not exactly comforting."

"Fair point." I popped a soggy french fry into my mouth. Once again, I'd lied to the cafeteria lady so I could get a free lunch. Now that I was unemployed, this would likely become an all-too-regular occurrence.

Amy had asked that morning if I needed lunch money, but I'd said no. She was already doing so much for me, letting me stay in her room, and I wouldn't take money from her, too. I told her I had a little cash saved. And, of course, she believed me.

"Trust me, though," I said. "This will work."

"I'm not sure what *this* is."

"Right. Okay." I pushed my empty tray aside and leaned forward with my elbows on the table. "So Ryder likes me, but he thinks I'm you. And he hates the me he thinks I am. Following?"

"Barely. But I'm confused. You chatted with him again after the first time?"

"Just . . . once," I said, cringing a little.

It had been more like half a dozen times.

"Oh," Amy said, clearly made a little uncomfortable by this. "That might have been nice to know. It would've explained why he kept waving to me in the hallway, if he thought we'd been chatting online. I wish you'd told me sooner."

"I know," I said. "But it just sort of happened. I didn't mean to do it again."

And again . . . and again . . .

"Well, I'm still not sure why you can't just tell him it's you he's been talking to."

"We've been over this," I said with a groan. "I've tried. He won't let me get a word out in person, and when I try over IM, he just logs off. And I'm scared if I tell him now or write it in an e-mail, he'll think I've just been screwing with him."

"So the alternative is . . . lying to him more?"

"Precisely. But for a good cause."

"A good cause," Amy repeated, dubious.

"My love life," I said. "It's in desperate need of some charity. Helping me would really just be doing a good deed."

"I don't know . . ."

"What's there not to know?" I asked. "It won't be hard and it won't take long. Basically, we just have to convince Ryder that it's me, not you, he's interested in. Really, it'll be beneficial to both of us."

"How do we do that?"

"I'm glad you asked, my dearest, *bestest* friend. It's simple. We start by making him warm up to me. I'll act like I'm just playing nice for your sake, and he'll agree because he's into you. But then, we convince him that you aren't at all the kind of girl he wants to be with, make him think he was wrong about you. By then he's gotten closer to me, realized just how charming I actually am, and bam! Ryder and I are making out in Gert's backseat while Boyz II Men plays on the stereo."

"Who?"

I gave her a disappointed stare. "You should really listen to that nineties playlist I made you. You'd understand so many more of my references."

Amy decided to ignore this and returned to the more important conversation. "I'm still not sure what you expect me to do," she said. "How do we make Ryder think I'm wrong for him?"

"Well, first, I won't IM him on your account again. And if he IMs you, you ignore him. Or say something rude."

Amy grimaced, as if the idea of being rude, even to someone she disliked, was physically painful.

"Or you can ask me to say something rude. Whatever."

"And what about in person?" she asked. "We go to school together. He thinks we've been talking this whole time — he's already trying to hang out with me."

"You blow him off," I say. "Act flaky. Or self-absorbed."

Even as I said it, I knew this was going to prove to be a challenge for Amy.

"I'll help you," I said. "You guys don't have any classes together, anyway. But when he does come up to you, I'll be your director. We're pretty much together all the time as it is, and I know exactly what it takes to piss off Ryder Cross. I might as well have a PhD in it."

"I'm still not sure . . ."

"Please, Amy." I clasped my hands together and gave her the biggest, saddest eyes I could manage. "*Please*. I need this."

"You really like him that much?" she asked.

"Yeah. I think I do."

I was not a particularly romantic person. Up until now, I'd only ever had two crushes in my life. The first was my childish obsession with Amy's brother. The second equally as unattainable crush was on Greg Johnson, the news anchor. A celebrity crush, if you will.

But Ryder was different. The fluttery feeling I got in my stomach wasn't based on how he looked (though staring at him in history class was not entirely unpleasant) or just because he was nice to me (because he wasn't always). My feelings for him had formed over the course of our instant message conversations — all of which had lasted hours. I'd never talked to anyone for hours

72

before, aside from Amy. We'd just *clicked*. He was smart and surprisingly funny.

Even if he was also a pretentious hipster.

"You hated him a couple of weeks ago," Amy said. "What if you change your mind about him again?"

"I won't," I assured her. "Believe me, Amy. He's not the asshole we thought. I mean, he sort of is, but not exactly. Ugh. I know I sound crazy. Just tell me you'll help. You have to."

She looked down at her half-eaten lunch. "I guess I will. As long as it doesn't go on too long —"

"Eee! Thank you!" I sprang across the table to throw my arms around her, my chest landing right in her plate of french fries. "I love you, I love you, I love you! You are my favorite human being, Amy Rush." And with that, I planted a kiss right on her cheek.

She blushed, either pleased or embarrassed. Then she said, "Um . . . Mr. Buckley just walked into the cafeteria, and he's giving us a very strange look. Probably because you're on top of the table, so . . ."

I laughed and pushed myself up and away from her, easing back into my seat. "I've done weirder things in class. He's used to it."

"I don't know if that's something to brag about," she said. Then her eyes widened. "Oh, no! Your shirt."

"What?" I looked down.

Ketchup.

On my white shirt.

All over my boobs.

"Fan-freaking-tastic," I said, even though I was laughing.

73

"Sorry," Amy moaned. As if it was her fault I'd launched myself across the lunch table.

"It's cool," I said. "I'll just tell everyone I'm dressed as a murder victim. I mean, we're only a few days from Halloween. No one will think twice."

The bell rang and we threw our trash out before heading to our third block classes.

"I have my gym clothes in my locker," Amy said. "You could borrow that T-shirt. It might be a little stinky, but there's no ketchup on it."

"It's fine," I said. "Maybe I'll start a new trend."

But my mind changed when I spotted Ryder heading down the hallway toward us. The reality of what I must look like hit me, and I was suddenly far less comfortable with it. I was supposed to be making a good impression, after all, and perhaps it wasn't best to start off with a giant red splotch across my breasts.

I ducked into an alcove, dragging Amy with me. We pressed against the wall and stayed quiet as he walked by, alone.

He was always alone.

My heart ached for him a little, almost overriding my embarrassment.

Once he'd turned the next corner, heading toward the library, I let out a breath I didn't know I'd been holding. Amy gave me a small, knowing smile.

"So . . . ," I said. "Yeah. About that stinky T-shirt."

8

"How do I look?"

Amy squinted two very sleepy eyes at me. She wasn't really supposed to be awake yet, but I was about to sneak out before her parents got up, and I needed her opinion on this crucial matter. So, with great effort, I'd shaken her out of sleep to show her the outfit I'd chosen. Jeans, newly clean and a little snug, and a hunter-green cowl-neck sweater with elbow-length sleeves.

It was the only nice top I'd brought to Amy's with me, and I'd been saving it for special occasions or, now that I was unemployed, job interviews. Interviews that, to my intense distress, had not yet occurred. It was my good-impression top, and today I needed to make a damn good impression.

"I don't think you've ever asked me that question before," Amy said.

"Well, I'm asking you now." I glanced at the full-length mirror that hung on the back of her bedroom door. My curls, despite my best efforts, were still a little wild, but they weren't *too* outrageous. "I've got to be friendly with Ryder today, and Snobby McSnobberson won't be so willing if I look like the homeless ruffian that I am."

"It's too early for you to use words like 'ruffian,'" Amy mumbled. She stretched her arms over her head and let out a huge yawn. "And if he's so snobby, why are you doing this?"

"Because he's cute and I want to kiss his face."

"Right."

"The problem is, he wants to kiss *your* face. So today is the beginning of our master plan to change that. Which means I need to look decent, so . . . how do I look?"

"Like a back-to-school clothing commercial."

"Perfect." I picked up my backpack, gave my hair one last check, and grinned at Amy. "Today, it begins."

"Mm-hm." She flopped back on the bed, eyes already closed.

I hurried out of the Rushes' house and down the street to where Gert waited. And, to my relief, she decided to run that morning.

I arrived at school with enough time to pop into the bathroom and give myself one more once-over before heading to Mr. Buckley's class. I was feeling uncharacteristically nervous.

I might have had a major crush on Ryder, but he still couldn't stand me. Which meant I had to ease him into it. If I could get him to tolerate me, it would only be a matter of time before he realized that I, not Amy, was the person he wanted to make out with.

This was the most crucial step of the plan, and I couldn't afford to screw it up.

The classroom was almost full by the time I slid into my seat behind Ryder. He didn't even look up as I walked past.

"Good morning," I said.

No response. But that wasn't a surprise.

I'd gone over and over the words I wanted to say to him, the phrasing I'd use to convince him to hear me out. But staring at the back of his head, at the hunched muscles in his shoulders, I felt myself start to panic. What if it just went down like last time? What if he didn't let me get a word out? What if I made him hate me even more?

What if this was all just a waste of time?

Before I could climb out of the doom spiral I'd begun to sink into, the bell rang and Mr. Buckley appeared.

"So," he said, walking to the whiteboard. "Who wants to talk about the Tudors?"

I sank back into my seat, the moment lost. I wouldn't get a chance to talk to Ryder again until the end of class, and that was only if he didn't rush out, in a hurry to get to his next class. The boy did put a lot of emphasis on punctuality.

Just when I started to think I'd wasted my nice sweater, an idea hit me.

Ryder and I may have had some communication problems of the face-to-face variety, but we were aces when it came to corresponding via text. Sure, he wasn't aware of that fact, but I was. And he couldn't interrupt me if my words were on paper.

I ripped a sheet from my notebook and pretended to take notes on Mr. Buckley's lecture while secretly scribbling a note to Ryder. It took me a few tries to figure out the right words, but eventually, I had it.

Hey. So, I know we have our issues, but you've been talking to Amy, right? She's my best friend, and as awful as you think I am,

I do want her to be happy. So can we play nice? Call a truce? For her, at the least. — S

I'll be honest — writing some of that made me nauseous. I had to fight the urge to rip up the paper and just write the truth, that it was me he'd been talking to. But I knew that would get me nowhere. He'd just think I was lying, ironically. Or that it had all been some mean joke.

Before I could second-guess my decision, I folded up the slip of paper, tapped Ryder on the shoulder, and tossed it into his lap. I watched him eye it for a minute, not touching the paper. Like he thought it might explode or contain anthrax or something.

"Don't be so dramatic," I whispered.

He sighed, just loud enough for me to hear, then picked up the note. Slowly, he unfolded it and began to read.

It took him *forever*. His eyes must have scanned over the words a thousand times. It was agonizing. But, at last, he picked up a pen and began to scribble his own response.

I held my breath as Ryder folded the paper back up, neater than I had, and quickly tossed it over his shoulder onto my desk.

I scooped it up and almost tore the paper as I scrambled to read.

Fine. For Amy's sake — truce.

I grinned as every muscle in my body relaxed, relieved.

Only to then go rigid once more as Mr. Buckley's lecture shifted away from some Henry or another and onto Ryder.

"Mr. Cross," he said. "Did I just see you pass Ms. Ardmore a note?"

"Uh . . ."

"Because I don't know how they did things at your old school in Washington, DC" — Mr. Buckley paused as some of our classmates chuckled — "but at Hamilton, we don't condone note passing."

"Mr. Buckley, I —" Ryder began.

"He wasn't passing me a note," I cut in.

Mr. Buckley and Ryder both turned to face me. But I was totally cool. Because while communicating with Ryder may have made me a nervous wreck, lying about it was something I could do in my sleep.

"Excuse me, Ms. Ardmore?"

"Ryder wasn't passing me a note," I said. I'd already swiped the paper off my desk and hidden it in my lap while Mr. Buckley was looking at Ryder. "He was . . . tossing me something else."

"Oh? And what's that?"

"I'm not sure if I should say, Mr. Buckley."

"You can either say it to me or the principal, Ms. Ardmore. Your choice."

"Oh, okay. Ryder was tossing me a . . . uh . . . sanitary napkin. It fell out of my purse and he was giving it back to me."

"A . . . oh." Mr. Buckley's face had turned quite red.

Ryder, however, looked confused. I wondered if he'd ever heard a pad referred to as a sanitary napkin. Since he hadn't grown up reading Judy Blume novels, I doubted it.

"Sorry about that, Ms. Ardmore," Mr. Buckley choked out. "I didn't mean to draw attention to . . . such a private matter."

"No big deal," I said. "It's just a pad."

Now Ryder had caught up. But, to his credit, he looked only slightly uncomfortable. Which was more than I could say for Mr. Buckley. While the class broke out into giggles, he looked totally mortified.

God, male teachers were so easy.

"Let's get back to England, shall we?" He turned to the board.

I sat back in my chair, fighting a smirk. It paid to be shameless.

After another half hour of taking notes, the bell rang. I leaned forward as Ryder shoved papers into his neatly labeled history folder.

"Sorry if I embarrassed you," I said.

"You didn't."

His voice was stiff, and he didn't look at me as he got to his feet. I stood, too, and for a minute, I thought he was going to walk out of the classroom without another word. But to my surprise, he turned to face me.

"Thank you," he said. "For the lie. The weird, slightly over-the-top lie that, nonetheless, kept me out of trouble."

Did he just use *nonetheless* in casual conversation? Oh, I knew I liked him.

"Hey, what are non-enemies for?" I asked. "Besides, it was my note. I couldn't let you take credit for my rule breaking. People might start thinking you were cool."

The corners of his mouth twitched, like his lips wanted to smile but his brain refused to let them.

I saw it, though. And somehow, I knew I'd just succeeded at something.

"See you around, Ryder," I said, my shoulder grazing his as I moved past him, heading for the classroom door.

I didn't look back, but part of me, the part that had seen a thousand bad romantic comedies, hoped he was watching me walk away.

Amy was waiting for me outside of the classroom, and we headed toward second block together.

"How did it go?" she asked.

I smirked up at her, Ryder's almost-smile flooding me with unexpected confidence. "He'll be mine soon enough."

9

Okay, so maybe I was a little overconfident. Just, like, a tiny bit.

But so far my plan was working pretty brilliantly. On Tuesday, I asked Ryder if I could borrow a pen, and he let me. And on Thursday, he helped me pick up my books after I accidentally-on-purpose knocked them off my desk.

Progress!

My plan had one fatal flaw, however, because while I was making Ryder not despise me, making him not adore Amy was proving to be impossible.

Ryder, obviously thinking he and Amy had a great cyber connection, kept trying to connect with her in real life. Over the next week, he walked up to her in the hallways at school, waved to her in the parking lot, and he continued asking her to sit with him at lunch.

Amy always gave an excuse, but that was the problem. Amy was so sweet, so polite, that no one would realize she was trying to avoid them.

"We've got to do something about this," I said. "Steering clear of him isn't going to be enough."

"I don't know what else to do," she said. We'd met in the

parking lot before school that morning and were walking into the building together. "And he keeps texting me the sushi emoji."

I laughed.

"I don't get it," she said.

"It's an inside joke. We had an emoji war once. It ended over emoji sushi."

"Well, I don't know how to respond to it."

"Don't," I said. "In fact . . . let me do it. You might be too nice to scare him off, but I'm not. Here. Give me your phone."

She pulled it from her purse and handed it over. "You can hold on to it," she said. "Like I told you before — the only people who ever call or text me are you and my brother. Well, and Ryder now, I guess, but he's actually texting you, so . . ."

I pocketed the phone and gave her a one-armed hug. "Thank you. Have I told you lately that you're the best, most generous, prettiest friend I have?"

"Yes. Last night when I let you borrow my nail polish."

"Right."

"And again five minutes ago when I let you have the last sip of my coffee."

"Noted. I'm a very appreciative person. You're lucky to have me."

"And you're so modest, too." She elbowed me with a grin. "But what are we going to do about Ryder? If me avoiding him isn't going to work, then —"

But before Amy had even gotten the question out, we found ourselves face-to-face with the devil himself. Ryder had just rounded the corner, and he was heading our way.

Amy only had time to mutter a nervous "Crap" before he was standing right in front of us.

"Amy," he said with a bright smile.

A smile that should've been for me. But I shook off the sudden, irrational pang of jealousy.

"Hi," Amy said, fidgeting next to me.

"How are you?" he asked.

"Okay." She glanced at me, her eyes begging for help. Only then did Ryder actually seem to notice that I was standing there.

"Oh, Sonny," he said. "Hi to you, too."

"Hey. Did you read the chapters for Mr. Buckley's class?"

"I always read the chapters." His voice was flat and obvious, without a trace of humor.

"Right," I said, feeling like an idiot for asking. Because of course he had. He was Ryder Cross. And despite the progress we'd made, apparently we weren't quite at small talk level yet. "Really interesting stuff we've been reading about. England and beheadings and all."

But his eyes were already back on Amy.

"Listen," he said. "I know you've been busy lately, but I was thinking maybe we could get together this weekend. There's an Iranian film that just came out, and I thought we could go see it together."

"Um . . . well." Amy looked at me again, as if I could somehow help her out of this one.

When I just shrugged, her eyes began searching elsewhere, and after a second she grabbed my arm.

"I have to pee," she announced. "Be right back."

And she promptly began dragging me toward the bathroom, leaving Ryder with a look of pronounced confusion etched on his face.

"Well, that's one way to make him stop worshipping you," I said once we were standing in front of the row of sinks. "Talking about your bodily functions."

"He keeps asking me out," she said. "And he's just going to ask again if I tell him I'm busy this weekend."

"I know," I said. "We've gotta come up with another way to . . . Wait."

"What?"

"I have an idea. Avoiding him isn't going to work, right? You're too nice and he just keeps trying. So maybe when you do have to talk to him, you could do things like what you just did."

"Talk about my bodily functions?"

"Among other things," I said. "Be weird. Be all the things he can't stand."

"I don't know what he can't stand," she said.

"Well . . . I know he doesn't like people who are flaky. Or people who are late for things. He hates when people are irresponsible and he's kind of a snob, so pop culture references get on his nerves."

"So . . . I should act like you?" she offered.

"Hey now."

"I'm kidding." She chewed on her bottom lip. "But . . . I don't know. I don't want to be rude."

"Yes," I said. "You do. For once in your life you do."

"Sonny . . ."

"It won't kill you," I assured her. "Come on. Please. Just be a little weird. And not cute, adorable weird. He'd probably be into that."

"I don't —"

"No time," I said. "Let's go."

I dragged her back out of the bathroom. As expected, Ryder was still waiting right where we'd left him. He smiled at Amy.

"Everything okay?" he asked.

"Oh, ye —" She stopped, glanced at me, and then cleared her throat. "No. I'm a little bloated, so . . ."

Ryder raised an eyebrow. "Okay . . . anyway. So about that date?"

"Can't," Amy said. "I, uh . . . There's a *Real Housewives* marathon on this weekend. I have to watch it."

"You watch reality TV?" As expected, he appeared to be disgusted by this revelation.

"She's obsessed," I said, chiming in. "Deeply obsessed. She's seen every season of *The Real World*, too. Even the old ones that came on back in the nineties."

Amy nodded. "Yep. So I'll be busy this weekend."

"Can't you record it?" Ryder asked. "The marathon?"

"I . . . um . . . No. I can't. I have to, uh, live-tweet it." But she couldn't resist adding, "Sorry."

"That's okay. Maybe another time. Next Saturday —"

"Amy, don't you need to get to class?" I asked. "The bell's about to ring. You'll be late. Again."

"Huh? Oh." She nodded. "Right. Late. I'm always late. Late Amy. That's what my teachers call me, so . . . Okay. Bye."

She took off down the hallway. Ryder frowned after her, then he turned to me. "That was . . . different. Is she okay?"

"What? No. She's always like that," I lied.

"She is?" Ryder looked skeptical. "That didn't seem like the Amy I know."

"You don't know her as well as you think."

"Hmm."

"Come on," I said, eager to change the subject. "We should get to class, too."

Ryder nodded and he fell into step with me as we headed for Mr. Buckley's classroom. Despite my failed attempt before, I tried to start a conversation with him again. I skipped the small talk, though, and went straight for the big guns.

"So how's your dad's campaign going?"

Ryder shrugged. "No idea. Why?"

"I'm just curious. Tuesday is election day, and I know he's running for reelection." But since Senator Cross didn't represent our region, I realized that might have been a wee bit strange, so I added, "Amy told me."

"My dad and I aren't exactly speaking right now. And I don't see that changing anytime soon."

"Oh. I'm sorry to hear that. I know his campaign is kind of a big deal. I just thought you might be going to DC to help him with it."

"I'm sure you and everyone else in this school would love that," he said as we entered the classroom and took our seats.

"No," I said quickly. "That's not what I meant. I was just wondering."

"Well, to answer your question, no. I don't particularly want him to win, so . . ."

"That's pretty harsh," I said, surprised. I knew what his dad had done, but I'd also done some research on Senator Cross. He was, without question, a shitty husband, but by all accounts, he was a good politician. He'd been the champion of several progressive bills over the past few years, and he seemed to be doing a lot to help the poor and middle class in Maryland.

Hot supermodel mistress aside, I would've voted for the guy.

"Nothing he doesn't deserve," Ryder said.

I wasn't sure how to respond to that, not when I technically wasn't supposed to know the details of the falling-out with his dad. I was saved the trouble, however, when the bell rang and class was underway.

An hour and a half later, I caught up with Amy as she left her first block class.

"If it isn't Late Amy," I teased. "You still bloated? Also, wow, that sounds like a pregnancy joke."

"Ugh." She groaned. "I didn't know what to say. That was so awful."

"No, it wasn't," I told her. We were weaving our way through the crowded hallway. For a school that barely had four hundred students, Hamilton High could get surprisingly congested. "Actually, you were perfect. Just do that every time you see Ryder, and he'll be over you in no time."

"But I don't want to do that," Amy said. "It was so awkward."

"It was supposed to be." I looped my arm through hers. "Don't worry. It'll be fine. Just a few more encounters with weird, flaky Amy and this thing will all be done."

Amy looked like she was about to protest, but then I realized something.

"Crap. I left my toothbrush in your bathroom this morning. You don't think your parents will go in there, right? And notice?"

"Notice your toothbrush?" Amy shook her head. "I doubt it. They have no reason to go in there. They have their own bathroom."

"Good," I said, relieved, as we slid into our seats in Mrs. Perkins's English class. "I've been getting sloppy lately. I left my shoes on the mat the other night, and two days ago I forgot to lock the front door on my way out."

"Well," Amy said, pulling out her textbook, "they haven't said anything to me about any of those things."

"Yeah. I know. I'm just paranoid."

"If you're really that worried about it, we could just tell them," she suggested. "They won't care that you're staying, Sonny. I've told you. If you just tell them you were kicked out —"

I shook my head. "No. It'll be too complicated. They'll want to talk to my mom and . . . just no. It's better if we keep things the way they are."

Amy sighed. "Okay," she said. "I still don't see what the problem is, but it's your choice. A few weeks ago I would've said there's no way we could keep it from my parents for this long, but clearly that's not the case."

"I am a magnificent sneak," I said. "The Russians should hire me as a spy. In fact, for all you know, maybe they already have."

"You *just* told me like three things that could've given you away," Amy pointed out.

"But they didn't!" I declared.

Amy shook her head, giggling.

"I should stop worrying about it, though," I said as Mrs. Perkins entered the room and began scribbling instructions on the whiteboard. "Your parents figuring things out, I mean. It's been a few weeks. If they were going to find out I was living with you, they would have by now. I'm probably in the clear."

10

"We know Sonny's been living here."

So maybe I'd spoken too soon.

It was the next day, Saturday, which meant I'd been secretly living in the Rushes' house for almost a month. I'd really thought I was in the clear, but when Mr. Rush had asked Amy and me to come talk to him and Mrs. Rush in the living room, I knew we were busted.

"What . . . what are you talking about?" Amy squeaked. Poor thing. The guilt was all over her pretty little face. She had the worst poker face I'd ever seen.

"We've known for a while," Mr. Rush said. "Contrary to popular belief, my wife and I aren't totally oblivious."

"You've left a few clues," Mrs. Rush pointed out. "And we've heard you sneaking in at night. You're not exactly the quietest person, Sonny."

"We also seemed to be running out of food faster than usual," Mr. Rush added.

"Why didn't you say anything before?" I asked. "If you've known . . ."

"We were hoping you'd come to us with whatever was going on when you were ready," Mr. Rush said. "But it was becoming clear that might not happen anytime soon."

I leaned back against the couch cushion, pulling my socked feet up and hugging my knees to my chest. I was holding down the wave of panic rising in my stomach.

"So now we have some questions of our own," Mr. Rush continued.

"Yes," Mrs. Rush agreed. "Like, Sonny, *why* have you been living here for the past few weeks? You know you're always welcome here, but you secretly moving in is something else entirely. We're concerned and we'd like to know what's going on under our own roof."

"I . . . I . . ." I swallowed. *Come on, Sonny. You got this. You're good at this. Just lie. Lie, lie, lie.* "I don't know. It's nothing, really. Home is just boring, so . . ." Damn it. Not my best work. But my heart was racing and my palms were all sweaty. "I'll just go home. It's fine."

But the idea of going back to my house made the panic even worse.

I started to stand up, but Amy caught my arm.

"No," she said. "Tell them, Sonny."

Mr. Rush raised an eyebrow while his wife frowned with confusion. "Tell us what?" she asked.

But I'd lost my words. I could always come up with an answer. I had a lie ready for anything. And I'd lied about this, about my mom, a thousand times over the years. It should've been easy. But this lie was a little bigger — it involved more people with more potential to poke holes in whatever I said — and I felt suddenly stuck.

I couldn't think of a lie to tell. Not one that wouldn't involve more questions. I needed a second to think.

Luckily, Amy bought me a little time.

"She was kicked out," she told her parents. "She didn't want to tell you, but her mom kicked her out. So she's been staying here."

"What?" Mr. Rush said. "Why would she kick you out, Sonny?"

I stared at my feet, the heat of embarrassment creeping up my neck. I couldn't see their faces, and I hoped they couldn't see mine as I shoved out the only lie I could think of.

"Pot," I muttered.

"Really?" Amy whispered. "You didn't tell me that part."

Amy had been begging, in her indirect sort of way, for details of my ejection from my mother's home for weeks. I'd always changed the subject or said I didn't want to talk about it or pretended I hadn't heard her ask. The less I talked about my mom, the better.

"Marijuana?" Mrs. Rush said. "That . . . doesn't sound like you, Sonny."

"No," Mr. Rush agreed. "It doesn't."

"I . . . I only used it once," I managed. "But my mom found out, and . . ."

"And she kicked you out," Mr. Rush finished the sentence for me. "Well, I wouldn't be thrilled if I were her either, but that seems like a bit of an overreaction."

"That's why she's been staying here," Amy said. "I'm sorry we didn't tell you two sooner. But can she keep staying here? Please?"

"Sonny's always welcome," Mrs. Rush said. "But I think we should speak to her mother about —"

"No." My head shot up. "No, that's a bad idea."

"It's been weeks since she kicked you out," Mr. Rush said. "Surely she's realized what an overreaction this is."

"We should talk to her. Try to convince her . . . ," Mrs. Rush began.

But I was shaking my head so hard it hurt. "No," I said again. "I've . . . I've tried. She's really strict about this stuff. She's not having it."

"Does she at least know where you are?" Mrs. Rush asked.

I nodded. "Yeah. I mean, where else would I be?"

Amy squeezed my hand.

"We should still call her," Mr. Rush said. "Just so she knows for sure that you're safe and —"

"I'll do it," I said quickly.

"Are you sure?" Mrs. Rush asked. "She might want to speak to us about —"

"If she does, I'll tell you," I said. "Just let me do it. Please. That is, if you're going to let me stay here?"

Amy's parents glanced at each other, then back at me.

"Sonny, of course you can stay here," Mrs. Rush said. "In fact, you should've told us sooner. We wouldn't have been upset."

"That said, we don't condone illegal substances in this house either," Mr. Rush said. "So if you are going to continue staying here, no pot."

"No problem," I said.

Truth be told, I'd never smoked pot in my life. Not for any

94

moral or ethical reason (clearly my morals were all over the place), but I just hadn't had much of an interest. I liked to be able to think quick on my feet. All the better for lying, my dear. A drug that slowed down the brain, even just for a little bit? No thanks.

"You have the same curfew as Amy, then," Mrs. Rush said. "All the same rules."

"And you have to call your mother. Right after we finish up here," Mr. Rush said. "I know you think she knows where you are, but I'd rather not leave her guessing. She still cares about you. She'll want to know you're safe."

I nodded.

But I wasn't so sure he was right.

Mrs. Rush got to her feet. "I better go get the guest room set up, then."

"That's okay," I said. "I don't mind staying in Amy's room."

"Are you sure?" Mrs. Rush asked. "It's got to be a little crowded in there for the both of you. A slumber party is one thing, but full-time . . ."

"We don't mind sharing," Amy assured her.

"Well, I'm at least going to clear the closet so she can hang her clothes up," Mrs. Rush said. "Good lord, Sonny. Have you been living out of a duffel bag this whole time?"

I nodded.

She shook her head and gave me a hug, as if this was the saddest thing she'd ever heard. Once she let go, she headed for the stairs. "Amy, honey, why don't you go put some fresh towels for both of you in the bathroom."

"Okay." Amy stood up, gave me a fleeting glance, then followed her mother up the stairs.

Which left only Mr. Rush and me.

There was a long silence at first, and it was so painfully awkward that I had to say something or my brain might explode.

"Thank you for letting me stay."

"Don't even mention it," he said. "You and Amy have been best friends for how long? We might as well make you living here official." He smiled, but there was a sadness in it. "Sonny, are you sure you don't want me to call your mother?"

"I'll do it," I said. "I'll tell her where I am."

He nodded. "But if you do need to talk about something, don't hesitate to come to Mrs. Rush or me. I know that probably goes without saying, but . . ."

"Thank you," I said. "I will."

"Good." He stood up. "I'm going to go get dinner started. Call your mother, okay?"

"Yes, sir."

I still had Amy's cell phone, and when Mr. Rush left the room, I pulled it out. I stared at the keypad for a long time before dialing the familiar number. One I'd dialed over and over and over again in the past few weeks.

"Sorry, but the number you have dialed is disconnected or is no longer in service."

I hung up and put the phone away, blinking back tears.

"The closet and the dresser are empty," Mrs. Rush announced as she made her way back down the stairs. "They're all yours."

"Thank you." I stood up. "I'll go put my clothes away."

"Did you call your mother?" she asked.

I nodded. "Yeah. She said she's not ready for me to come home yet, but she's glad I'm okay. She says thanks for letting me stay."

Mrs. Rush smiled and touched my shoulder. "Good," she said. "Let me know if you need anything, okay?"

"I will. Thank you."

I couldn't say it enough. Thank you for letting me stay. Thank you for not asking more questions. It was more than I deserved. More than most people would give their daughter's delinquent best friend.

I wasn't actually a delinquent, but based on the lies I'd just told, they thought I was. But still, they were letting me live here. That's just the kind of people the Rushes were.

I went up to Amy's room and grabbed my bag. I took it to the guest room and started tossing my wrinkled clothes into drawers and putting the nicer things (i.e., my one nice sweater) on hangers.

I was almost done when Amy's phone buzzed in my back pocket. I looked at the screen and saw that it was a text from Ryder.

My dad knows I know about the model and now he won't stop calling. I never answer. He won't take the hint.

I was supposed to respond with something obnoxious or bizarre. Something to make him question why he'd ever like Amy. That was why I had the phone, after all. But just then, with my

mother's silence ringing in my ears, I couldn't hold back the words
I really wanted to say to him.

Answer him. He might be a dick, but at least he wants
to talk to you.

It only took Ryder a second to respond.

That wasn't the reply I expected. Is everything okay?

Not for the first time, I found it was easier to be honest in text
form than in real life.

Not really.

Is it your mom?

Yes.

*Do you want to talk about it? I'm here to listen. You've
listened to me complain plenty about my parents.*

Actually, I'd rather talk about anything but that right now.

We can do that, too.

We shouldn't have. I shouldn't have.
But we did.

*　　*　　*

The next day, my hunt for employment finally paid off.

I got an e-mail from the bookstore at the mall, inviting me for an interview.

I sat down with the manager after school on Monday, but only for a few minutes. I got the sense they would hire pretty much anyone.

"It's retail," the manager, Sheila, said. "We get pretty busy around the holidays."

"So this would just be seasonal?" I asked, a little disappointed. Any job would do, but I was going to need one well past the end of the year.

"Yes," Sheila said. "But there's always potential for you to be hired on in the new year, too."

"Potential is good."

"So you're in?"

"Definitely."

While I felt a little guilty about mooching off the Rushes, at least now I'd have money to pay for my gas and lunch without having to lie or borrow from Amy. I could also start saving up for new clothes, since I hadn't packed many winter outfits when I left my house.

"Also," Amy said when I told her the good news that night, "you can get me a discount on books."

"Because you don't have enough of those," I said, gesturing to the overflowing bookcase next to her desk. "Have you even read all of those? Or even half?"

"It's more about the collection," she said.

I rolled my eyes. "One day, you're going to be on a reality TV show, buried under your collection and needing a serious mental health intervention."

"And you'll be the concerned friend who, instead of finding me the help I need, decides to get me on TV."

"Hey, girl. I need my close-up, too."

We both burst into giggles, for once not worried about being too loud or waking her parents. I have to admit, it was nice to be done with the sneaking around. Between that and the new job, a huge weight had been lifted off my shoulders.

Unfortunately, there were still a couple more I couldn't seem to shake.

11

I had this recurring nightmare that started when I was eleven, when things with my mom began going south.

Or more south than they'd already been.

The dream began in my bedroom back home. I was doing something — homework or reading, I was never really sure — when I heard the front door slam. From there, it was always the same. I'd get up and call out to my mom, but there would only be silence. Thick, unnatural silence. Even the birds outside my window seemed muted all of a sudden. So I'd leave my bedroom and find that the house was nearly pitch-black. The sun, which had been shining through my bedroom window, vanished. I'd keep calling for my mom and hunting for a light switch, but they weren't where they were supposed to be. And neither was the furniture. I'd reach to put my hand on the counter or go to sit on a chair and find nothing there. Eventually, I'd go to my mom's room, sure she'd be there. Sure she'd be able to fix whatever had happened to our house.

But the door to her room was like the entrance to a black hole. The darkness was thicker. Darker than black. I screamed for Mom, but the hole swallowed it up.

That was when I'd wake up, shaking and desperate for a sound, any sound, just to know I wasn't alone.

Sometimes I'd go months without having the dream, and sometimes it happened every other night.

It had been a while this time. I guess Amy's snores had chased any nightmares of silence away. But the day after I got my new job, the nightmare came again.

I woke up with another scream on my lips, and I had to bite it back. The room was so dark that, for a minute, I couldn't remember where I was. Next to me, Amy snored, loud and long. It was a small comfort, but after a few seconds of deep breaths and calming thoughts, I still couldn't relax, let alone get back to sleep.

"Amy," I whispered, nudging her arm and feeling only a little guilty about disrupting her beauty sleep. "Hey, Amy."

Apparently, I wasn't interrupting anything tonight because all she did was snort and roll away from me.

Don't be stupid, I thought. *You're not alone. She's right there, even if she can't hear you. Go back to sleep, Sonny.*

But the room seemed too dark, and the idea of closing my eyes, of adding another layer of blackness, made my heart thump uncomfortably in my chest.

"Screw it," I mumbled, throwing the blankets off of me. I climbed over Amy, grabbed her cell phone from the dresser, and tiptoed out of the room.

The minute the light in the rec room flickered on, it was instantly easier to breathe. Like the darkness had actually been pressing down on me, crushing my chest. I walked over to the couch and flopped down on my back, Amy's phone still in my hand. One of the benefits of borrowing her phone while mine was out of commission: She had a smartphone. Which meant games. I'd already downloaded a few free ones, along with some humorous, inappropriate text tones that Amy hadn't found quite as funny as I had.

But even silly phone games with their bright colors and funny sounds couldn't chase away the lingering nightmare. Or the knowledge that, even though the rec room was bright and familiar, I was still alone in here.

I can't explain what I did next. It was stupid and self-destructive and wrong on many, many levels I didn't care to think about. But I was lonely, and I needed to talk to someone. Anyone would have done, really. But there was only one person I knew might be awake at one in the morning on a school night. Which just so happened to be the first Tuesday in November. Well, I guess technically it was Wednesday now. Whatever.

So did your dad win the election?

Ryder had texted a few times in the past couple of days, but I'd either not responded or just replied with emojis that made no sense in the context of his comment or question. And when he sent back a question mark, I didn't reply. How was that for flaky? Honestly, it was probably pretty good progress on the make-him-think-Amy-was-a-weirdo front, but here I was.

Messing it all up again.

Just as I'd expected, he was awake, and it only took him a second to text me back.

He did. Unfortunately.

Not so unfortunate for his constituents, though. I looked him up. He seems to be doing some good things.

Sure. When he's not doing the model.

Before I could respond, Ryder sent another message.

He still wants me to come visit for Thanksgiving.

Will you?

Of course not.

But don't you want to visit DC? I know you miss it.

I don't think I do anymore. I'm pretty sick of DC.

I frowned. I knew things were bad with his dad, but this was a sharp turnaround for the guy who'd compared every little detail of Hamilton to the infinitely superior Washington, DC, since he'd arrived. But, thinking about it, I had seen far fewer snarky Facebook statuses since he'd learned the truth about his dad. Still, DC was his home. It was where he'd grown up. It was where his old friends were, even if they had drifted apart some. I would have expected him to take any opportunity to visit, even if for only a day or two.

He didn't seem eager to talk about that, though, because he sent another message straightaway.

I know it's only been a week, but I've missed these late-night chats.

Yeah. Me, too. I've been keeping my insomnia mostly at bay. But I couldn't sleep tonight. Nightmare.

What about?

It wouldn't make any sense if I explained it.

Try me.

I almost didn't reply. I almost ended the conversation right there. I should have.

I'd never told anyone about my nightmare. Not even Amy. I'd called her in the middle of the night a few times, panicked and desperate to hear someone's voice, but I'd always glossed over what the dream was about. I'd just say something like, "Something bad happened to my mom" or "I was trapped in a dark house." I never went into details. I didn't want to open that door. To expose that dark, broken place inside of me where all the bad things lived.

But for some reason, I wanted to tell Ryder. Maybe because — and yes, I knew this was sick — he wouldn't know it was me. There was security in knowing he'd think it was Amy's nightmare. Amy's dark, broken place.

I was still freaked out and didn't want to cut off the contact with another person just yet, so I found myself writing out the dream, taking up several long texts to do so. When I hit SEND on the last one, the one that explained my mother's bedroom, I felt a pang of regret.

Too much, I thought. *Too honest. Too close.*

I didn't think he'd reply. Maybe this would help him get over Amy once and for all.

But then:

Things really are bad with your mom, aren't they?

Yeah.

I'm sorry about the nightmare. But they say if you talk about it, you won't dream it again.

Does that count with texting?

I guess you'll find out.

I smiled. Actually, I did feel a little better having it off my chest. The shaking had stopped and my heartbeat had slowed down. I might even manage to fall back to sleep if I tried to.

But right now, for better or worse (definitely worse), I wanted to keep talking to him.

Thanks for letting me share.

Of course. I just wish I was there with you.

I felt a mischievous smile tugging at my lips as I typed my response.

Oh, yeah? Why? What would you do if you were here?

For a minute, he didn't respond, and I was worried I might have scared him off. I should've known better, though. At the end of the day, he was still a guy.

Are we really doing this?

Do you WANT to do this?

I do, but I have no idea how. I've never done it before.

You never sent sexy texts to Eugenia?

No. Have you?

No, I have never sexted with Eugenia.

You're hilarious.

I know.

Pause.

*If I were there, I would lie on the bed next to you and
pull you into my arms.*

I'm actually on a couch right now.

Are you TRYING to make this difficult for me?

No. Sorry. Continue.

Then I would . . . kiss your neck?

I snorted.

You seem unsure about that.

*You make me nervous. I'd be nervous if I were there
with you.*

I felt my heart pound harder. There was something so sweet
about him saying that. About the snobby, confident Ryder admitting he'd be nervous if we were alone together.

I'd be nervous, too.

Here's another truth: I was a virgin. Not only that, but in
seventeen years, I'd only been kissed one time, by Davy Jennings
at the ninth-grade homecoming dance. His breath tasted like
root beer and it had been enough to kill our fledgling romance.

Most of what I knew about sex came from copious amounts of television, unintentionally hilarious *Cosmo* articles, and my inter-rogation of Amy, who had swiped her V-card at summer camp last year.

That's something I doubted anyone would expect. That out of the two of us, I was the virgin with virtually no sexual experience while goody-goody Amy was not.

But right now, trying to think of things to say to Ryder, I found myself wishing I had more experience to pull from. He was right. This was difficult.

It's your turn.

BRB. Googling how to do this.

LOL! So you give me a hard time, but you don't know what you're doing either.

OK, some of these sexting examples are hilarious. So that was no help.

We don't have to do this if you don't want to.

No. Now I am determined to type at least one sexy thing, damn it.

I took a deep breath and closed my eyes. I had to be overthink-ing this. I went to my imagination, where Ryder was lying next to

me. Where he'd just nervously kissed my neck. What next? I tried
to let the scene play out.

I'd slide my hand down your chest. Slowly.

I don't know why, but I felt like everything sounded a little
sexier when you added *slowly*.
I held my breath, my face scorching red, as I waited for Ryder
to respond.

I'd reach for the hem of your nightgown . . .

Nightgown? You think I sleep in a nightgown? What
century is this?

I don't know what girls sleep in.

Well, right now I'm in just a baggy T-shirt and
underwear.

Wow. That's actually hotter than a nightgown.

We went on like this for about an hour, fumbling our way
through texts that were usually more awkward and funny than
seductive. But I was left giggling and feeling fluttery nonetheless.

We'll get better at this eventually.

It wasn't until I read that message from Ryder, though, that the dirty feeling began to sink in. Not fun, I've-been-sending-sexy-texts dirty either. The gross, I-need-a-shower dirty that came with suddenly remembering that all those messages, all those things he'd imagined us doing, had been for Amy. Every virtual kiss and touch, he'd imagined doing to my best friend. He'd pictured her hands, her long, thin body. Her dark, curly hair. Her face. Her lips.

And he thought we'd get better at it. That we'd do it again.

I thought I was going to be sick.

I didn't write back after that. I didn't say good-bye or good night. Instead, I went through and deleted every single text we'd sent over the past hour, knowing Amy would kill me (and have every right to) if she saw those messages.

When I crept back into Amy's room, she was still snoring. I crawled over to my side of the bed and pulled the covers over my head, wishing I could hide from the guilt and the shame of what I'd just done.

12

The Ardmores had never been big on Thanksgiving. Or any holiday that involved gathering, really.

My dad wasn't close to his parents. I'd only met them once, when I was five, and now all I knew about them was that they lived in Florida somewhere. My maternal grandmother had passed away a few months after I was born, and my grandfather had died when I was nine. He might have left his house to his only child, my mom, but before that, he'd been the cold, unfriendly sort. Mom never saw the point of making a fuss over a dinner for three people, and after my dad was arrested, I guess it seemed even more pointless.

The Rushes, on the other hand, loved Thanksgiving.

There were a few years a while back where Amy's parents weren't home much. They jetted from one business trip to another, and Amy spent most of the time at her grandmother's. But even then, when the family seemed to be drifting apart, Mr. and Mrs. Rush always came home for Thanksgiving. They made a big deal out of it: a huge turkey, the best stuffing you'd ever tasted, and enough side dishes to feed an army of hungry soldiers. They also invited everyone they knew: their extended family, their friends, their kids' friends. Which meant I got to be a part of the annual feast. It was always a highlight of my year, and it was always hard to go home, full and happy, to a dark, quiet house.

This year was different, though. This year I was able to experience the Thanksgiving festivities from the time I woke up in the morning until I went to bed that night.

I was incredibly excited about this, and even Mrs. Rush's request to invite my mom couldn't bring me down.

"There will be more than enough food. I know things are rough with you two right now, but she's always invited to Thanksgiving dinner and we'd be here to serve as a buffer. It might be good for both of you," Mrs. Rush said as I helped her clean the house that morning.

"I'll see," I said. "But I think she'll probably have to work today. You know how retail is these days. . . ."

Mrs. Rush shook her head. "Forcing people to work on Thanksgiving is just terrible."

I nodded, relieved when there were no follow-up questions.

After that, the day was fabulous. Good food, lots of people, the Macy's Thanksgiving Day Parade on in the background. The Rushes celebrated Thanksgiving all day.

And into the next morning, too.

Because the Rushes not only loved Thanksgiving, they also loved Black Friday.

"I don't understand," I told Amy as we stood on the sidewalk outside of Tech Plus, an electronics store (the only non-grocery store in Hamilton) at four a.m. I had to work at the bookstore later that afternoon and knew I was gonna regret being up this early.

113

"You're loaded. Isn't Black Friday meant for poor people like me? So you all can watch us fight to the death, Hunger Games style, over a half-price iPod?"

"We're not loaded," Amy said.

"Excuse me. What kind of car do you drive?"

"A Lexus."

"And your brother?"

She sighed. "A Porsche."

"I rest my case."

She shrugged. "I guess my parents like deals."

At that moment, Mr. and Mrs. Rush were in Oak Hill, waiting outside the mall to do some hardcore Christmas shopping. As much as I hated being awake before seven (okay, let's be real, I hated being up before noon if I could help it), I couldn't complain much. Amy and I did have the easiest of the Black Friday tasks. We just had to run in, grab the newest video game console, and get out.

"Your brother better know I was a part of this gift," I told her. "I may not be contributing financially, but it is a testament to my affection for him that I got my ass out of bed for this."

"And here I thought it was so I wouldn't be fighting the crowds alone," Amy said.

"Nah. Why would I ever do anything for you?"

She giggled, then let out a huge yawn. "What time does the store open again?"

"Five."

She whimpered.

"I know," I said, patting her on the back. "It's cruel to have sales start so early right after everyone's loaded themselves with sleepy turkey chemicals."

To make matters worse, it was also cold. We were bundled up in our sweaters and coats, but they didn't do much to deflect the occasional gust of wind that blew into our faces. The amazing part about this was that Amy's hair still looked flawless. Four a.m., cold and windy morning, and she still looked like a model with a classy, curly updo.

I wasn't the only one who noticed either.

"Oh my God. You *have* to tell me how you did that."

Amy and I both turned when we heard the voice behind us. There was a girl there, drinking Starbucks. She couldn't have been much older than us, and she looked a little familiar. Probably a Hamilton High grad. She was wearing some amazing black boots over multicolored leggings that I only wished I could pull off.

"Sorry?" Amy said.

"Your hair," the girl said. "You have to tell me how you did that."

It was only then that I noticed her own curls. Brown corkscrews, even tighter than mine or Amy's. They were a little frizzy because of the wind, but they still looked ten times better than mine. Damn it.

"Oh," Amy said, patting her hair self-consciously. "It's really easy. You just need a hair tie and a few bobby pins."

"And by 'easy,' she means impossible for us commoners," I said.

"Right?" The girl laughed. "Bobby pins and hair ties just leave me with a rat's nest on top of my head."

"It's really not that hard. You just —"

"Chloe!"

Two more people were coming our way: a girl with straight black hair and a cute boy I recognized as Cash Sterling, a former player on the Hamilton High soccer team. (Soccer was the only sport I kept up with. Mostly because it was an excuse to stare at boys with really nice legs.)

"Sorry we're late," Cash said to the curly-haired girl, Chloe.

"You're not. The store hasn't opened yet."

"I know," Cash said. "But according to Lissa, we were supposed to be here by four. So I was told to apologize for making her late."

Lissa, meanwhile, was too busy digging in her purse to argue with Cash. "I have a map," she said. "I drew it last night. I figured out the best route to get back to the TVs when the doors open."

"Oh dear God," Chloe moaned. "We have to do this?"

"If I have to do Black Friday," Lissa said, "I'm doing it efficiently." She sighed. "Why does my stupid brother want a TV for a wedding present? Why couldn't he just ask for a blender like everyone else?"

"He's gonna need a TV to drown Jenna out," Cash said. "I still can't believe they're getting married."

"I just can't believe he's getting married before I had a chance to hook up with him."

"Ew, Chloe. I can't deal with you lusting after my brother right now. I'm already freaking out over the crowd here. Ugh. It's gonna be awful in there. Here. Let's study the map."

Amy and I glanced at each other, then turned around, clearly no longer a part of this conversation.

"We should've made a map," Amy whispered.

"I don't think we're neurotic enough for that," I whispered back.

The minutes lurched by as the line got longer and longer on the sidewalk behind us. There was no doubt about it — when those doors opened, we were in for a freaking stampede.

"Ready?" Amy asked when there was only a minute to go.

"Why do I feel like I'm about to go to war?" I asked.

But she didn't have time to answer because right then the front doors of Tech Plus swung open.

And everyone charged forward.

I ran, tripping over my own feet in order to avoid being trampled. With my relatively short legs, this was not easy. But after a lot of pushing and shoving and cursing at complete strangers, I made it inside the doors. It was still a madhouse, but people spread out, running for the items they'd come to buy.

"Okay, where are the game consoles, Amy?"

But when I turned to look at her, Amy wasn't there. She wasn't anywhere near me.

"Shit," I muttered, realizing too late that we'd been separated by the crowd. Finding her in this chaos, especially when I wasn't all that familiar with the layout of Tech Plus, was going to be impossible.

Maybe packing a map wasn't as neurotic as I'd thought.

I wove my way through the crowd, hoping to spot a tall, curly head somewhere. A few times, I popped up on my tiptoes so I could look over the heads of the people around me. Unfortunately, with my neck craned and my balance compromised, I ended up falling flat on my ass in front of an iPod display.

"I'm so sorry. Are you okay?"

I looked up at the person who'd just slammed into me and was met with two very surprised green eyes.

"Sonny," Ryder said. "I didn't recognize you."

"I'm sure I look different from this angle," I said. "Help a girl up?"

"Sorry." He took my hand and pulled me to my feet. I wanted to relish that moment of having his hand in mine, but it was over so fast I barely got to enjoy it. "Are you all right?"

"I'm fine. Just surprised to find you here."

Lie.

Confession Time: Ryder, not Amy or Wesley, was the reason I was at Tech Plus that morning.

It had been a couple of weeks since our little texting tryst (which still made me feel icky when I thought about it) and Ryder had been sending messages almost every day since. I'd ignored most of them, knowing that responding was counterproductive. That last conversation had, apparently, given him the confidence to approach Amy in person again. Luckily, I was with Amy pretty much any time she wasn't in class, which meant I was able to shut down the conversation and hurry her away before she found out about the texting.

I knew I shouldn't risk giving him more encouragement to pursue Amy, no matter how temping it was to reply to his messages. We were making some progress in person, but not as quickly as I'd hoped, and texting was the only way I really got to talk to him.

I'd been holding on to my last shred of willpower, fighting my self-destructive urges, but Thanksgiving break meant not even seeing him at school, and when he sent a text about needing a new iPod, I couldn't help suggesting he go to Tech Plus on Black Friday. I knew Amy would be going, and it would make perfect sense for me to join her.

So here I was, in the middle of Black Friday madness, all so I could run into a guy who didn't even know he liked me.

"I'm surprised to find me here, too," he admitted. "But my iPod broke and Amy said this place would have them on sale, so . . . Hey, if you're here, is she?"

"Um, yeah. Somewhere. I've lost her."

And I sort of hoped she stayed lost. At least until Ryder and I had had a few minutes together.

Not that this was the most romantic setting, but I'd take what I could get.

"Oh. Do you think we should go look for her?"

"No, no. She had some shopping to do. I'm sure I'll find her soon." I cleared my throat. "So. A new iPod? What sort of music do you listen to?"

"If I told you, you'd probably call me a pretentious hipster."

"Yeah . . . probably. But I already do that."

He laughed. "At least you're honest."

Not something I heard often.

"So indie stuff no one else has heard of, then? Like Goats Vote for Melons, maybe?"

Ryder's eyes widened, shocked. "You know Goats Vote for Melons?"

"I've heard a song or two."

I'd checked out some of their stuff after Ryder had raved about them. As expected, it was pretty terrible for the most part. All acoustic, no catchy hook. Yes, I was part of the masses. I admit it. I loved bad pop music, especially if it was released in the nineties, and grunge, of course, but that was awesome. GVM just went way over my head.

They did have one decent love song, though, inexplicably titled "Of Lions and Robots," which I'd been listening to a lot lately.

"Well, I'm also trying to broaden my musical horizons."

"Oh, yeah?"

He nodded. "I've been exploring some other genres. Kind of getting into nineties grunge, actually."

The grin that split my face was almost painful. Grunge! He was broadening his musical horizons because of me! I wanted to squeal. To hug him. And then to make out with him, right here, in the middle of this crowded electronics store.

But I couldn't.

Because, in Ryder's mind, we were little more than acquaintances.

Sometimes I had to remind myself of that.

"Grunge is great," I said. "What albums have you tried? Anything you really like?"

He opened his mouth to respond, but his answer was drowned out by another voice.

"Sonny!"

I groaned, and then felt awful for it.

Amy had found us. She was coming up behind me, a box tucked under her arm. "There you are," she said. "I'm so sorry we got separated. I didn't mean to lose you. I looked —" She stopped midsentence when she noticed Ryder. "Oh. Hi."

"Hey, Amy," he said, his face totally lighting up.

And now I wanted to shake him.

Even if his continuing affection for her was sort of my fault.

"You play video games?" he asked, gesturing to the box under her arm.

"Huh? Oh. No. This is for my brother."

"Hey, speaking of shopping," I said, my voice louder than I'd intended. "You should probably get that iPod, Ryder. You don't want them all to be taken."

"Good point. I'll be right back."

He walked a few feet away, disappearing into a crowd of desperate people clambering to get their hands on Apple products.

I grabbed Amy's arm. "When he comes back, do something."

"Something like what?"

"I don't know. Something weird. Something he won't like."

"Sonny, you know I'm bad at this."

"You're not. You'd be a great actress if you tried."

"But I don't have a script here," she pointed out. "I don't know what to do. I don't know how to be weird."

"You're the only teenager with that problem." I glanced around, searching for inspiration, and found it standing a few feet away.

There was a guy — blond, early twenties, built like a Ken doll — on the other side of the aisle. And he was totally trying to catch Amy's eye. "Perfect," I said.

"What?"

I jerked my head toward the stranger. "Him."

"What about him?"

"When Ryder comes back, go flirt with him. Right in front of Ryder," I whispered. "It'll make him think you're super flaky and kind of mean."

"Sonny, I don't want to do that," Amy whispered back. "That's too much. It's cruel to Ryder and to that guy."

"Please. You'll be making the other guy's day. Plus, he's cute. So it could be worse."

"But —"

"Here he comes. Get ready."

"I don't —"

"Got the iPod," Ryder announced as he moved toward us. "Some guy with a mullet tried to take it right out of my hands, but I managed to hold on to it."

"Glad you survived," I said.

"Me, too." He glanced over at Amy, as if waiting for her to say something.

And I elbowed her. Hard.

She let out a tiny squeak. "I, um . . ." She looked at me, her eyes desperate.

Go, I thought, staring back at her. *Just do it already.*

Amy turned to Ryder, a forced smile on her pretty pink lips. "Just a second," she said. Then she walked over to the Ken doll, who was checking out some tablets now, just down the aisle. His face brightened when he saw Amy approaching. And even though her greeting of "Hey . . . you" was super awkward, he didn't stop smiling.

"Hi," Ken Doll said.

The rest of their conversation was drowned out by a pack of women nearby, shouting at a Tech Plus employee about a guy who had taken one of their items before they could check out. But we could still see what was happening. The guy leaned toward Amy; she giggled, batted his arm. All the typical obvious flirting moves. Actually, it was probably more convincing this way, with Amy's inevitably embarrassing words on mute.

"Does she know that guy?" Ryder asked, frowning as Ken Doll took a step closer to Amy.

"No," I said. "That's just Amy. She's always flirting with someone."

"Oh."

We both watched the scene for a minute longer, then Ryder, face fallen, took a step back. "I should go pay," he said. "I'm pretty exhausted."

Even though I knew this was in both of our best interests, I felt bad for him. He thought he had a connection with Amy, and here she was, seemingly apathetic to that and hitting on other dudes right in front of him. It had to sting.

It was supposed to sting.

"It was nice running into you," I said. "Literally."

"Yeah. Sorry about that. Anyway . . . tell Amy I said good-bye."

123

"Okay."

He gave Amy one last glance before turning away, disappearing into the crowd.

As soon as he was gone, I ran over to Amy, interrupting her conversation with the Ken doll.

"Hey," I said. "He's gone. We're good."

"Excuse me?" Ken Doll asked.

"Hey. Sorry. She's seventeen, so this isn't gonna happen for you. Thanks for playing." I grabbed Amy's arm and dragged her away, toward the checkout counter. Though I made sure to take a different route than Ryder had so as not to risk crossing paths.

I fully expected Amy to scold me for how I'd talked to Ken Doll. To point out how rude it was.

But she didn't.

She didn't say anything.

In fact, she was silent the rest of the time we were in the store and the whole way back to her house.

Her parents still weren't home from their own Black Friday adventure by the time we pulled into the driveway. Amy grabbed the console and carried it into the house, me trailing behind her.

"Do you want me to help you wrap that?" I asked.

"No. I can do it," she mumbled.

"Okay . . . Hey, thanks for your help. I think it may have worked. Ryder seemed pretty upset."

"I didn't want to do that, Sonny," Amy said. She put the game console down on the coffee table. "It was awkward and embarrassing. And gross. You made me flirt with a guy I didn't know and didn't like."

"I know," I said. "I'm sorry, but —"

"I don't think you do know," she said. After a pause, she shook her head. "I'm tired. I'm gonna go take a nap."

She went upstairs to her room, and for once, I had the strong sense that I wasn't supposed to follow her.

She just needs her space, I thought. *She needs some time to herself, and it'll be fine.*

But I knew, deep down, that it was more than that. That, without me realizing it, I'd crossed a line that day.

And for the first time ever, in over a decade of visiting the Rushes' house, I didn't sleep in Amy's bedroom when I got home from work that night.

Or the night after that.

13

The next time I ran into Ryder outside of class wasn't the result of any scheming — for once. This time, on a chilly Saturday in the beginning of December, we both ended up at the Hamilton Public Library by sheer coincidence.

I was walking around the first floor, scanning the shelves, when a familiar voice called my name. I looked up and saw him sitting at one of the wooden tables in the corner, a legal pad and a huge, leather-bound book in front of him. He was wearing giant retro-style headphones. When he raised a hand to wave me over, my heart began pounding just a little too hard.

"Hey," I said, approaching the desk. "What are you doing here?"

"Research," he said, tugging his headphones down so they hung around his neck. "For the history essay, actually." He tapped the leather-bound book next to him. "Taking some notes on the French Revolution."

"Yay guillotines."

"A sentence that has oft been uttered."

I smiled and picked up the book. It was massive and heavy. "Are you actually reading this whole thing?" I asked. "You know, they have this new invention. It's called the Internet. It contains all of this and more — without the paper cuts."

"Paper cuts are like battle scars for the academic," he said, smiling back. "I guess I'm old school. I like to get my information from a real book, and I take my notes by hand."

"I, on the other hand, am best friends with *Wikipedia*."

"You know that site is woefully inaccurate a lot of the time, right? Because anyone can change the information."

"Yep. I'm the girl changing the information to make it woefully inaccurate."

"So half the high schoolers around the country have you to thank for their failing grades on research papers."

"Yes, sir. I'm practically a celebrity. Or, I would be if it wasn't anonymous."

He laughed, and even though there were still butterflies in my stomach, I felt relaxed. This felt natural. It felt like it had when we were instant messaging all those weeks ago. Like it did in our text messages, which, admittedly, I'd been sending again.

I hadn't slept in Amy's room since the Black Friday debacle, and the silence of the guest room had contributed to my insomnia. And to my recurring nightmare, which I'd had at least three times in the past two weeks. When I woke up, panicked and alone, it was easy to text him. To reach out and know someone else would answer.

I kept telling myself I would stop soon. Or that it wasn't actually detrimental for the plan — that maybe, somehow, it made Amy seem even flakier to be texting him when she was so weird in person.

127

I'd told myself so many lies, I didn't even know what to believe anymore. I just knew that I liked him. A lot.

And finally, after more than a month of inching closer and closer, we were having that same connection face-to-face.

"So what are you doing here?" he asked. "If you're such a denizen of the twenty-first century."

"Dropping off some books for Amy," I said. "My one day off from the bookstore job and I still find myself surrounded by books."

"Is that a bad thing?" Ryder asked.

"No. Just ironic. I actually applied for a job here, too. Unfortunately, I was informed that the last time the librarian hired teenagers to help her, they were caught making out between the shelves . . . multiple times."

"Interesting," Ryder said, tapping his chin with the end of his pen. "Who knew the Hamilton Library was such a scandalous place."

"Right? I should hang out here more often."

He nodded, and then we just stared at each other for this long, intense moment. At least, I thought it was intense. A little voice in my head was silently calling out to him: *See me. Figure out that it's been me all along.* Of course, that would be a disaster. It had been long enough that any hope of Ryder not being pissed that I'd been sort of, accidentally, and then deliberately catfishing him was out of the question.

I didn't want him to know that it was me sending all those messages.

I *did* want him to know that I was the girl he should be with.

If I hadn't been sabotaging myself with those text messages, maybe he would have by now.

"Hey," he said, after a second. "Would you want to get out of here? Go for a walk or something?"

I thought my brain might *explode*. He wanted to go somewhere *with me*. He wanted to take a walk *with me*. There was no Amy, no reason we should talk about school. It was just Ryder asking me to hang out with him.

Finally.

"Yeah," I said. "Sure. Let's go."

However, my exuberance faded pretty much as soon as we stepped out into the cold afternoon and Ryder said:

"I was hoping to talk to you about Amy."

Fuck.

Of course.

What was wrong with this boy? As far as he was concerned, Amy had been leading him on for over a month with IMs and texts, only to be a completely different person (literally) in real life.

I knew it was partly my fault for keeping up the correspondence, but come on. Was that really enough to keep him clinging to the idea of her? They hadn't even kissed. Hell, they hadn't even *touched*.

"Amy. Right." I shoved my hands deep into the pockets of my old, battered coat. "What about her?"

"It's just . . . I'm confused. Really confused." He kicked at a pebble on the sidewalk, and I watched as it rolled away from us, wishing I could follow it, away from this conversation. "Do you know why she avoids or ignores me when we're in the same room?"

I shrugged. "That sounds like a question for Amy."

"I've asked," he said. "A thousand times. I never get a straight answer."

It was true. Ever since our first bout of texting back at the start of November, Ryder had sent multiple messages, asking why I (read: Amy) didn't talk to him in person. Why they hadn't been on a date yet. Why things were so different in texts and IMs than they were in real life.

Most of the time, I ignored these messages. They'd come mid-conversation, and they'd serve as the end of the correspondence. Sometimes I'd respond with something vague — a simple *I don't know* or a blatantly untrue *I don't avoid you!*

I was hoping all the inconsistencies would scare him away from Amy.

But he just kept trying, in real life and via text message.

"You're her best friend," he said. "I figured if anyone would know what's going on with her, you would. And since you and I are friends now. . . ."

Friends.

He thought we were friends. A smile fluttered onto my lips, and I had to hurry to hide it. At least it hadn't all been in vain.

"Do you have any idea why she'd avoid me?" he asked. "Does she . . . does she even like me? No. No, I know she does. Of course she does. It's just that when we're together, she's so . . . different."

"I don't know," I said. "She seems pretty normal to me."

"She doesn't act like the Amy I know."

"Then maybe you don't know her that well."

130

"I do, though," he insisted. "Or I think I do. When we're texting or talking online, she's so . . . She's great. She's funny and smart and it's so easy to talk to her. The virtual Amy is incredible."

I got all shivery when he said that, and not just because it was cold.

"I just wish the Amy I saw in real life was more like that."

My hands balled into fists in my pockets. I wanted to tell him. I wanted to come clean so bad. That person he thought was "incredible," the person he'd fallen for, was standing right here.

Instead I said, "I'm sorry, Ryder. I don't know what to tell you."

"Why are you friends with her?" he asked.

I was taken aback. "Excuse me?"

"Why are you friends with her? What do you like about Amy?"

"Well . . ." I probably should have said something vague. Or something shallow. Something to reinforce this image of the flaky, bizarre Amy he couldn't figure out. But this, Amy, was one thing I couldn't lie about. "She's generous, for one thing. She'd do anything for the people she cares about. Hell, she's letting me live with her right now. She's always been there when I needed her."

He nodded. "What else?"

"She balances me out. I'm the loud, dramatic one and she's the quiet, practical one. She's my other half, in a lot of ways. People talk about soul mates in a romantic way, but I think if soul mates do exist, Amy would be mine. I think I'd be lost without her."

I had to shake off a pang of guilt. Since Thanksgiving break, I'd been telling myself things were fine between us. Me sleeping in the guest room was just a natural progression. We couldn't sleep in the same room forever, after all. Amy didn't act mad at me. She was still sweet and giggly and we still hung out. But something was different.

"I like the way you describe her," Ryder said. "Why doesn't she show that side when she's around me?"

I didn't answer. There were only so many times you could say "I don't know."

"Do you think it has something to do with her mom?"

"What?"

"She's told me a little about her mom."

It took me a minute to understand what he was talking about. Mrs. Rush was amazing — what would Amy's weirdness have to do with her? But then I remembered. I'd talked to him about *my* mom. Great. Another subject I'd rather not discuss.

"Oh. Yeah. Her mom."

"She said once that she thinks her mom might regret even having her," Ryder said.

"Yeah," I said. "Amy's mom is . . . Well, she's interesting. Complicated. That relationship has definitely screwed her up in a lot of ways."

"I know how she feels," he said.

I shook my head. "I don't think you do." Seeing an opening to change the subject, though, I added, "But, hey, congrats on your dad winning the election."

"Thanks," he said, voice flat. "It's official: My parents are getting a divorce."

That seemed like a good thing to me. At least things were being decided. But I couldn't say that because I wasn't supposed to know the backstory. So instead I replied, "I thought they were already divorced?"

Ryder shook his head. "My dad's been holding out. Asshole. He's still waiting a few months so it doesn't look like he was just waiting until he got elected. Even though that's precisely what he was doing."

"That sucks," I said.

"God. He's such a cliché. Cheating on my mom with some young model," Ryder said bitterly.

"Then as shitty as it is, maybe the divorce is for the best."

"He's still a dick. And I'm done talking to him."

Guess Ryder and his dad hadn't resolved their issues yet.

We were passing the elementary school, and without even saying a word, we both started walking toward the empty playground.

"What does your mom have to say about that? About you not talking to him?"

"I don't really talk to her about Dad," he admitted. "She gets upset about it. Mad, even. I can't blame her. She's a great person, and he screwed her over."

I wanted to point out that, not long ago, Ryder was (rightfully) upset that she'd dragged him all the way to Illinois without even asking how he felt first.

But Sonny wouldn't know that; Amy would. So I had to bite my tongue.

"What about you?" he asked as we made our way toward the swings. "What's your family drama?"

I shrugged and sat down on one of the swings. The leather was cold, even through my jeans. "It's pretty boring."

"That seems unlikely," he said, sitting on the swing beside mine. "You just said you're living with Amy. Doesn't sound too boring to me. Where are your parents?"

I'd already had to move the conversation away from my mother, and I wasn't eager to return to it. So instead, I blurted out something I hadn't talked about in years:

"My dad's in prison."

"Oh." Ryder looked startled, and I couldn't help but notice the way he moved away from me a little. Like he suddenly remembered that I wasn't the rich, beautiful girl he wanted.

I was poor white trash.

At least by his standards.

But, to my surprise, Ryder shifted again on his swing, his hands wrapped around the chains, and swiveled to face me. And he didn't look disgusted at all. "How long?"

"In and out since I was seven. But I haven't seen him in . . . I don't even remember the last time I saw him. My mom stopped taking me to visit after she divorced him, when I was still in elementary school."

"Does he ever try to write to you?" Ryder asked. "Or call?"

"No," I said. "Although I've moved since the last time I saw him. My granddad died and we moved into his old house. Plus, I don't have the same cell phone number. So I guess I don't really know. I just assumed he hadn't because my mom always told me what a deadbeat he was. Not that she's the most reliable . . ."

I shook my head, and before he could ask about my mother, I started talking again.

"I've thought about him some. I've considered writing him a few times, but I always talk myself out of it."

"Why?"

Ryder's green eyes were watching me, glued to me. Intent. It sent a shiver up my spine. And yet . . . it was easy. Telling him all this. Being honest about something I usually wasn't.

"I'm scared." It was something I'd never said out loud. "I'm scared he'll let me down . . . or that he won't want me. And I figure maybe it's easier if I just don't give him the chance."

"Sonny." He reached out and put a hand on my arm. It was like a bolt of electricity shot through me, starting where his palm touched my arm. Maybe he felt it, too, because he pulled back and wrapped his hand around the chain again. "Sorry," he said.

I wasn't sure if he was apologizing for touching me or for everything I'd said about my father.

"It's okay," I said, deciding I'd rather he apologized for the latter. "He probably is the deadbeat I've always imagined. Chances are I'm better off."

"Maybe."

We sat on the swings for a while, not talking. And that was okay, too. As much as I liked talking, or typing, to Ryder, it was kind of nice to just sit with him and watch as the sun began to set in the distance.

"We should get going," he said after a while. "It's about to get dark."

"Oh, yes," I said. "Because elementary school playgrounds are known to be a hotbed of crime and debauchery after sundown."

"I meant because it's going to get even colder, smart-ass." He stood up and offered me his hand. I took it and he pulled me to my feet. Our fingers stayed locked together for just an instant longer than they should have, and when he let go, my hand felt too cold.

I shoved both hands in my pockets and followed Ryder toward the sidewalk.

We walked back to the library in silence, our shoulders brushing lightly against each other.

"This is me," I said when we reached Gert. I slapped the old clunker on her hood. "Sweet ride, huh?"

"Is it going to start?" Ryder asked, raising an eyebrow.

"Isn't that the million-dollar question." I pulled my keys from my purse and unlocked the driver's side door. "It was nice hanging out with you today, Ryder."

"You, too."

I expected him to walk away, but when he didn't, I looked at him again.

"You should write to your dad," he said.

I frowned at him. "Why? I told you, he's probably the deadbeat loser my mom always told me he was."

"But he might not be," Ryder said. "It's been years, you said it yourself. And if you've been thinking about him anyway . . . Maybe it's worth a shot."

"But . . . but what if he doesn't care about me?" My voice trembled a little on the last words. "What if he lets me down?"

"You won't know unless you try," he said. "If there's one thing I've learned since moving here, it's that sometimes people surprise you, if you let them."

He was looking right at me when he said this, and the butterflies swarmed in my stomach once again.

He took a step back and started moving toward his car. "See you at school, Sonny."

I nodded, but I didn't get in the car. I just stood there, in the December cold, and watched him walk away.

That night, alone in the guest room, I couldn't sleep.

I lay there, replaying everything that had happened with Ryder. The way he'd smiled at me. The way he'd looked at me, like for once he was actually seeing *me*, not just his dream girl's annoying best friend.

But, mostly, I kept thinking about what he'd said about my dad.

Sometimes people surprise you, if you let them.

I hadn't seen my dad in years. I hadn't even mentioned him to anyone in years. Not until today. But I'd thought about him. A lot.

He used to push me on the tire swing in our backyard when I was little. He used to bring home big gallons of cookies-and-cream ice cream because it was my favorite. He used to say, "Quiet. You'll wake up Sonny," when Mom raised her voice during a fight, even though, most of the time, I was still awake.

Then he got arrested for the first time.

And then the second.

The first time it was for boosting cars, but I only knew that because I'd heard some people in town talking about it when I was little.

"Isn't that the Ardmore girl? You hear about her dad? Goddamn thief."

That's when I started lying, telling people he was an international businessman, not an inmate.

I didn't know what he'd been charged with the second time. Or any of the times after that. All I knew was that Dad hadn't spent more than a couple of weeks out of jail since I was seven.

Mom took me to see him every week until she didn't anymore. He was an asshole. He was a deadbeat. That's what she said. That's what I believed.

Maybe it was true, and maybe it wasn't. Ryder had me questioning all of it now.

My dear friend insomnia wasn't going anywhere, so I peeled myself off the bed and headed downstairs. Mr. Rush kept an office on the first floor, but Amy and I were welcome to use it if we needed the desktop. And since I wasn't sure how welcome I was to Amy's laptop these days, it seemed like a more suitable option.

It was 1:12 a.m. when I opened up the Word document. And it was 1:36 a.m. before I managed to type the first word.

It was a short note. But it felt like pulling teeth. Each word was scary and raw. Each word made me vulnerable. What if it was easier to just leave him out of my life than to reach out and have him hurt me?

I choked back all the fears as my cursor hovered over the PRINT button. I swallowed once, twice, closed my eyes, and clicked.

Before I could change my mind, I found an envelope in Mr. Rush's desk. I shoved the letter inside, scribbled the to and from addresses, and smacked on a stamp. I'd ask Mr. and Mrs. Rush permission to give their home number tomorrow morning. If they said no, I wouldn't send it.

But if they said it was okay, I didn't want any excuse not to drop the letter in the mail.

I put the envelope on the breakfast table, where I wouldn't be able to hide from it come morning, then I ran back upstairs, buried my face in my pillows, and spent the rest of the night panicking.

14

I had hopes of sleeping in on the first day of Christmas break. There was no school and my bookstore shift didn't start until the afternoon.

Amy, however, had other plans.

The guest room door burst open at eight-thirty that morning. "They got here early!" she squealed as she dashed past my bed to the window, which looked out onto the Rushes' driveway.

"Mmmm," I groaned, but I forced myself to sit up. Amy hadn't been this excited about something in a while, especially not since the awkward flirting incident a few weeks ago. "Who's here early?"

"Wesley and Bianca!" She hopped up and down as she watched a car pull up outside. She turned and made a dash for the door. "Come on!"

I dragged myself out of bed and followed her downstairs.

Very few things in life got Amy this animated. In fact, only three things: puppies, private Shakespeare recitations, and Wesley.

My feet had just touched the bottom step when the front door opened and a pack of Rushes, plus one, spilled in, along with a burst of cold December wind. Amy shrieked and threw herself at the tallest Rush, who greeted her with open arms.

When Amy detached herself from her brother, she turned and repeated the performance with the shorter, auburn-haired girl at his side.

"Hey, Amy," Bianca said, patting her awkwardly on the shoulder. "It's good to see you, too."

At first glance, Bianca didn't fit in with the Rush family. She was a good half foot shorter than even Mrs. Rush, who was the smallest member of the family. She wore tattered jeans, T-shirts, and faded red Converse, where they wore polished, expensive clothes most people in this town couldn't afford.

At first glance, Bianca seemed . . . more like me.

But if you looked closer, at the way they welcomed her, at the way Wesley looked at her, it made perfect sense. Bianca was smart and funny and, from what Amy had told me, she'd played a role in bringing the family back together a few years ago, when it had all but fallen apart. And now, she was part of it.

I didn't know her that well, but it was clear she belonged with this family.

Meanwhile, I suddenly felt like an intruder. Just some kid mooching off their generosity. Which was why I stayed put on the stairs. As glad as I was to see Wesley, I couldn't bring myself to interrupt the family reunion happening before me.

But Wesley, who towered over everyone else in the family, only took a second to notice.

"Sonny!" he called, waving me over for a hug. "So Amy finally convinced our parents to let her keep you, huh? It's about time."

I laughed and accepted the quick hug. "It's nice to see you, Wesley."

"Is it?" he asked. "I've texted you a few times, but you never replied. I thought maybe you were too cool for me now."

"Oh, I am," I assured him. "But, also, my phone is broken. I've been using Amy's."

Which reminded me that I had a few text messages from Ryder to delete.

"It's nice to see you again, Sonny," Bianca said.

"You, too. How's New York?"

"Cold."

"Luckily, she's got me to warm her up," Wesley said, putting an arm around her. Bianca rolled her eyes.

"Well, I hate to cut this short," Mr. Rush said, glancing at his watch. "But I'm sure Bianca's father will be eager to see her. We can't hog all her time."

"I'll take her home," Wesley said, grabbing a set from the hook by the door. The keys to his beloved Porsche.

He hadn't taken it with him to New York. I guess there wasn't much of a need for it there. But he was clearly excited to get behind the wheel now that he was home.

"Come back over soon," Amy said. "We have to catch up."

"Obviously," Bianca said.

And as quickly as they'd arrived, Wesley and Bianca swept back out the door, while Amy, her parents, and I migrated to the kitchen for breakfast.

"I'm so glad they're home," Amy was saying as she poured herself a bowl of cereal. "It's nice to have the whole family together again."

"It is," Mrs. Rush agreed.

A knot twisted in my stomach, and I found myself blinking back sudden tears. I cleared my throat.

"Um, Mr. Rush? Has there been any mail for me?"

Mr. Rush had just filled a mug with coffee. He looked at me over the rim, his eyes knowing. He'd been the one to put my letter in the mail, so he knew exactly why I was asking.

"No, Sonny," he said. "I'm sorry."

"Are you expecting something?" Amy asked.

"Yeah," I mumbled, the ache in my chest growing as I watched the Rushes bustle around the kitchen, laughing as they bumped into each other and tripped over one another's feet. "But I probably shouldn't be."

Amy raised an eyebrow, and I knew she'd be asking me about it later. I still wasn't sure if or what I was going to tell her.

"Sonny," Mrs. Rush said, "why don't you invite your mother for dinner on Christmas Eve? I know she had to work on Thanksgiving, but hopefully she has Christmas Eve off."

"Maybe," I said. "I'll see. I'm sure she'd appreciate the invitation."

Lie, lie, lie.

"Ryder."

It was embarrassing how surprised I sounded, but he was the last person I expected to find on the Rushes' front porch. Well, okay. Maybe not *the last*. That title most likely belonged to the Queen of England or the reanimated corpse of Edgar Allan Poe.

Or my mom.

143

But Ryder was unexpected, nonetheless. He was wearing an army-green utility jacket, his nonprescription black glasses, and a beanie. He looked hot in that awful hipster way I'd somehow grown to appreciate.

"Hey, Sonny," he said, smiling at me.

There *may* have been a little bit of fluttering in my stomach. Maybe. Just a little. Unfortunately, it was quickly drowned out by the awful realization that I looked like shit.

I'd only gotten out of the shower ten minutes before the door-bell rang. I was dressed, thank God — though maybe if I hadn't been, he'd have other, more interesting things to look at than my hair, which was wet and tangled and pulled back from my face with a tie-dyed headband I used whenever I put on a face mask. Which I'd been only seconds away from applying when the door-bell rang.

So as timing goes, it wasn't as bad as it could have been.

But why, *why* hadn't he chosen to come by on a day when I looked amazing? Or when I was wearing some sort of sexy yet classy lingerie? I didn't even own lingerie, but that seemed like an excellent scenario, and one that would likely go a long way toward furthering progress on my master plan.

Ryder didn't seem to notice my unflattering hairdo, however.

"Hey. Is Amy home?" he asked.

I managed to keep my composure despite my disappointment. "Nope. She went out to *run some errands* this morning, and she insisted it would be boring and I didn't have to come." I smirked. "You know what that means, right?"

"What's that?"

144

"She's out buying my Christmas present."

"Oh?" he asked. "What do you think she'll get you?"

"Well, I asked for a pony," I informed him. "And I'm not sure I could settle for anything less."

"Any good friend would get you a pony," he agreed.

Then we were grinning at each other, and those fluttery feelings made their triumphant return.

"Do you want to come in?" I asked. "It's just me here. Everyone else is out doing last-minute shopping."

Mortification crept over my face as I realized with a start exactly what I was offering. Me and Ryder. In a giant, empty house. With infinite rooms just begging to be made out in.

Or, you know, we might just watch TV.

Although, knowing Ryder, he probably hated television.

But for a full second, I thought he was going to say yes. His mouth opened to speak, but then he snapped it shut. He looked at me, then looked away, shaking his head as if shaking water from his face.

"That's okay," he said. "I'd better get going." I tried not to let the disappointment show, but I wasn't strong enough to hide it when he said, "But will you give this to Amy?"

It was only then that I noticed the thin, rectangular box, covered in green wrapping paper, tucked under his arm. It was the sort of box clothes were always given in on Christmas, and it was for Amy.

"Of course," I said, taking the box from him. "No problem." And then, spotting an opening to push my plans along a little, I added, "But I'm sorry. I don't think she got you anything."

Ryder shrugged. "That's okay," he said, only a tiny bit crest-fallen. "You never know. Maybe she'll pick me up something while she's out buying your pony."

"Maybe."

We stared at each other for another long moment. In the silence, I had the sudden urge to tell him about my letter to Dad, but I shoved the impulse away. I hadn't heard from Dad yet, and I might not. If he never called or wrote back, I wasn't sure I could stand having to answer questions about it later.

Ryder did that same head shake he'd done a minute before and finally turned, moving toward the front steps. "Merry Christmas, Sonny," he said over his shoulder.

"Merry Christmas."

But at that moment, the gift box feeling heavy and cruel in my arms, it didn't seem all that merry.

As much as I didn't want to know, I was *dying* to know what was in the box Ryder had given to Amy.

"Why didn't you just open it?" she asked when she got home that evening.

"Because it's for you." The words came out harsh and bitter. And yes, I knew that wasn't fair. Amy hadn't asked for this. But damn it, if she wasn't so irresistible, we wouldn't be in this situation.

Was it really too much to ask for a shrew as a best friend? I didn't think so.

"Not really," she said, but she picked up the box anyway and sat down on the bed with it in her lap. She peeled off the green paper, careful not to tear it. Where I would have just shredded it, Amy was always neat about the way she unwrapped gifts, as if she might want to reuse the paper later. (She never did, though.)

Once she'd finished with that task, she began working at the tape that held the white box closed. It took her a second, but then the lid was flipping open and she was pulling out a shirt.

A red buffalo plaid flannel shirt.

My heart swelled, then promptly sank.

Because, as I kept reminding myself, it wasn't for me.

"Oh," Amy said, examining the shirt, which was clearly not at all her style. "It's . . . cute."

"It's flannel," I said.

"Uh-huh."

"It's for your future nineties grunge band."

Amy blinked at me. "Excuse me?"

"Nothing. It's stupid." I stood up and moved toward the door. "Enjoy the shirt."

"Sonny, you can have it," she said. "Obviously. It's not really for me."

"It's not for me either," I said. "You're the one he thinks would look cute in flannel."

"I'm going to disagree with him on that." She put the shirt back in the box before looking at me again.

My hand was on the door, but I was watching her. Or maybe I was glaring at her. Unintentionally.

"Are you mad at me?" she asked.

"No."

I was, though. And I hated myself for it. This situation with Ryder wasn't Amy's fault. It was mine. I was being an asshole.

It wasn't just about Ryder, though. It was this stupid holiday. It was a constant reminder that Amy had everything I didn't. A family, a future, a home . . . and now Ryder. She had people who loved her. People who wanted to buy her gifts and spend time with her. And I had no one.

No one . . . except her.

I felt myself deflate, my shoulders slumping forward as the anger seeped out of me, replaced by the weight of guilt.

"No," I said again. "I'm not mad at you. I'm sorry."

"You can have the shirt," she said again, holding the box out to me. "It's really for you."

"That's okay. It probably wouldn't fit me anyway." But I still took it from her. After a second, I forced a smile, and even though it wasn't real, I knew it was believable because, well, it was me. "Your brother brought home some of those cookies with the icing we love. I'm stealing one. Should I grab two?"

Amy's fake smile was more transparent. "Sure. Wanna play a game of pool in the rec room?"

"You're on," I said.

15

Bah, humbug!

Between the gift drama with Ryder, the lingering awkwardness between me and Amy, endless shifts at the bookstore, and my general lack of a family to spend the holidays with, I had become a scrooge. Every commercial featuring a happy little kid opening gifts with their loving parents made me want to karate chop the Rushes' flat-screen TV. Every Christmas song on the radio gave me road rage. And I was no longer allowed to answer the front door for fear of what I might do to some unsuspecting caroler who might come knocking.

I'd even gotten reprimanded by Sheila for scowling too much at work. Dealing with the general public day in and day out while forcing a cheery attitude was torture. And even though I needed the money, I'd called in sick a couple of times just to keep myself sane.

Suffice it to say, I was not particularly eager to go downstairs on Christmas morning.

Don't get me wrong, I knew the Rushes would be nice. They'd probably even gotten me a small gift — some assorted lotions or a new sweater, all of which I would have been incredibly grateful for — but I wasn't the person they wanted to see today. They'd invited me into their home and never let me feel unwelcome for a moment, but in the end, I was their guest. And Christmas was a day you wanted to spend with family.

Amy and I would exchange gifts later that day. I would let the Rushes have the morning to themselves.

At least, that was my plan.

Until Wesley threw open my bedroom door at eight in the godforsaken morning.

"Merry Christmas!" he bellowed. "Time to get up."

I groaned and smushed my face into the pillow. "No."

"Come on, now. Where's your holiday spirit?" I heard his heavy footsteps move quickly across the floor, then my curtains were thrown open and blinding sunlight filled the room. "Rise and shine, Sonny. Come downstairs and see what Santa brought you."

I sighed and rolled onto my back, squinting against the light. "If you honestly think I still believe in Santa, we need to have a conversation, Wesley."

"Let's have it downstairs," he said. "Come on. Everyone's been waiting on you to open presents for almost an hour."

I frowned. "Waiting on me? Why?"

"Because they didn't want to wake you up. Thought it would be rude. I, on the other hand, have no such reservations."

That wasn't what I'd meant, though.

Before I could clarify, Wesley grabbed my wrist, pulled me to my feet, and began dragging me toward the door. Thank God I was wearing Amy's frog pajamas.

"Okay, okay," I said, having to jog to keep up with his long strides. "I'm coming. No need to use brute force."

"I get aggressive about presents."

"Clearly."

He released my wrist and I followed him downstairs. The rest of the family was sitting around the huge living room, all in their pajamas. Mr. Rush had a mug of coffee in his hand and Amy was munching on a frozen waffle. They looked up when Wesley and I entered.

"We told you not to wake her up," Mrs. Rush scolded.

"If we waited for Sonny, we wouldn't be opening presents until noon," Wesley argued.

"So?" Mrs. Rush asked.

"Mother, that is unacceptable. Even you know that."

"Sonny, I'd like to apologize for my son. His manners are obviously lacking."

But I barely heard her. I was too busy staring at the mantel over the fireplace, where five stockings had been hung. They hadn't been there when I'd gone up to bed the night before. But there they were. Five.

One for each member of the Rush family.

And, right in the middle of them, one that said *Sonny* in glittery, hand-painted letters.

It was a small thing, on the surface, but it felt huge. I had to swallow a lump that had risen in my throat. I had never had a stocking with my name on it. Mom had never hung them. Hell, we hadn't even had a Christmas tree in at least five years.

"Sonny," Mr. Rush said, calling my attention back to the family. "Come sit down. We have to pass these presents out before Wesley's head explodes."

I nodded and migrated over to the couch to sit between him and Amy, who offered me a warm smile.

"Merry Christmas," she said.

"Merry Christmas," I replied, beaming back at her.

Wesley passed out the gifts, but none of us opened them until every package under the tree had been given to its rightful owner. Then we were free to tear in, though no one did this with quite as much enthusiasm as the eldest Rush child.

"You're nearly twenty-one years old," Mr. Rush reminded his son as Wesley impatiently shredded the paper on one of the gifts — the game console Amy and I had picked up.

"The Christmas spirit doesn't have an age," Wesley assured him.

As for me, I had a small pile of gifts, pretty much as I'd expected. A new red sweater from Mr. Rush (was that cashmere? I didn't even know what cashmere felt like) and a box of lavender-scented lotion, body wash, and perfume from Mrs. Rush. Wesley had gotten me something, too, though the present itself confused me a little.

"Oh, thank you," I said, looking down at the smartphone case that had clearly been custom designed with my name in pink, swirly letters. I didn't have a smartphone, but I did have the ability to fake enthusiasm. "It's really cute."

"That actually goes with another gift," Mrs. Rush said. "Go check your stocking."

"Uh, okay." I stood up and walked over to the mantel. Carefully, I reached my hand inside the Sonny stocking and pulled out the only item. And gasped.

A smartphone.

A brand-new, working smartphone.

"That's from all of us," Mr. Rush said.

"But it was Amy's idea," Mrs. Rush informed me. "We know your phone's been broken for a while, and we figured it was time for an upgrade."

"We added you to our phone plan, too," Mr. Rush said. "We transferred your old number and everything."

That lump was back again. Persistent bastard. I just shook my head, barely managing to choke out the words, "I-I can't accept this."

"You can, and you will," Wesley said.

"It's a little selfish on our parts," Mrs. Rush added. "We want to be able to keep in touch with you while you're living here, and you and Amy can't *always* be attached at the hip. So this is for us, too."

"I'm sure it'll also make it easier for your mother to get ahold of you if she needs to," Mr. Rush said.

"Do you like it?" Amy asked. She was grinning at me, her eyes wide and bright.

I nodded. "I do. I do — thank you. Thank you so much."

"You're welcome," Mr. Rush said. "And thank you for spending Christmas with us. We're glad to have you here, Sonny."

I smiled at him. "I'm glad I'm here, too."

I may not have been as filled with holiday joy as Wesley (I doubted I ever would be), but if I was going to spend Christmas with anyone, there was no other family I'd rather be with.

Except, maybe, my own.

The only call I got that day wasn't on my new cell phone: It was on the Rushes' house phone, and it was collect.

"Yes, I'll accept the charges," I said, feeling a little guilty despite their insistence that they'd be okay with paying the fees when I'd originally asked them about it.

I had a feeling this was the first time the Rush house had received a call from a prison.

"Sonny?"

I hadn't heard his voice in years, but I recognized it immediately. It was deep, but light. You could hear the smile in it. In all my memories of my father, he was always smiling.

"Hey, Dad," I said, my own voice a tad shaky. "Merry Christmas."

"You sound so grown-up," he said. "You're probably too old for me to call you Sonny Bunny now, huh?"

"Maybe a little," I said. I was surprised by how normal he sounded. How confident and pleasant. Somehow, I'd expected prison to rob him of that. He just . . . didn't sound like a criminal. "It's been a while."

"I know. I was so happy to get your letter."

"You were?"

"Of course, Sonny Bunny. I've tried to call and write before, but I could never get in touch."

"We moved a few years ago," I said. "Into Granddad's house. And Mom never got a house phone. And her cell number has changed a few times, so . . ."

"Your mother," he said, a slight laugh in his voice. "She's a piece of work."

"Yeah . . . So that's why I gave you this number. I'm at my friend's house right now. Her parents said I could take your calls here."

"Oh," Dad said. "Well, tell them thank you for me." He paused. "How is your mom, anyway?"

Time to lie.

"Great," I said. "She's got a good job right now and she's seeing someone, so that's good for her. We had a great Christmas this morning, and then I came over to my friend's house for dinner."

"That's great," Dad said. "I miss you, Sonny Bunny."

"I miss you, too."

I didn't know the words were true until they left my mouth. Despite everything I'd said about him over the years, despite all the anger and hurt I felt, I'd missed him. Especially now.

"Listen," he said. "I know you're busy, but I'd love to see you if you ever want to come for visitation —"

"I will."

"Yeah?"

"Yeah," I said. "I mean, I don't know when, but I'll come soon."

"That would be great, Sonny. You can come make fun of me in my very fashionable orange jumpsuit." And even though his voice was still confident, I could sense that little touch of relief. No one else would have caught it, but I did.

I had to remind myself of that. My dad might not have sounded like a criminal, but he was one. There was no disputing that. Maybe he'd changed over the years. Maybe he wasn't the asshole my mother had once claimed. But for all his charm, he was a liar.

Just like me.

The question was, how much was he lying about?

There was a chance that letting him back into my life was a mistake. But Ryder said Dad might surprise me if I gave him a chance, and he already had just by calling.

"You still there, Sonny Bunny?"

"Yeah," I said. "I'm here. But I can only talk for a few more minutes. The phone charges are kind of . . ."

"I understand," Dad said. "But, if you have a few more minutes, I'd love to learn a little more about this grown-up you."

I smiled. "What do you want to know?"

"Everything," he said.

I wouldn't give him that. I couldn't give anyone that. But for the next five minutes, I told him as many true things as I could.

16

"Are you freaking kidding me?"

I slammed my fist into Gert's steering wheel and jumped at the resounding *honk!* it elicited. Because, despite all logic, it had somehow surprised me.

I'd just managed to pull my piece-of-shit car onto the shoulder of the road as it groaned and creaked to a stop. But now I was stuck, stranded on the stretch of highway between Hamilton and Oak Hill on the day after Christmas.

And I was going to be late for work.

"Please just be the battery," I muttered as I climbed from the car and went to open the hood. "Please just need a jump."

I may have had a job now, but between gas money, Christmas presents, and buying some new winter clothes, I didn't have the money to fix Gert. I knew the Rushes would pay for it if I asked, but I still felt guilty about letting them give me a new cell phone.

I pulled open the hood and stared down at the tangle of machinery inside, suddenly remembering that I knew absolutely nothing about cars. I wasn't even sure why I'd popped the hood other than that was just what you were supposed to do when you were stranded on the side of the road.

"Damn," I said, looking down at what I thought might be the battery.

I reached into my back pocket and pulled out my new cell phone, which only had a handful of numbers programmed into it. I tried Amy, but there was no answer. She'd gone to the library to work on an essay for her college applications, so maybe she'd put it on silent. Then I remembered that I hadn't given Amy her phone back yet — it was still in my room. So I tried Wesley next.

"Hello, Sonya."

"Not funny," I said. "Hey, are you busy?"

"We're just watching a movie. Why?"

I heard someone laughing in the background, and I realized he must've been at Bianca's house.

"Gert's dead."

"Who?"

"My car."

"Oh . . . okay. Where are you?"

I gave him directions and he assured me they were leaving immediately. I hung up and shoved my phone back into my pocket with a sigh.

"Damn it, Gert," I said, resting my hand on the hood. "Get your shit together, woman."

I dialed the bookstore's number, but there was no answer. I was about to try again when I heard someone call out to me.

"Hey. You all right?"

I looked up and noticed a Honda slowing to a stop next to me. A guy with messy brown hair stuck his head out the window.

Beyond him, I could make out a pretty brunette in the passenger's seat. Neither of them were much older than me.

"Fine," I said. "My car just sucks."

He turned the Honda onto the shoulder, just a few yards in front of my car, making room for other cars to speed past us. Then he and the brunette both climbed out and started walking toward me.

I stiffened, thinking that this was exactly how every horror movie began and hoping that Amy would avenge my murder, regardless of the weirdness between us at the moment, but then I realized we were on a busy highway in broad daylight and any smarter serial-killing team would not be so careless.

"Sorry," the brunette said, noticing the uneasy look on my face. There was something vaguely familiar about her, but I couldn't place it. "Nathan here has a Good Samaritan complex. We promise we're not going to, like, kidnap you."

"That's just what any good kidnapper would say," I pointed out.

The girl, who was wearing a University of Kentucky sweatshirt, snorted, and her blue eyes twinkled just a bit.

"It's not a Good Samaritan complex," Nathan argued. "It's called being a decent person. Try it sometime."

"I'll pass. Thanks."

They stared at each other for a moment, both smiling, and suddenly I felt as though I was intruding on something. Worried they might start mauling each other in front of me, there on the side of the road, I cleared my throat.

"Yeah," I said. "I'm fine. Just a craptastic car. My friends are on the way."

"See. She doesn't want our help," the girl said. "Let's leave her alone. I'm freezing."

"Does the heat work in your car?" Nathan asked me. "Do you want to wait in our car with us?"

"Oh, I don't —"

"I was trying to convince her that we *weren't* trying to kidnap her," the girl said. "You're not helping my case here."

Nathan laughed. "Sorry. Whitley's right. We aren't trying to kidnap you."

"Wait," I said, looking at the brunette. And suddenly I realized why she looked so familiar. "Whitley? Whitley Johnson? You're Greg Johnson's daughter?"

Whitley stiffened a little. "Yeah."

"Oh my God," I said. "Okay, I swear, I'm not usually a squealing fangirl, but your father is *amazing*."

"So I've been told."

"He paid for my gas once."

Whitley met this comment with the same lack of enthusiasm I had received from Ryder. She just gave a vague, placating smile, and I realized what an idiot I sounded like.

Nonetheless, I was suddenly way more willing to wait in their car until Bianca and Wesley arrived.

The three of us climbed into the Honda, me sliding into the backseat, and Nathan cranked up the heat. I listened with curiosity as he and Whitley talked about other things — school, plans for the weekend, some awkward family Christmas drama — only then remembering that these two were not only a couple but stepsiblings.

That had really gotten the rumor mill stirred up a few years ago, shortly after Greg Johnson moved to Hamilton. His daughter, Whitley, already had a reputation for being a party animal, but the gossip only got worse when she started dating her stepmother's son. Talk around town had mostly faded after the two went off to college, but sometimes flared up again when Whitley and Nathan were back for school breaks.

This was my first time meeting either of them in person, and I was fascinated by how a relationship like that would work.

I also wondered if my love life was more or less screwed up than theirs.

Probably more.

"Are those your friends?" Nathan asked as a Porsche eased onto the side of the road, right behind Gert.

"Yeah," I said, though I was mildly disappointed to be ejected from this riveting couple's presence.

I hopped out of the Honda and saw Wesley and Bianca approaching. Whitley and Nathan spotted them, too, and to my surprise, they also climbed out of the car.

"Hey," Nathan said, beaming.

"Hey." Wesley grinned. "Long time no see."

"You guys know each other?" I asked.

"Sort of," Bianca said. She and Whitley gave each other a polite nod.

"Whitley here stole my best friend," Wesley explained. "How is Harrison, anyway? I haven't heard from him in ages."

"That's because he has a new boyfriend," Whitley said. "He's spending Christmas in Los Angeles with Antonio. I'd be mad at him for it, but they're disgustingly cute together."

"Good for him," Wesley said. "Bianca and I were talking about going out to visit him if he doesn't come home this summer."

They kept talking until Bianca noticed me standing there shivering and cleared her throat.

"Well, we just came to pick up the stray." She jabbed a thumb at me. "Thanks for keeping an eye on her."

"I'm not a puppy," I said.

"We discussed kidnapping her," Whitley said. "Just so you know."

"Glad you didn't," Wesley said. "Then I'd have to find my sister a new best friend, and those can take forever to housebreak."

I rolled my eyes. "Ha-ha."

Whitley and Nathan said good-bye and climbed into their car, then Wesley, Bianca, and I headed back over to Gert.

"So what's the problem?" Bianca asked, tapping the hood.

"I don't know," I admitted. "It stopped running. I'm hoping it's just the battery. Do you guys have jumper cables?"

Wesley opened his mouth to answer, but Bianca just popped open the hood. "Let me take a look first. I have plenty of experience with crappy old cars."

"Be my guest."

She poked her head around inside while Wesley and I watched. After a second, she took a step back and slammed the hood shut.

"We'll need to call a tow truck."

I groaned. "What's wrong with Gert?"

"Your alternator. The belt is totally just hanging there. It'll need to be replaced."

"The alternator," Wesley said, nodding. "I mean, obviously."

Bianca rolled her eyes. "For someone with such a nice car, you know so little about them."

"How much is that going to cost me?" I asked.

"Hard to say," Bianca admitted. "If it's just the belt, it won't be that bad. If it's the actual alternator . . . a little more."

"More that I don't have," I muttered. "And I don't get paid until next week."

"Don't worry about it," Wesley said. "I'll take care of it."

"I can't let you do that," I said. "Or your parents. You guys have already done way too much for me."

"Don't be silly," he said. "We don't mind."

"But I do," I argued.

Bianca put an understanding hand on my shoulder. "Maybe you could consider it a loan, then," she said. "To be paid back when you can."

I still wasn't thrilled about this, but it wasn't as if there were a ton of options. So, reluctantly, I nodded.

"Deal," Wesley said. "I'll even charge interest if you like."

"Let's negotiate that in the car. Where it's warm," Bianca suggested.

It took about twenty minutes for the tow truck to arrive, and by then, I was super late for work. Poor Gert and her broken alternator were hauled off, and I silently promised her I'd come to rescue her soon.

"So where were you headed?" Wesley asked as he steered the Porsche back onto the highway.

"The mall," I said, checking the time. "My shift started half an hour ago. My boss will be so pissed. And now I have no way to get home after . . ."

"We can come pick you up," Bianca said.

"You don't have to do that," I said.

"Of course we do," Wesley said. "You don't think we'd leave you stranded, do you? Just give me a call when your shift ends."

"Thank you," I said. "Really."

Wesley smiled at me in the rearview mirror. "Anytime."

17

Well, this was some serious déjà vu.

"Sheila, come on," I begged. "I told you. My car broke down. I had to wait for the tow truck."

"You could have called," she said.

"I tried," I said. "No one answered."

"Why didn't you try again?"

Fair question.

"We had to call someone else to cover your shift," she said. "The day after Christmas is always busy, and you weren't here."

"I told you. My car —"

"You always have an excuse," she said.

To be fair, the excuses about Gert had been true. I'd had more problems with her lately than usual. I seriously needed a new car. But that required money. Which required a job. Which Gert was making it incredibly hard to hold on to.

Well, Gert, and my hatred of the holidays.

"Look," Sheila said as she rearranged a few picture books that had been tossed around by some kids a few minutes before. I was following her around the store like a pathetic, lost dog. "You were seasonal anyway. We were probably going to be laying you off in two weeks as it is."

But that was two weeks' worth of pay that I needed. Especially now that I owed Wesley for Gert's repairs.

I just stood there, staring at her.

"Sorry, Sonny," she said. "But you're fired."

I stormed out of the bookstore, pissed at Sheila and at Gert and at myself. I thought of calling Wesley, asking him to turn back around and come pick me up. But I took a deep breath and decided to be more proactive.

I was already at the mall, so I might as well start my job hunt right away.

I sighed as I headed toward the food court, remembering the day Amy and I had come here when I was first applying for new jobs.

Some days I felt like a rat on a wheel, running and running and running and never getting anywhere.

"Sonny?"

I was walking out of Daphne's, a vintage-inspired clothing store, after dropping off my application. Ryder was standing a few yards away, a shopping bag in his hand and his green utility jacket slung casually over his shoulder. He looked like a model. Like a picture any one of these stores would have loved to have advertising their brand.

"Hey, Ryder," I said.

"What're you doing here?"

We said it in unison, then laughed together.

"If I was seven, I would yell jinx right now."

"Yeah," I said. "Such a shame we're too old for — JINX! You owe me a soda."

Ryder rolled his eyes. "Seriously?"

"Of course. I take these things *very* seriously. I prefer orange soda, by the way. Though I will also accept grape. No root beer, though. Disgusting."

"Noted." He glanced down at the stack of applications still tucked beneath my arm. "So, back to my question. What are you doing here?"

"Seeking employment."

"I thought you worked at the bookstore?"

"No longer."

"Oh. Sorry to hear that."

"What about you? What brings you to the mall on this fine winter's day?"

"Something just as fun." He lifted up the shopping bags. "Returning unwanted gifts."

"Unwanted gifts? That's an oxymoron, Ryder."

"You've never been honored with a present from my grand-mother, then."

"That bad?"

"She gave me suspenders once."

"Well, I mean, those are making a comeback. Especially among hipsters like yourself."

"I'm not a hipster," he said. "And do I look like someone who wears suspenders?"

"I mean, maybe . . ."

"Bright purple ones?"

I giggled, trying to picture it. Ryder in his expensive blue jeans, red Goats Vote for Melons T-shirt, and bright purple suspenders. "No, not really. Though I would pay money to see it."

"Yes, well, pay all you like. It's not going to happen." He sighed. "Luckily, I've been able to trade things in for items I *would* wear, so at least it wasn't a waste of a nice gesture."

Without saying anything, without planning it, we started walking. Together. Our shoulders nearly touching as we wove our way past families with strollers and seniors in tracksuits.

"So did Amy get you that pony?" he asked after we'd passed a few stores.

"Sadly, no. I'm very disappointed. We're no longer on speaking terms because of it."

"That's a shame. You know she . . ."

I looked at him as he trailed off. My heart was already beginning to sink. Back to Amy. Barely a minute together and that's what he wanted to talk about. I hadn't even been texting him from her phone lately. At least, not much. Just a couple of times, once or twice, when the guest room felt especially lonely. But I'd definitely slowed down since the start of Christmas break. Especially after he brought her that gift. As far as he knew, Amy had never even thanked him for it. Yet he still wanted to talk about her.

He shook his head. "You know what? Never mind."

Or maybe he didn't.

"So where else do you have to drop these off?" Ryder asked, taking the applications from me and thumbing through them.

After Sheila fired me, I'd gone around the mall, picking up applications, then filled them out in the food court. Now I was just dropping them off.

"The candy shop. The smoothie place. And that sporting goods store on the other side of the building. You know, that one where all the middle-aged men in camo stand around comparing fishing poles for hours?"

Ryder grimaced. "You're going to put an application in there?"

"My car broke down on the way here, and I have to pay for the repairs, so I can't afford to be picky." I took the applications back from him.

"Your car broke down on the way here?"

"Yeah. I had to call a tow truck. Thankfully, Amy's brother was able to pick me up, so I wasn't stranded long." I slowed as we neared the candy store, and Ryder followed me in. He was quiet as I handed my application to the lady behind the counter, who wasted no time informing me that they weren't hiring right now, but that they'd keep my application on file.

"Listen," Ryder said as we were leaving the shop. "I was about to leave here, but I'd be glad to give you a ride home if you need one."

"That would actually be great," I said, surprised. "If you don't mind. It would save my friends another trip out here."

"I don't mind at all."

How had I ever thought this guy was a jerk?

I dropped off my last few applications, including, yes, one in the sporting goods store. After I handed it to the man at the counter, I sent a text to Wesley, letting him know I had found another ride home. Then I went in search for Ryder, who had wandered off somewhere in the few seconds I wasn't looking. I found him looking at bright orange hunting jackets and vests.

"Thinking of changing your wardrobe?" I asked.

"Marveling at the fact that my grandmother hasn't gotten me one of these yet," he said.

"A blaze-orange vest would go splendidly with those purple suspenders."

"My thoughts exactly." He turned to me with a smile. "Are you ready to go?"

"Not until you try one of those on."

"Ha-ha. You're hilarious."

"I'm serious," I said. "If you do it, you'll no longer owe me a soda."

"No."

"Oh, come on, Ryder," I said, punching his arm playfully. "Be a little spontaneous for once."

He hesitated, but I must've been persuasive because he sighed, resigned, and put down his shopping bags. "Give me your phone."

"What? Why?"

"Because I don't want you taking pictures to use as blackmail, that's why."

"Oh, that's a great idea. But I don't have a phone, remember?"

"You didn't before, but you do now. I saw you using it a second ago. Hand it over."

I sighed and passed him my new cell phone. He looked at it and chuckled. "Your name is on the case and everything. Worried you'll forget who it belongs to?"

"Just shut up and put on the jacket."

He shoved my phone into his pocket and turned to the rack of orange attire. After a second, he selected a coat. He tossed me his jacket, then slid the bulky orange monstrosity onto his arms.

It was impossible not to laugh.

"Please can I have my phone back?" I choked through the giggles.

"Absolutely not."

"You just look . . . so different." And he did. He didn't look bad — hell, if all hunters looked like this, I'd be up in a deer stand in a heartbeat. But he didn't look like Ryder at all. It was funny how one item of clothing could completely change a person.

"Looks great on you, kid," one of the employees said as he walked past us. "You're ready for deer season now!"

Embarrassment flooded his face. I doubted he'd ever been hunting in his life.

"He's also in the market for a new fishing pole!" I called to the employee.

Ryder shoved the jacket off his shoulders, hung it back up, picked up his bags, and grabbed my hand, pulling me to the exit as I laughed, leaving the store employee looking very bewildered.

His hand was warm against mine, and it sent a spike of adrenaline through me.

"Happy now?" Ryder asked when we were away from the store, but I could tell he was holding back a laugh, too.

"Oh, very," I told him. "Extremely, even."

"Good. Then let's get out of here before you try to make me play dress-up anywhere else."

We stood there for a minute, our hands still locked. I waited for him to let go and hoped that he wouldn't all at the same time. But, after a moment that lasted an instant too long, he did. And maybe it was my imagination, but I think he was just as disappointed to lose that contact as I was.

I traded his jacket for my cell phone and we headed outside, to his car. It wasn't late, but it was already dark out. We walked close together, our heads ducked against a wind that had picked up in the hours since Gert had broken down. And as I climbed into the front seat of his car, shivering, I realized that the last time we'd been in a car together was in October, on another day when Gert had given me trouble and I'd been fired.

The day all of this had started, really.

We'd come a long way since that day, but not nearly as far as I'd hoped.

"It'll warm up in a second," Ryder said after he started the car. The engine had a purr so quiet I barely noticed it.

"So. This is the Rydermobile, eh?" I looked around at the leather interior. It was spotless. Other than the shopping bags he'd just tossed into the backseat, there was really nothing in it. No discarded water bottles or forgotten fast-food wrappers. I knew Gert was a mess, but jeez. This car was almost scary clean.

As if he'd read my mind, Ryder said, "Yeah. My mom's always on me to keep it clean. She's a little anal about stuff like that. Probably because my dad was such a slob." The disdain in his voice was undeniable. "But there are worse things than a clean car, so I don't complain."

Though somehow, I knew he would have before the truth about his father came out. He would have thought his mother was a tyrant back then. Back before he decided she was a saint.

I wasn't going to bring that up, though. Instead, I decided to bring up my own dysfunctional family unit.

"Hey. I've been meaning to tell you . . ." We were pulling out of the parking lot now, smoothly turning onto the highway that would lead us back into Hamilton. "I, um . . . I wrote to my dad."

He glanced at me before turning back to the road. "You did?"

"Yeah. After we talked at the park that day. What you said, about letting people surprise you . . . Well, anyway, I wrote to him. I didn't want to say anything unless something good out of it. I didn't want to be embarrassed —"

"You wouldn't need to be embarrassed," he said. "If he didn't write or call you back, he's the one who should be embarrassed."

"Well, actually, he did. Yesterday. He called me."

"Really? That's awesome, Sonny."

"It was just a short call. Who knows what kind of guy he really is. You can't tell from a call, but . . . but it's the first time I've talked to him in years, and I didn't realize how much I'd missed him." I wrapped my arms around myself, suddenly feeling naked. That was too much. Too honest. Too close.

But then Ryder's hand was on my arm, and everything inside me relaxed a little. He gently tugged my arm free and his fingers slid down to circle my wrist, leaving a trail of electricity in their wake. Then he placed his palm against mine and held my hand again, the way he had in the mall, only this time his fingers laced with mine.

"I'm glad you wrote to him," he said, his eyes never leaving the road.

"Yeah. Me, too. . . . And I wouldn't have done it if it weren't for you. So, thanks."

We were silent for a minute, and I was keenly aware of his hand, still wrapped around mine. I was giddy and nervous and eventually, I had to say something.

"Anyway . . . bad gifts aside, how were your holidays?"

"Fine," he said. "Quiet. Mom hasn't really felt like doing much celebrating. Instead, she's been much more concerned with me spending the break filling out college applications."

I grimaced. "Ugh. I don't even want to think about that."

"I know what you mean," he said. "My mom went to Stanford and my dad is a Princeton alum, and they expect me to attend a top school as well. At my old school, I pretty much would've been a shoo-in wherever I wanted to go. But now that we've moved here, I'm a little worried about my chances." He paused, then quickly added, "That's not me complaining about Hamilton, by the way. At least, not intentionally."

"No," I said. "I know. And it makes sense. Hamilton's not exactly a prep school."

"It's grown on me, though." He cleared his throat. "So why are you stressed about college?"

"Because I don't think I can go."

It was the first time I'd said it out loud, and doing so made it feel so much more real and scary. I'd been ignoring the issue — or trying to — for months, but now, with only a semester left in my senior year, I was running out of places to hide.

"But you're in AP classes," he said. "That seems like a lot of stress for someone who isn't college-bound."

"I know," I agreed. "It's not that I don't want to go. But, I mean, how could I afford it?"

"Loans?"

"I don't even live with my parents, and I just lost my shitty part-time job. Who in their right mind would give me a loan?"

"So what are you going to do after graduation?"

"I have no fucking idea."

Once again, I was scared I might have said too much. That he'd realize I was a girl from a Podunk town with no future. But, just like in the park a few weeks ago, he didn't seem fazed by this. He didn't even let go of my hand. In fact, he gave it a soft, reassuring squeeze.

"Don't tell anyone," I said. "You're the first one I've admitted that to. I haven't even told Amy. She still thinks we might be able to go to school together, and I haven't been able to let her down yet."

"I won't say anything," he said.

"Thank you."

His hand stayed in mine as we drove through the darkness. And it was still there when we pulled into the Rushes' driveway ten minutes later.

"Thanks for the ride," I said.

He was still holding my hand.

"Thanks for the fun afternoon," he said.

He was still holding my hand.

"So you had fun playing dress-up, then?"

"Don't tell anyone."

He was *still holding my hand*.

It may have been the dead of winter, but it felt like the hottest summer day in that car. Every nerve in my body was on end. Every muscle I possessed was tense. Ryder and I were in a dark car, holding hands, and he was looking at me. Really looking at me. Staring at my eyes.

At my lips.

He had some nice lips himself.

He was about to kiss me. I knew it. I started to lean toward him. My eyes started to slip shut. And then —

He pulled his hand free, turned his head, and scooted away from me so fast that I wasn't sure if I'd imagined everything that had come before.

"So . . . do you know if Amy has any plans for New Year's?"

It was like he'd dropped a bucket of ice water over my head.

I was mortified.

And pissed.

I sat back in my seat and used my now empty hand to undo my seat belt. "Um . . . yeah. I think we already have plans. Sorry." My voice was cold and brittle.

"Oh. Too bad." He wasn't looking at me. In fact, it looked like he was focusing very, very hard on the steering wheel.

"Right. Well, see you at school, Ryder."

Before he could say another word — not that he would have — I got out of the car and hurried inside, slamming the door behind me.

18

"We should do something," Wesley said as he slid into the seat across from me.

"Could you be more specific?" Bianca asked. She was sitting next to him, sipping a Cherry Coke.

It was a couple of days after Christmas, and the four of us — Wesley, Bianca, Amy, and me — were spending an evening at the Nest, a local hangout popular with *some* of Hamilton's high school population.

Amy and I definitely weren't too keen on the place, but Wesley had insisted we go for "old times' sake." His old times, not ours. But alas, we'd caved in.

Wesley plucked a french fry from the basket in the middle of the table. "Winter break's not that much longer. We should do something fun before we have to go back to New York."

"I thought we were *here* because you thought it would be fun," I said.

"It is."

"We will agree to disagree."

"Oh, come on. This place is great," Wesley said. "They're hiring, you know. Don't you need a new job?"

"There's not enough money in the world," I said, cringing as a group of freshman girls squealed with delight as they ran through the front door.

"I'm with Sonny on this one," Bianca said.

"Amy's with me, though, right?" Wesley looked at his sister, who didn't disagree but also refused to meet his eyes, which was telling enough. "Something is wrong with you three. Everyone else here agrees that this is the best place to hang out in Hamilton."

"There's not exactly competition for that title," I pointed out.

Wesley ignored me. "You know," he said, a wicked grin spreading across his face as he put an arm around his girlfriend, "this is the first place Bianca and I ever kissed."

Bianca snorted, almost spitting out her Cherry Coke. "Um, it's also the first place I ever threw a drink in your face."

"Has that happened enough times to warrant a 'first'?" I asked.

Bianca nodded, and Amy and I both burst out laughing. Wesley, however, pressed on, undeterred.

"I was serious before, though," he said. "About doing something fun before school starts again."

"Like what?" Amy asked.

"Like maybe we could throw a party?"

Bianca rolled her eyes. "Again," she said. "Fun for who?"

"I don't see you coming up with any better ideas."

"Actually," she said, "I think I have one. My granddad has a cabin down in Tennessee, in the Smoky Mountains. Mom is constantly nagging me to bring some friends down to stay there for a long weekend. We'd have the place to ourselves."

"Oh," Amy said, perking up. "*That* sounds fun."

"Actually, it does," Wesley admitted.

I looked down at the surface of the table. It had been carved up over the years, names and dates and curse words cut into the wood. I focused on it, pretending to read as the three of them discussed plans to head down to Tennessee in a few days. I tried to think of something else, of my own plans for New Year's Eve, but the pulsing rhythm of the electronic dance music kept my brain from getting too far.

"We'll leave on Thursday, then," Bianca said. "A few days in the mountains. I'll let Mom know. She'll be thrilled that someone is finally using the place."

"Is there a hot tub?" Wesley asked.

Bianca didn't answer. "It'll be cold, but it's a gorgeous place to hike. So pack some boots if you have them."

"I just got a new pair," Amy said.

"Excellent. What about you, Sonny?"

My head jerked up. "Huh?"

"Boots," Bianca said. "Do you have some? If you don't, I have an extra pair that might fit. What size shoe are you?"

"Oh. Size seven, but . . ."

The truth was, as close as I felt to Wesley, I didn't know Bianca that well. I'd met her several times over the years, sure, whenever she and Wesley were home for holiday breaks, and I liked her a lot. We'd hung out plenty, but it was always with Wesley and Amy. She knew me through them, and I doubted she saw me as a friend. More like an occasional, not-entirely-unpleasant tagalong. I wasn't someone she liked well enough to invite to her grandfather's cabin.

179

I'd assumed this discussion related strictly to the two Rush siblings at the table.

"But what?" Bianca said. "You're coming with us, aren't you?"

"If you want me to," I said. "I just figured it would be the three of you. A family trip or something."

"You are family." Wesley said it like it was the most obvious thing in the world. Like it was something no one could deny. The sky was blue, the Earth revolved around the sun, and I was family.

I felt an embarrassing, unexpected lump rising in my throat. Luckily, Bianca chimed in before I had to.

"Of course you're invited," she said. "Do you think we're assholes who would talk about the trip right in front of you if you weren't?"

"No, but —"

"Besides," she said, cutting me off. "Everywhere Amy goes, you go, right? You two are like a package deal."

I glanced at Amy, who was selecting a french fry from the basket. Maybe we were a package deal, but lately, it hadn't been a pretty package. She was still acting a little distant, and she practically shut down any time I mentioned Ryder, giving monosyllabic replies until she found a way to change the subject or a reason to leave the room.

Maybe getting away from it all, taking this trip with Wesley and Bianca, would be good for us.

"Okay," I said. "I'm coming."

Bianca smiled at me.

"Excellent," Wesley said, a twinkle in his eyes. "Someone will have to keep Amy occupied while Bianca and I sneak off to —"

"Ew!" Amy and I both shrieked.

"Perv," Bianca said, but she was laughing.

"I was going to say *to go hiking*," Wesley said, all mock inno-cence. "It's you three who have your minds in the gutter."

"Sure. Whatever you say." Bianca popped the last fry into her mouth. "Now can we go? I'm almost twenty-one. I feel like a creepy old lady in here."

On our way out, I risked a glance over at Amy. She caught me and gave a small smile. It wasn't fake, but it wasn't quite real either.

I told myself I would fix it. That a few days in the mountains would bring us closer again.

Unfortunately, things got worse before they got better.

"Hey, Sonny?"

I looked up from the suitcase I was packing to find Amy standing in the doorway of the guest room. There was a sweater slung over her shoulder and a pair of boots in her hand, and I knew she must've been packing, too. We were set to leave for Tennessee early the next morning. We'd be gone only a few days, but Bianca had warned us that it would be cold in the mountains, so layers were required. Pretty much my entire wardrobe was folded into the suitcase, plus a pair of snow boots I had borrowed from Mrs. Rush.

"What's up?"

"Nothing. I was just wondering if I could get my phone back from you?" she asked. "Now that you have one, I figure you don't need mine anymore."

"Oh, right." I stood up and glanced around, trying to remember where I'd left it. "I'm sorry. I completely forgot to give that back."

"No big deal. It's not like I missed any calls."

I found it in the pocket of some dirty jeans, wadded up on the floor. I held the phone out to her and she took it with her free hand.

"Thanks," she said. "Are you almost done packing?"

"Yep. Got everything but my toothbrush."

"Definitely don't forget that."

"Amy, are you saying I have bad morning breath?" I asked, feigning insult. "I'm devastated."

She gave a little giggle, but I noticed she didn't deny my accusation either. "I'm looking forward to this," she said. "This trip, I mean. I think it'll be good to get out of Hamilton for a few days. Just the four of us, you know? No school. No distractions."

No Ryder.

She didn't say it, but she didn't have to. I knew what she was thinking.

"Me, too," I said.

"Well, I should finish packing. Thanks for the phone."

"Yeah. No problem."

When she was gone, I went back to my suitcase and began to zip it shut. I'd only moved the zipper a couple inches when I heard the little trill from down the hall. The familiar sound of a text message coming through on Amy's phone.

Amy's phone.

Amy never got text messages.

Except from Ryder.

Then I realized with horror that I hadn't deleted the last few text messages we'd sent. They were from a few days ago — before Christmas, before our almost-kiss in his car — and, to make matters worse, they were of the sexier variety.

"Oh, shit!"

I jumped to my feet and sprinted down the hall, flinging open Amy's bedroom door.

But it was too late.

She was holding the phone, staring down at the screen with wide eyes.

"Amy," I said slowly, my heart racing.

She looked up at me, her shock melting into an expression I'd rarely seen her wear.

Fury.

"You've been texting him?" she asked. "You've been texting him these messages and pretending to be me?"

"I can explain," I said. Because that's what everyone said in a situation like this. In reality, though, I didn't even have a good lie to cover my ass.

"I don't think you can," she said. Her voice was so calm, so quiet, that it sent chills up my spine. The sharp contrast between her tone and her blazing eyes was terrifying. "You were supposed to be making him *not* like me. You were supposed to be scaring him off so he'd like *you*. So we could be done with this. But all this time you've been . . ." She looked down at the phone again. "He thinks I sent these?"

"Amy . . ."

She threw the phone on the bed and turned away from me. "I have to finish packing."

"Amy, I'm —"

"Just go, Sonny." She wasn't looking at me. "Just . . . Just get out of my room."

It was the first time she'd ever kicked me out of her room. Before it had been my choice, my decision to give her space. But this time . . .

This time she was telling me to leave.

And she had every right to.

Because I'd really fucked up this time.

19

It was an almost-seven-hour drive from Hamilton to Bianca's grandfather's cabin in Tennessee.

And it was possibly the most painful seven hours of my life.

Though I would say the feeling was mutual for everyone in the car, for one reason or another.

To start with, Wesley insisted on taking the Porsche.

"There are four of us," Bianca argued. We were standing outside the Rushes' house the next morning, ready to go.

Amy hadn't said a word to me since she'd kicked me out of her room the night before.

"There are four seats," Wesley said.

"Are you actually counting that backseat as a seat?" Bianca asked. "Because, having sat back there before, I'd beg to differ."

"Well, we can't take your car," he said, picking up her duffel bag and tossing it into the trunk. Although, is it called a trunk when it's at the front of the car? I was really confused about this, but it didn't seem like the appropriate time to ask. "You *still* haven't gotten that heater fixed. And I know Sonny's car is out of the shop, but do you really trust that thing to get us across state lines?" He picked up my little suitcase and shoved it into the trunk, too.

It was a really small trunk, and I wasn't sure all of our stuff would fit.

"What about Amy's car?" Bianca asked.

Wesley put the last bag into the trunk and, with what seemed like great effort, shut the hood. "Too late," he said. "We're already packed."

Bianca groaned. "You're such an ass."

"An ass with a nice car."

"A nice, impractical car."

"And having a broken heater for three years is practical?"

"I'm hardly ever home to drive the thing!"

I glanced over at Amy, who — rather pointedly, if I may say so — did not look at me.

Since Bianca and I were the vertically challenged members of this foursome, we were placed in the, as previously noted, tiny-as-hell backseat. My knees were cramping within ten minutes, and we had a long way to go.

And in a car that small, there was no hiding the tension between two best friends who were not on speaking terms. Particularly when the other two passengers were of a bantering nature.

"Oh my God, Wesley," Bianca said. "We are not listening to this shit all the way to Tennessee."

"Billy Joel is hardly 'shit,' thank you."

"I like Billy Joel, but not seven hours of Billy Joel." Bianca turned to me. "He's been obsessed with 'New York State of Mind' for *months*. I can't anymore. Sonny, Amy, back me up."

But Amy just shrugged, and I felt too weird arguing with either Bianca or Wesley, even if it was in jest. My gut was telling me to keep my mouth shut for once. At least around Amy. My foolish hope was that if I was quiet long enough, she'd cool down about last night's little discovery. I didn't want to fan the flames by saying something unintentionally infuriating.

"Silence?" Wesley asked. "Really? From you two?"

"Seriously," Bianca said. "Are you guys okay?"

"I'm fine," Amy said. But there was that little inflection, that slightly clipped tone, that told me she definitely wasn't.

"Me, too," I mumbled.

"Okay . . . ," Wesley said.

I noticed his and Bianca's eyes meet in the rearview mirror.

This went on *forever*. And Bianca and Wesley just didn't know when to give it a rest.

"No, that wasn't our exit, Bianca. I'm positive."

"Excuse me? Who in this car has actually been to this cabin before?"

"And who has the worse sense of direction?"

"I do not."

"You got lost in midtown Manhattan. This year. You've been going to school there for how long?"

"It could happen to anyone."

"The streets are numbered," Wesley pointed out. "It's a grid."

"I might trust you more if you used the GPS on your phone to get us there."

"I can't. The voice is annoying."

"*Your* voice is annoying," Bianca snorted.

"Aw. I love you, too."

She laughed. "Okay, let's ask the rest of the car. Ladies, who do you trust to get you to the cabin safely? The person who has been there before —"

"And who gets lost in her own dorm building."

"Shut up. That's not even true." Bianca cleared her throat. "The person who has actually *been* there, or the cocky jerk who won't even use a GPS?"

But all they got were shrugs.

They made a few more attempts before finally giving up on convincing Amy or me to speak.

They talked a little more, but eventually even they fell silent, swallowed up by the potent blend of hostility and unease filling the cab of the Porsche.

Even as my knees ached, I stayed as still as possible, worried my movements may jostle the back of Amy's seat. It was dumb, I knew. It wasn't like nudging her a little to get comfortable would make her hate me any more than she already did, but the fear had crept up inside of me and wrapped itself around my chest like a boa constrictor.

The wide, flat highways eventually turned into narrow, winding back roads that twisted their way through rolling, faintly blue hills. My anxiety and aching knees aside, it was a beautiful drive.

At long, long last, Wesley made a turn onto a gravel driveway that twisted through tall trees before coming to a stop in front of a quaint little cabin.

It was small but well kept. The front porch had a swing in one corner, and a layer of snow covered the roof. Honestly, it looked like the picture you'd find on a Hallmark Christmas card.

"Oh, thank God," I heard Bianca mutter under her breath as Wesley shut off the ignition.

Ditto, I thought.

The four of us climbed out of the car and retrieved our stuff from the front-trunk. Bianca found the hidden key beneath the doormat and unlocked the door.

The interior was pretty plain, but cozy. There was an old box TV, a fireplace, and a hallway that led back to the bedrooms.

Of which there were only two.

Which meant I was back to sharing with Amy.

"This will be your room," Bianca said, opening the door to the smaller of the two rooms. It was plain, too, with a small closet and a queen-size bed shoved up against the far wall.

Amy and I glanced at each other, then back at the small room.

"Yeah," Bianca said slowly. "I'm gonna let you two settle in." And then she ducked out of there so fast she might have been mistaken for a cartoon character on the run.

I shut the door behind her before turning to Amy and offering a small smile.

"Cute house," I said.

"Yeah."

"It'll be a fun trip."

"Mm-hm."

"Nice to get away for a few days."

"Definitely."

That was all I could get out of her: one-word answers.

But it wasn't as if she was like this with everyone. As the first night and next day wore on, I caught her talking to Bianca and to her brother, laughing with them, even. But the minute I entered the room, her mouth shut.

She'd been distant since Black Friday, but nothing like this.

And with no cell phone service and nowhere else to go, it didn't take long for the silence to start getting to me.

It was freezing in the mountains.

Although it was far colder inside the cabin than out.

Bianca and Wesley tried to fill the silence with banter and mock arguments. Or maybe not "mock" arguments. It was always hard to tell with them. I wasn't sure how aware they were of the intense teen angst that was brewing, but I had to give them some credit for attempting to defuse the awkward.

Still, I spent most of my time outside, hiking in the snow and bitter wind. Melancholy mood aside, I couldn't deny how pretty the mountains were. They were blue and misty, and more low and rounded than I'd realized. They'd been quite aptly dubbed the Smoky Mountains, because they really did look like billowing puffs of smoke.

On the afternoon of New Year's Eve, I headed out of the cabin for another hike. My skin was dry and cracked from all the hours I'd spent in the freezing cold over the past few days, but it was the only way to keep from going insane.

So I put on my boots and pulled a hat down over my curls before heading out the door.

And ran right into Bianca and Wesley.

Making out on the porch.

"Jesus," I said as they broke apart. Bianca looked appropriately sheepish. Wesley, on the other hand, just grinned. "You two have your own room. In the house. Where it's warm."

Bianca cleared her throat and shook the car keys in her hand. "I was just . . . on my way. You need anything from the grocery store, Sonny? I'm getting lots of snacks for the ball drop."

"Thanks, but I'm good. Not really feeling that festive."

Bianca and Wesley glanced at each other, then she started backing off the porch. "Well, give me a call if you change your mind."

"There's no cell reception," Wesley reminded her.

"Then I hope you don't change your mind. I'll be back."

She hopped off the porch, her feet crunching in the snow, and unlocked Wesley's car before sliding inside.

"You let her drive the Porsche?" I asked him.

"I let her do whatever she wants," he said.

I wasn't sure if there was a lascivious note in that response or not.

We watched as the Porsche drove off, disappearing down the long, winding driveway. Once it had gone, I started down the wooden steps. "See you later."

Wesley followed me. "Where are you going?"

"On a hike."

"I'll join you."

It wasn't a question.

We made our way around the side of the cabin, toward the thickest part of the woods and some of the best trails. Snow clung to the bare, skeleton trees, some higher than any I'd ever seen. Neither of us spoke for a few minutes, and I started to think that this walk might actually pass in silence. But, of course, this was Wesley. He wasn't known for being quiet.

Or for minding his own business.

"So what's going on with you and Amy?"

"What do you mean?"

But even I, convincing as I typically was, couldn't play dumb on this. Especially not with Wesley, who'd known both of us since we were toddlers.

"Come on," he said, rolling his eyes. "You've barely spoken since we got here. Amy might be the quiet type, but you are most definitely not."

"That doesn't mean there's something wrong with me and Amy."

"Yes, it does," Wesley said. "She's acting weird, too. Come on. Just tell me. I'll nag you until you do."

Unfortunately, I knew he wasn't bluffing. I also knew that if I didn't tell him on this walk, he'd get Bianca in on helping him and I'd never escape. Might as well get it over with.

I shoved my hands deep into the pockets of my coat. "It's . . . it's about a boy."

Wesley raised an eyebrow. "Seriously? A guy is what's coming between you two?"

"No," I said. "Well . . . yes. But not in the way you think. It's complicated. Amy doesn't like him. I do."

"So what's the problem, then?"

"It's complicated."

"As you've said. But we have lots of time to hike. Which means lots of time for you to explain."

God, he was persistent. How the hell did Bianca put up with it?

I ducked under a low-hanging tree branch, both to avoid his eyes and to save myself from getting smacked in the face. "He's new in Hamilton, and he's kind of a tool. I thought I hated him, but then I got to know him and he's not so bad. . . . He's kind of great, actually."

"Doesn't sound too complicated so far."

"Well, here's where it starts, then, because he likes Amy."

"Oh."

"Yeah."

Wesley thought about this for a long moment as we wove between the trees, our feet sinking deep into the snow. "Does this guy — this kind of a tool, kind of great guy — know that you like him?"

I shook my head.

"So how do you know that he doesn't like you?"

"Please excuse me while I have horrifying middle school flash-backs triggered entirely by this conversation."

He laughed. "Fine. Better question. Why do you like him?"

"He's . . ." I smiled a little as a snowflake drifted down and landed on the tip of my nose. "He's a lot like me. He gets me in a way a guy never has before. And I think I get him, too."

Wesley grinned. "Wow," he said. "That's shockingly senti-mental coming from you. I've never heard you say something so heartfelt about anyone besides Amy."

I might have blushed if my face wasn't moments from becom-ing an ice cube.

"You should tell him how you feel," he said. It was so noncha-lant. So casual. Like what he was suggesting was the simplest thing in the world.

I had no idea he was so dumb.

"I can't."

"Why not?"

"It's complicated."

"We've already established this."

I bit my lip.

"From what you've said, it sounds like he might feel the same way about you."

"I've barely said anything," I pointed out. "And, no. He likes Amy. She's sweet and gorgeous and I'm . . ."

"You're what?"

He wasn't letting me off the hook.

"And I'm . . . not Amy."

Wesley stopped and put his gloved hand on my arm, turning me to face him. I had to tilt my head up to meet his eyes.

"Okay," he said. "Listen to me. First, stop comparing yourself to Amy."

"There's no comparison —"

"Stop." He glared at me, daring me to speak again. I didn't, and he continued. "You've got to stop sizing yourself up. I know it seems like it matters now — I used to think so, too — but it doesn't. Trust me."

I rolled my eyes. That was easy for him to say. He was a Rush. He was gorgeous and well liked. And it wasn't like I thought I was hideous or anything. I just knew that someone who found Amy attractive probably wouldn't be as interested in me.

"Second," Wesley said, drawing my attention back. "Are you really going to let this get between you and my sister?"

Guilt twisted my stomach, and I swallowed. "I don't want it to."

"Then don't," he said. "This guy might be as great as you say, but you two have something special. You've been inseparable from the minute you met. Like peanut butter and jelly."

"Ew."

"Right. I forget you don't like peanut butter and jelly . . . but Amy never forgets. Did you know that when our parents took you two to the beach as kids, Amy would make your sandwiches herself? Dad would always forget and make peanut butter and jelly for everyone. So Amy would make you a different sandwich and pack it herself."

I looked down at my feet. I didn't know that, but it didn't surprise me.

"I don't know exactly what's going on with you two," he admitted. "I don't know how this guy figures into it. But I do know that both of you will regret it if you don't fix things."

"She won't talk to me," I said. "How can I fix things if she won't talk to me?"

"Be patient with her," he said. "You know Amy. She's not like you and me. Sometimes it takes her a while to put words to what she's feeling. She'll come to you when she's ready."

"Yeah," I said, sighing. "You're right."

"I know. I usually am."

I snorted. "Whatever you say."

"Come on. Let's head back to the house. Bianca will kill me if I die of frostbite at her grandfather's cabin."

"But you'd already be dead, so . . ."

"That wouldn't stop her."

We got turned around a few times on the way back — in our conversation, both Wesley and I had forgotten to pay attention to where we were going. Just when morbid thoughts of the Donner Party were starting to pop into my head, we spotted the cabin and made our way toward it.

We rounded the corner of the cabin just as his Porsche began making its way up the driveway.

"Hey, Sonny. Seriously, just tell the guy how you feel," Wesley said, even though that conversation had long since been dropped.

"But —"

"And don't assume you know how he feels," he said firmly. "You can't read his mind. Give him a chance. He might surprise you." He smiled, watching Bianca as she climbed from the car.

"Hey," she yelled, waving him over. "Are you gonna come help me with these groceries or not?"

His smile turned to a grin as he hurried to her, our conversation clearly completely vanishing from his mind. "What's in it for me?" he asked as she rolled her eyes and shoved a bag into his hands.

I hung back, watching them for a long moment. Wesley's words had left me a little a stunned. Ryder had said almost the exact same thing when he encouraged me to contact my dad.

And he'd sort of implied it about me.

Maybe Wesley was right. Maybe Ryder would surprise me if I just gave him a chance.

And as for Amy, I just needed to be patient. She'd come to me eventually, and we'd work things out when she did.

20

Bianca hadn't disappointed when it came to snacks for the night. She bought candy, popcorn, and a gallon of chocolate-swirl ice cream. Not to mention more Cherry Coke than a person could or should even drink in two days, which was all that remained of our Appalachian adventure.

The four of us piled into the living room, the fireplace blazing, to watch the ball drop. Amy stayed quiet, as she usually did when I was in the room now, but I tried to keep my spirits up. Partly because of what Wesley had said — knowing that when Amy was ready, she'd talk to me — but mostly for Bianca's sake. This trip had been her idea, after all, and I hadn't been the most pleasant guest.

"You sure you don't want any ice cream, Amy?" Bianca asked.

"No, thank you," Amy said.

"Not everyone likes ice cream in the dead of winter," Wesley said.

Bianca shut him up by shoving a spoonful of ice cream in his mouth. He reeled back, cupping his hands over his head. "Oh, I'm sorry," Bianca teased. "Brain freeze?"

Wesley took a few deep breaths, then looked up. "You're going to pay for that," he said just before leaping on top of her. She shrieked as he began to tickle her sides.

It was too disgustingly adorable, and I had to look away. Which was when I caught Amy's eye.

She was watching me, I realized. I gave her a small smile, but it fell fast when she looked away.

"I think I'm gonna go to bed," she said, getting to her feet.

Bianca and Wesley sat up, both still laughing.

"It's only eleven-thirty," Bianca said. "Are you sure?"

"Yeah. I'm a little tired. I'm sorry."

"Okay, well . . . we'll see you in the morning."

"Good night, Amy," Wesley said.

"Good night." She started down the hallway, toward our little room, then stopped and looked back. "Hey, Sonny?"

I turned to her, surprised and a little hopeful. "Yeah?"

"Will you come talk to me for a minute?"

"Sure," I said. "Of course."

I stood up, then looked over at Wesley, who was giving me a very I-told-you-so look.

"Night," I said, and left Bianca and Wesley alone in the living room, waiting for the ball to drop.

I followed Amy into our room and quietly shut the door behind me. Amy sat down on the bed, chewing on her bottom lip. I remained standing, leaning against the wall.

"So, I've been thinking . . . about this whole Ryder thing," she said.

"Amy, I'm so sorry about the texts," I said, unable to hold it back. "I know it was wrong. I knew it even when I did it, and you have every right to be pissed at me. But I swear, it won't happen again."

"I appreciate that, but ——"

"I mean, you have your phone back now," I said. "And I haven't IMed Ryder in forever, so the catfishing is over."

"Good . . ." She took a deep breath. "But it's more than just that."

"I know," I said. "The texts were kind of dirty and that's weird for you, and I'm really ——"

"Sonny, no," she said. "I mean, yes. It's weird. But that's not what I'm trying to say."

"Well, then, say it."

"I'm trying." She sighed. "I know you really like him. And I know you didn't mean to upset me. You'd never mean to do that. But . . . this whole thing has gone on a lot longer than I thought."

"What whole thing?"

"Your plan," she said. "To make Ryder like you and not like me. Me acting weird and rude around him. I just . . . I really don't feel comfortable doing it."

"I know," I said. "I know. But we're so close." I moved to sit on the bed beside her. "Really, really close, Amy. It won't take much longer."

"You've said that from the start," she said.

She wasn't wrong about that.

"But, Amy ——"

"Wait. Just . . . let me finish." She tugged on a curl and stared at the wall for a second, silent. "I know you like him," she said again. "But I don't think I can do this anymore. I can't keep lying.

200

I'm not good at it the way you are. And I don't like being rude. And I don't like him thinking I've been sending those texts —"

"I told you. I don't do that anymore."

"But it's already been done," she said. "And he thinks it was me who sent them."

"So . . . what are you saying?" I asked.

"I guess I'm saying that I want out," she said. "I don't want to do this anymore."

"But you said you'd help me."

"It didn't feel like I had a choice," she admitted. "And I didn't think it would go this far. I'm sorry, Sonny. I just . . . I can't." She wrung her hands in her lap and took another deep breath. "And . . . and I want you to tell him the truth. That none of it was me."

"Oh." I hadn't seen that last part coming.

"I just . . . I think he should know," she said. Every word seemed to cost her something. "And I need him to know. It'll be better for all of us."

I nodded, but inside I was a mess of feelings. Anger at Amy, guilt, regret, heartbreak. Because for all the good things Wesley had said on our hike that day, about Ryder maybe surprising me, I knew it didn't matter now.

If Amy wasn't going to play along anymore, I didn't have a choice. I was going to have to come clean, and that meant I had no chance with Ryder. All of our progress had been for nothing.

"I'm sorry," she said again.

"I understand," I said.

And I did. As upset as I was that she was bailing, I knew why she wanted out. This scheme had gone on a lot longer than either of us had expected, and I'd known for a while she wasn't happy about it. I'd just hoped that if I pressed on, things would get better.

They hadn't.

"So . . . you'll tell him?" she asked.

"Yeah," I said. "I guess I will."

"Thank you." She wrapped her arms around my shoulders and rested her head on top of mine. "Thank you for understanding."

As we changed into our pajamas and climbed into the bed, I tried to look on the bright side. Everything was about to crumble with Ryder, but at least I had Amy back.

That's what really mattered, right? It was like Wesley said. Amy and I had been together forever. We needed each other. It would be crazy to let a guy — even a great guy like Ryder — come between us.

That didn't make what she was asking easy, though.

In the other room, Bianca and Wesley cheered as the television counted down. "Three! Two! One!"

"Happy New Year, Sonny," Amy whispered.

"Happy New Year."

21

I was dreading history class on Wednesday morning, the first day back from break.

Not only would it be my first time seeing Ryder since our almost-kiss in the Rushes' driveway *and* my first contact with him since I'd promised Amy I'd tell him the truth, but we were also beginning our unit on World War I, which I — personally — found super boring.

I hadn't figured out yet when or how I was going to confess my myriad of lies to the boy of my dreams, but I had a feeling that doing it at school, with everyone around, was a bad idea. While part of me was glad to have a little more time, another part just wanted to rip off the damn Band-Aid and get it over with. It was going to be ugly no matter when I did it, and I knew, without a doubt, that it would end any hope I'd had of winning him over in the long run.

Which was why seeing him smile up at me when I walked into class that morning was so incredibly painful.

"Hey, Sonny," he said, swiveling in his seat to face me as I sat down behind him. He gave me a slightly nervous smile and adjusted his thick-framed glasses. "How was the rest of your break?"

"Good," I mumbled as I pulled out my textbook. "How was yours?"

"It was fine."

There was a long, awkward pause. I fidgeted in my seat and fiddled with the pages of my book. Finally, I looked up and caught him watching me. I expected him to ask about Amy, but he didn't. "You okay?" he asked. "You seem a little . . . off."

He was right. Sonny Ardmore wasn't known for avoiding people's eyes. Or for mumbling. Today I was definitely "off."

I shook my head. "I'm good. Just . . . trying to get back into the swing of things. It's always hard after a long break. . . . And you *know* how much I hate talking about World War One."

He laughed. "Yes. I think the whole class does. You've been pretty vocal about it. You actually asked Mr. Buckley if we could skip the whole unit last semester."

"And I'm going to ask again," I assured him. "Persistence is a virtue."

"I thought patience was a virtue."

"A virtue I lack."

Oh, no. I was doing it again. Sinking into the rhythm of our conversation, letting myself get swept up in it. I needed to stop this. I couldn't let myself fall any harder for him. Not when it was all about to go up in flames. Time to get started on that Band-Aid.

"Hey, listen, Ryder," I said. "Are you . . . are you busy this weekend?"

He raised an eyebrow, and I realized with a jolt what my question must have sounded like.

"Just to hang out . . . as friends," I added. I almost told him that I needed to talk to him about something, but I knew that would just solicit too many questions. I wanted to tell him on the weekend, sometime when he wouldn't have to see me the next day. I figured it would be kinder to the both of us.

"Actually," he said, brightening, "I was going to invite you to a party. I've somehow managed to acquire an invitation to Chris Lawson's on Friday night. I guess my efforts to be less of an asshole have paid off."

A party wasn't exactly the scenario I'd had in mind — again, too many of our classmates would be around. But at least the music would be loud enough that, hopefully, no one would hear him screaming at me. Or maybe I could pull him into a bedroom or somewhere outside. Or, even better, I could get him drunk before I told him the truth.

Or maybe I just secretly wanted to go to a party with Ryder Cross at least one time before this all fell apart.

"That sounds great," I said. But then, knowing what he might say next, I preemptively added, "I don't think Amy can come, though. She's got plans this Friday. With her parents."

"Oh," he said. But he didn't look as disappointed as I'd expected. I tried not to read too much into that. "Well, that's fine. We can still hang out, right?"

"Yeah," I said. "Sure. If you're okay with that."

"I am," he said. He smiled. "It'll be fun. I'm actually excited to go to a party here. Maybe finally make some friends. Show people I'm not a pretentious snob."

"Oh, Ryder." I sighed. "You are a pretentious snob . . . but you have a few redeeming qualities. Namely that you're rich."

"Ha-ha," he said. "I was wrong. You're not off today. You're very Sonny."

"And by 'Sonny,' you mean delightful?"

Mr. Buckley walked in then, and Ryder had to turn back around in his seat. I was relieved, honestly. The more I talked to Ryder, the less I wanted to tell him the truth. And not telling the truth wasn't an option anymore. I'd promised Amy, and I was going to follow through on it. No matter how hard it might be.

Or how much it might break my heart.

"So you're telling him tonight?"

"Yep."

It was Friday, which meant I'd survived the past two days seeing Ryder in class, knowing the end was coming. But here we were, an hour before the party, and I could almost hear the countdown in my head, ticking away like one of those time bombs on TV.

Amy stood up and grabbed the pick from my hand. "You're going to rip your hair out," she said. "It's gonna be okay, Sonny."

I stared at the mirror over Amy's dresser as she took a section of my hair and began combing through the curls herself. I'd already done my makeup twice, but it still didn't look right. Probably because I never really wore makeup. But waiting for the party for hours after school was too nerve-racking. I needed something to do with my hands. Something I could do and erase and redo to perfection. Not that I'd achieved makeup perfection.

"It won't be as bad as you think," she said, moving to another section of hair.

"He's going to hate me, Amy."

"No, he won't."

"Just because you're so forgiving doesn't mean everyone else is." I tugged on the sleeve of my sweater. It was too tight and the turtleneck was choking me. "He'll never speak to me again."

Amy didn't say anything as she finished with my hair. Under her careful guidance, my curls actually looked nice. She smiled at her handiwork, our eyes meeting in the mirror.

"Thanks," I said.

She wrapped her arms around my shoulders and pulled me into a tight hug. "I know this is hard, but it means a lot to me."

I nodded and leaned my head on her shoulder. "I should've done it a long time ago. I'm sorry I dragged you into all of this. I really didn't think it would go this far, but . . ."

"But it ends tonight," she said. She released me and brushed a few of my curls behind my ear. "And you'll feel so much better afterward."

I nodded, though I knew it wasn't true.

"And who knows?" she said. "You two have a connection. You've said so yourself. Maybe once he learns the truth, he'll recognize that. Maybe he'll understand and you two will finally —"

"Don't," I said, shaking my head. "Don't give me false hope."

"I reject and deny the notion of 'false hope.' Hope is never false." She put her hands on her hips and lifted her chin. "If he's smart, he'll listen. He might be mad, but he'll hear you out and realize how perfect you are for him."

But I knew Ryder. He may have been smart, but he held a grudge. He'd gone from practically worshipping his father to wanting nothing to do with him. What his father had done was awful, no doubt, but he was still his family. And who was I? The best friend of the girl he thought he liked? The annoying girl from history class? He owed me no loyalty.

Amy wouldn't hear it, though, so I just nodded and sat down on the bed to tie my sneakers. It was seven-thirty, and the party started at eight. The Rushes had curfew set at eleven on weekends, so at least this would all be over in three and a half hours.

Which would likely be the worst three and a half hours of my life.

"Just so you know, I told Ryder you had plans with your parents," I said. "I know you're tired of the lying, but if I hadn't said something, he'd expect you to be there, so . . ."

"It's okay." She sat down next to me on the bed. "It's the last lie you'll tell in all of this." She sighed. "I know this is hard for you, but I'm really glad it's going to be over tonight. I'm no good at lying, and always keeping an eye out for Ryder at school — ducking into bathrooms and around corners — I'm way too tall and awkward to be a superspy, Sonny."

I laughed, despite myself. "You can say that again." I got to my feet. "Okay. How do I look?"

"Adorable," Amy said. "Love the blue turtleneck. Is that mine?"

"Yep. Don't tell, but I had to stuff my bra a little bit to make it look right on me. I like to think that if I look nice enough, Ryder might be like, 'Yeah, I'm super pissed, but you're hot, so all is forgiven.'"

"Seems totally plausible to me," Amy said. "But if that doesn't work out, I'll be waiting here with ice cream and Audrey Hepburn movies."

"You know I'm more of a Marilyn girl."

"We're not having this fight again."

"Another time," I assured her. "But now, I'm off to my doom. Enjoy your evening."

I exited the bedroom with dramatic flair, which was somewhat undercut by Amy following me downstairs.

"Hey," she said as I slid on my coat by the front door. "Can I say just one more thing?"

"You never have to ask me that."

"He's probably going to be mad at first," she said. "But if he doesn't realize how great you are, despite this little kerfuffle —"

"'Kerfuffle'? Oh my God, you've been around me too long."

"Shut up and listen." But her lips twitched toward a smile. "Despite this *kerfuffle*, if he doesn't see how awesome you are, Sonny, it's his loss."

"Thank you," I said, accepting another hug that I definitely did not deserve.

She was wrong, though. If — *when* — Ryder rejected me and refused to speak to me again, the loss would be entirely my own. The guilt twisted in my stomach, and I wished, not for the first time, that I'd found a way to tell him the truth earlier, when the lie first began as just an accident. But now, it had gone way too far.

"See you later," I said, opening the front door and stepping out onto the porch.

"Good luck," Amy called.

I dragged my feet down the driveway. When I finally reached Gert, I pulled out my keys and sighed. "It's gonna be a long night, girl," I said, sliding into the driver's seat. "Let's get it over with."

22

Chris Lawson wasn't one of those popular jock types. But man, he wanted to be. He was constantly trying to be the cool guy, seemingly unaware that cool people were cool because they didn't try.

And Chris's party was kind of a reflection of himself.

It wasn't bad as far as parties go. It was just trying too hard.

The speakers were blasting loud rap music when I walked in. People were milling about the living room, red Solo cups in hand, though no one seemed quite as enthusiastic about the party as Chris, who darted over to greet me.

"Sonny!" he shouted. "Awesome! Glad you came!"

"Thanks, Chris."

"You should go dance! Everyone's dancing!"

No one — not a single person — was dancing.

"Maybe later," I said.

"Wanna watch me do a keg stand?"

"Sure, but not right now. I'm actually looking for someone. Is Ryder here yet?"

"Who?"

"Ryder Cross."

"The new kid?" Chris asked.

Ryder had been in Hamilton for more than a semester, so I wasn't sure "the new kid" was still an appropriate title, but I nodded nonetheless. "Yeah. Is he here yet?"

"Yep. Saw him walk back into the kitchen a few minutes ago."

"Great. Thanks."

"No problem," he said. "Enjoy the party, Sonny! We're gonna blow this place up!"

"Uh-huh. Definitely."

As promised, I found Ryder in the kitchen, a red cup in his hand.

"You drink?" I asked, a little surprised.

He looked up and smiled when he saw me. "Sometimes," he said. "But not tonight. This is water. I don't have enough friends here to know I'll have a ride home."

Damn. I was sort of hoping to get him inebriated before the truth came out. Why did he have to be so mature and responsible?

"You can drink, though," Ryder said. "I know Amy isn't with you, but I can give you a ride home later if you wanted."

"And leave Gert here? Where anyone might steal her?"

He snorted. "I have the feeling no one wants to steal your car."

"Hey, don't dis Gert. She's vintage."

"Is that what we're calling it now?"

The truth was, I would have loved for Ryder to drive me home. To maybe, possibly, go through with that almost-kiss from a couple of weeks ago. But I knew that, after what I was about to tell him, there was no way he'd want to be stuck in a car with me. In fact, he'd probably be more than happy to strand me here at Chris's party.

Ryder finished his water and tossed the cup into the recycling. "It's for the best," he said. "I'm sure the beer here is no good."

"Oh, great. Are you a beer snob, too?"

"No," he said defensively. "I just prefer PBR."

I snorted. "Of course you do. I should've known."

Ryder looked a little sheepish.

"You know," I said, "this is something you and I may have in common. Pabst Blue Ribbon might be the drink of hipsters, but it's also the drink of my people — poor white trash. It was always my dad's favorite beer."

"Don't call yourself white trash," he said. He was suddenly very serious, and looking at me in a way that he hadn't before. In a way that made me catch my breath.

Now was the time to tell him. Get it over with and go home. I opened my mouth to begin the confession, to finally tell him the truth, but the words that came out weren't at all the ones I'd intended to say.

"Do you wanna dance?"

Ryder blinked at me. "What was that?"

Take it back, I thought. *That's not why you're here.* My mouth and my brain seemed to be at war with each other.

"Let's dance," I said, already trying to justify it. I had a few hours. Might as well have a little fun before I broke the news, right?

"But . . . no one else is dancing."

"Perfect. Then you can be a hipster about it later. *We were dancing before dancing was cool*," I said, doing a fake Ryder voice.

"I do *not* sound like that."

"Whatever you need to tell yourself to sleep at night." I grabbed his arm and started pulling him into the living room. "Come on. Be spontaneous."

"The last time you said that to me, I ended up in a bright orange hunting jacket in the middle of the mall."

"And wasn't that fun?"

The answer must have been yes, because Ryder didn't argue. Instead, he grabbed my other hand and spun me into the living room. The heavy bass hip-hop wasn't exactly the right jam for spinning and dipping a girl, but Ryder didn't seem to care. He twirled me like a ballroom dancer, and somehow managed to keep us in rhythm with the music.

"Wow," I said when he swung me back into his arms, his hand resting on my hip. We were so close, closer than we'd ever been before. And I felt like I was on fire. And then there was the fact that everyone was staring. "This is how you dance at parties?"

"My mom made me take ballroom classes in middle school," he confessed. "It's the only way I know how to dance. Sorry. It's pretty embarrassing."

"No," I said, shaking my head. "It's the opposite of embarrassing. It's fantastic. These idiots *wish* they could be us right now."

Ryder smiled and gave me another spin.

We danced until we couldn't anymore. Until our feet hurt and we were short of breath, either from the exertion or from standing so close to each other. For me, it was definitely the latter.

"Do you want some water?" Ryder asked.

I nodded, and we made our way back to the kitchen, stumbling despite our sobriety.

Ryder grabbed us each a red cup and began to fill them with tap water. I hopped up onto the counter, taking some of the pressure off my feet. "Damn. That was —"

"That. Was. Awesome!" Chris announced as he charged into the living room. "You two killed it out there! Everyone's talking about it!"

"The same way everyone was dancing earlier?" I asked as Ryder handed me my cup.

Chris didn't seem to hear me. "Ryder, dude, that was wicked! I thought dancing was lame, but all the girls out there ate it up! You've gotta teach me your moves!"

I snorted into my water as I imagined Chris trying to dance the way Ryder did. He'd probably get a little too into it and end up giving some poor girl a concussion.

"I'll put on whatever music you want if you guys want to dance again!"

"Maybe in a little while," Ryder agreed. He looked over at me, those green eyes meeting mine in a way that made me shiver. "If Sonny's up for it."

We held each other's gaze for a long moment.

"Sweet!" Chris said. "I better get back out there. Gotta keep things under control."

"What was out of control?" Ryder murmured so that only I could hear.

I laughed, and Chris ran back into the living room.

"You know," Ryder said, "we probably were the highlight of this party."

"Are you kidding me? I'm the highlight of every party."

Ryder smiled. "I don't doubt that."

Again with the shiver.

Everyone must've finished their beers at once, because all of a sudden the kitchen became a high-traffic area. Ryder took my cup from me so I could hop off the counter without spilling. He gestured for me to follow him, and we wove our way through the pack of thirsty partyers, darting into the hallway to avoid another run-in with Chris.

Somehow, we ended up in an empty bedroom.

I took my cup back from Ryder and sat down on the edge of the bed. "So," I said. "What's the verdict on your first Hamilton party?"

"Not too shabby," he said.

"But I'm sure it doesn't even compare to the parties back in DC, right?"

"This party is much better than the ones in DC."

"Oh, come on," I said, setting my cup on the nightstand. "That's not even remotely possible. You partied with politicians' kids. I watch enough TV to know it gets wild. Plus, you've got money. Which means better booze, at the very least."

"Maybe the parties back home had some advantages," he agreed, putting his own water down before sitting next to me.

Really close to me.

"But," he continued, his eyes on me in that way again. That way that gave me chills and made my face burn all at once. I was suddenly very aware of where we were — an empty bedroom, on a bed. "The company here is much better."

"Ryder," I said, even though every inch of me was fighting me, trying to keep me silent. But I couldn't put it off anymore. "I need to talk to you . . . about Amy."

He shook his head. "Amy is the last thing I want to talk about right now."

I'd been dying to hear those words for months. Dying for him to look at me the way he was right now. But it was too late. I'd promised Amy, sworn I'd tell him the truth tonight.

I swallowed. "Listen —"

"Sonny, wait," he said. "I just . . . I need to . . ."

Then he kissed me.

And his mouth definitely didn't taste like root beer. It was mint.

One of his hands was on my neck, the other on my knee. I didn't move — couldn't breathe or think — as his lips moved over mine. I was stunned. Paralyzed.

But when he pulled away, even just an inch, it felt like I might die.

"Was . . . was that okay?" he asked. "Should I not have done that?"

No. He definitely shouldn't have. Because I needed to tell him the truth.

Now.

Just say it, I told myself. *Before this goes any further.*

217

"Sonny?" His voice was quiet, nervous. "I'm sorry. I should've asked. Or just not . . . I didn't know I was going to do it until —"

"Shut up," I said. I grabbed him, a hand on either side of his face, and pulled him back toward me for another kiss. My heart was pounding and everything I'd wanted over the past few months was spinning in my head.

This time, when our lips met, I wasn't paralyzed at all.

Amy was already in bed when I slipped in that night, but she wasn't asleep.

"Hey," she murmured as I climbed over her and into my side of the huge bed. I'd been sleeping in here again since coming back from Tennessee. "How did it go?"

"Great," I said.

We'd made out in the bedroom for a while before Chris walked in on us. And then, when Ryder walked me out to my car, he kissed me again. I was sure it was supposed to be a quick good-night kiss, but it had lasted much longer, my back pressed against Gert's driver's side door, my arms around Ryder's neck.

I'd had to speed home to make curfew.

I could still feel the ghost of Ryder's lips on mine, his phantom hand on my hip. I shivered and hid my face in the pillow, though in the darkness, Amy could never have seen my blush.

"Really?" Amy asked, her tired voice going up an octave with excitement. "That's a relief. So you told him the truth?"

Everything was going right. Amy wasn't mad at me anymore. Ryder had kissed me. Like, a lot. I had everything I wanted.

Everything I'd been hoping for since this started in September. But it all could've fallen down with a little gust of wind. One wrong move, and I would lose everything.

So I did what I do best. What I always did when I was scared.

"Yeah," I lied. "I told him everything."

23

By Monday morning, I was dealing with some serious post-make-out regret. Not regret about the kissing specifically — that had been awesome — but about how it had come to pass. Namely, me wussing out on telling Ryder the truth.

And now that I knew exactly what I was going to be missing, telling him would be even harder.

But I had to. Because that hot make-out session didn't change anything.

So when I walked into history class that morning, I was determined to do the right thing. No matter how anxious the whole thing made me.

"Hey," I said, sliding into the seat behind his. "So . . . we should talk about what happened Friday."

Ryder had already swiveled in his seat so we were facing each other. "I was actually thinking the same thing."

For a moment, my heart sank. *He regretted the kiss, too*, I thought. But for completely different reasons. He probably couldn't believe he'd done it. He probably didn't like me that much. I was poor and less attractive. But we'd been dancing and laughing and then we were alone in a stranger's bedroom . . .

I was sure he was going to say it never should have happened.

But then —

"Why don't you come over this afternoon so we can discuss it."
And in case I hadn't noticed the slightly arched eyebrow or the
suggestive tone in his voice, he added, "My mom won't be home
until late."

"Oh."

Or maybe he didn't regret it at all.

This shouldn't have made me happy, particularly because it
made what I was about to do so much harder, but it did. That little
grin on his face gave me butterflies and thrills and all those other
silly middle-school-crush feelings.

And it *would* be easier to tell him at his house, with no one else
around to overhear. I just had to stay away from his bed. And his
couch. And his lips.

No, I thought. *Don't do this again. Tell him right now.*

"Look, Ryder, I actually —"

"All right, class," Mr. Buckley boomed as he entered the room.
"Let's talk about Germany."

And there went my chance.

I felt bad for feeling so relieved.

Ryder had passed me a note with directions to his place, which was
only a few minutes south of Amy's house. When I pulled into the
driveway around three that afternoon, I was surprised to find a
fairly small brick house. I guess I'd expected something more
extravagant just because I knew he came from money. But then, it

was only him and his mom sharing the place, so it didn't need to be huge.

He was waiting for me on the narrow front porch and smiled when I started walking toward him. The sunlight hit his eyes in just the perfect way, making the green seem even brighter. The way he looked at me took my breath away.

I tried to swallow back the panic rising inside me. He was so beautiful and so amazing and I didn't want to lose him.

When I reached him, he gave me a quick kiss.

"Come inside," he said, taking me by the arm and escorting me through the front door. "Welcome to my humble abode."

"Humble?" I repeated, staring at the living room, the furniture that most definitely showed where the money had gone. Everything was brand-new and shiny. The TV was huge. The sofas were lush and fancy. And the place was immaculate.

Ryder took my coat, his fingers skimming across my shoulders as he slid it off my arms. "It's humble compared to where we came from," he said.

"Ha. If this is humble, then you should see where I live."

"Don't you live with Amy?"

"Right. Well . . . where I used to live."

"Yeah. I've been meaning to ask you about that." He hung my coat on a hook by the door. "Why do you live with the Rushes? I know about your dad, but . . . what about your mom?"

I meant to lie. The same lie I'd told Amy and her parents. *She kicked me out, end of story.* But instead, I found myself saying the truth. At least, part of it.

"My mom . . . is kind of a mess." I followed him into the living room, but when he sat down on the couch, I stayed standing. "There've been some problems at home, so Amy was nice enough to let me stay with her."

He scoffed. "That surprises me."

I frowned. "What's that supposed to mean?"

"She just doesn't seem like the caring type," he said, his voice bitter. "She's so . . . inconsiderate. And rude. Plus, isn't she too busy dealing with her own mom issues?"

It took me a second to remember that last time I'd talked to Ryder about my mother, he'd still thought he was talking to Amy. "Hey," I said, feeling defensive even though that was exactly the image I'd wanted him to have of Amy. "She gets it, okay? Besides, she's my best friend."

"I know," he said. "I just don't know why. You've said she's great, but I don't see it."

"You saw it before," I pointed out. "In fact, it wasn't that long ago that you said the same thing about me. That you couldn't see why Amy would be friends with someone like me."

He shrugged. "I was wrong. I thought she and I had something, but it was IMs and text messages. In person, there was nothing. She wasn't the person I thought. It just took me a while to accept it. But with you . . ." He looked up at me and smiled. "There's always been something there, I think. Even when we were fighting in Mr. Buckley's class, there was this . . . energy. Chemistry, I guess. I just didn't realize it. And then on Friday . . ."

"Yeah." I looked down at my feet. "Look, about Friday, things were a little crazy and —"

"I don't think it was crazy," he said. His hand folded over mine, and he pulled me toward the couch. "In fact, I think kissing you may have been the most sane thing I've done since I moved here."

I rolled my eyes, because — let's be real — that was a cheesy line. Even if it did kind of give me butterflies.

I was standing right in front of him, my legs touching his as he looked up at me. My heart was pounding and I'm sure my face was beet red.

"You barely know me," I said.

But that wasn't true. Ryder knew me better than most people did. He saw more of me than I'd let anyone see. He just didn't know it.

"I know that you make me laugh," he said. "I know that you think faster on your feet than anyone else I've ever met. I know that you use SAT words in everyday conversation."

"So do you," I said. "Only I do it to be cute and funny. You do it because you're a prep-school snob."

"I know that you named your car because you love it, even though it's a piece of junk," he continued. "I know that your real name is Sonya."

"What? Who told you? I'll kill them."

He laughed. "I know that you're smart. And witty. And incredible."

Incredible.

It wasn't the first time he'd used that word to describe me. Before Christmas, he'd called the person behind the IMs and texts

224

"incredible." He thought it was Amy, sure, but those were my words. I was the one he thought was incredible.

"Well, um . . . did you know I'm also a serial killer?"

"Why do you do that?" he asked.

"What?"

"Anytime things get serious or sentimental, you deflect with humor," he said. "Why?"

"I don't know," I said. "I guess because I'm nervous."

He smirked. "I make you nervous?"

And, despite my better judgment, I told the truth.

"Very."

There was a flicker of recognition in his eyes, and I suddenly remembered that text message conversation back in November, where we'd admitted to making each other nervous. For a second, I thought he might figure it out. Might realize that it had been me all along.

I held my breath, not sure if I wanted him to figure it out or not.

But the moment passed as quickly as it had come. He gave my hand a little tug, and I fell into his lap. And then, even though I'd tried to avoid it — sort of — we were making out again.

I still hadn't gotten the hang of this whole kissing thing. I wasn't always sure what to do with my hands or which way to tilt my head. We bumped noses more than once, but Ryder just laughed, like my clumsy kissing skills were more adorable than annoying.

With his hands in my hair and his tongue sliding into my mouth, I made a decision.

I wasn't going to tell him the truth.

He liked me. He was totally over Amy, and he wanted to be with me. He thought I was incredible.

Part of me still wanted to compare myself to Amy. How could Ryder go from wanting someone as beautiful as her to someone like me? She was gorgeous and rich, and I was . . . average. And definitely not rich.

But that wasn't how he looked at me. Or how he treated me.

Maybe Wesley was right. Maybe comparing myself was a waste of time, and Ryder saw me as more than just the moderately attractive, somewhat obnoxious best friend.

My plan — though it had taken months — had worked.

This was what I'd wanted. What I'd been hoping for all along.

I wasn't going to tell him.

He didn't need to know.

After a while, the necessity of breathing drove us apart. But only long enough for Ryder to ask:

"I was wondering: Do you want to go out this weekend? On a real date?"

"Maybe," I said, my nose touching his. "What were you thinking?"

"Dinner and a movie?"

"Sounds fun," I said. "Oh, actually, there's this new romantic comedy that just opened. I think Rachel McAdams is in it."

Ryder wrinkled his nose. "Ugh."

"You don't like Rachel McAdams?" I asked, appalled. "What's wrong with you?"

"It's not her," he said. "I just . . . don't really like mainstream Hollywood films. I was thinking that we could go see that new Korean film that just opened at Cindependent."

"Oh my God," I said, rolling my eyes. "Everything you just said is so wrong."

But that didn't stop me from kissing him again.

24

"You've been spending a lot of time with Ryder lately," Amy said. She was sitting on her bed, watching as I applied a little bit of lipstick in the vanity mirror. "Where are you guys going tonight?"

"A movie," I said.

It was the next Saturday, a week since our first kiss, and it had been one of the most blissful weeks of my life. Suddenly, I was glad to be unemployed. We'd spent almost every afternoon together — sometimes doing homework at the library, sometimes making out in his bedroom — doing whatever we felt like that day. We were always either laughing or arguing, which usually led to laughing.

Yes, my life, for once, was awesome.

Even if he had won the movie debate.

"It's a Korean film," I told Amy as I put the cap back on the lipstick — a lipstick I'd stolen from her, actually. "And you know how I feel about subtitles. Ugh. I'm sort of hoping we can be normal and just make out in the back of the theater. Knowing Ryder, though, he'll likely think that's far too pedestrian."

I laughed and turned to face her, but Amy only gave a small smile.

"What about you?" I asked. "What are you doing tonight?"

"I'm not sure," she said. "Probably finishing up a few college applications."

"You party animal," I teased.

She laughed. "Well, I'm almost done. I've already mailed off my applications for Brown, Cornell, and Dartmouth. I'm hoping to get the others in the mail by Monday. What about you?"

"What about me what?" I asked.

"Have your applications yet?"

"Um, yeah," I lied. "Most of them." I turned back to the mirror, checking my outfit one more time, and tried to ignore the sinking feeling in my stomach. I still hadn't figured out what I was going to do after graduation, or how I was going to tell Amy that college wasn't an option.

Honestly, I couldn't believe she thought it was.

"Good," she said. "Because there's not much time left. Where did you apply?"

"Oh, you know," I said, tugging on the hem of my sweater. It was the one that the Rushes had given me for Christmas. "Mostly the same places as you."

"Great," she said. "We'll definitely get into at least a couple of the same schools. Wouldn't it be great if we could be roommates? I'm not sure if I could share a dorm room with anyone else."

"I know what you mean."

"We should go shopping soon," Amy suggested. "We could go ahead and pick out some stuff for our future dorm room. I was thinking we could decorate the room in green and —"

"That sounds great," I said, even though every word she said was killing me. "But I better get going. I have to pick Ryder up in a few minutes."

"Why isn't he picking you up?" Amy asked.

"Got to challenge those gender norms," I said. "Also, if I have to see a foreign film, he has to be seen riding around in Gert."

"I guess that seems fair."

"Have fun with your applications," I said, grabbing my purse and heading for the door. "Don't wait up, darling."

"Yeah," she said. Her voice was quiet as I headed out the bedroom door. "You have fun, too."

I may have begun my relationship with Ryder with limited kissing experience, but I was most certainly making up for lost time.

For the next few weeks, Ryder and I could hardly keep our hands off each other. We were making out in his car, in mine, at his house — occasionally in the hallways at school. Sitting behind him in AP history was torturous, because all I wanted to do was lean forward and press my lips into his neck.

I had a feeling Mr. Buckley wouldn't take too kindly to that.

There was only one thing that could distract us from kissing when we were alone together.

"We're not making out to a Goats Vote for Melons song," I said, turning my head so that Ryder's lips hit my jaw instead of my mouth.

We were horizontal in Gert's backseat, parked out beneath some trees on Lyndway Hill. Ryder's car may have been fancier (and cleaner), but Gert boasted a larger backseat. Victory for Gert.

He groaned and sat up a little, propping himself on his elbows. "What's wrong with Goats Vote for Melons?"

"It's not sexy. We need to get some Boyz II Men playing up in here."

"Who?"

"Ugh. I'm surrounded by uncultured idiots."

"Funny. I often feel the same way."

I shoved at his shoulders, forcing him up and off me. He moved too quickly, though, and his head slammed into Gert's roof. "Ow!"

"Serves you right," I said as I reached for his iPod. "Let's see. What else do we have on here? Hipster band, hipster band, hipster band . . . Oh, grunge. That's a nice change."

Next to me, Ryder seemed to deflate slightly. For a minute, I was confused; then I realized that, to him, I wasn't the grunge girl. Amy was. That was her music, and she was the reason he'd given it a chance.

Part of me wanted to correct him on this. To tell some story about how I was the one who loved grunge and had pulled Amy into it. But really, Amy was the last thing I wanted to talk about right now.

So I cleared my throat and went back to skimming through the songs on his iPod. Eventually, I gave up on finding anything decent and selected "Of Lions and Robots," the only GVM song I didn't hate.

Ryder, having regained his composure, gently removed the iPod from my hand and tossed it into the front seat, out of reach.

"Make you a deal," he said, kissing just beneath my ear. "I'll add some better make-out music to my collection, if you drop it for the moment. . . ." His lips traveled down my neck, sending chills up my spine.

"*Fine,*" I said, as if this was some great sacrifice on my part.

He eased me back down onto the carpeted seat, and I wrapped my arms around his neck. He kissed his way up to my mouth, tugging slightly on my lower lip with his teeth. I giggled and arched my back, pressing myself tighter against him.

But then Ryder shifted slightly, and I was suddenly less focused on his mouth and more keenly aware of his hand, which had begun creeping beneath my shirt.

Despite the constant making out, we hadn't quite reached second base yet. Not that I was at all opposed to it.

But the higher his hand crept, the more nervous I began to feel. What if he managed to get my bra off only to be disappointed? What if my boobs were too small or weird looking or something? Amy's were much bigger than mine and probably perfect. Though, admittedly, I wasn't really sure what made boobs perfect or weird. It didn't stop me from worrying.

"Hey," Ryder said, pulling away a little. "Is this all right?"

The minute his eyes met mine, I felt myself relax. His expression was so soft, so gentle, and it eased some of my worries.

Stop comparing yourself to Amy, I thought. *He doesn't want her, he wants you.*

"Yeah," I said. "Definitely."

He smiled, then went back to kissing me.

And to trying to unhook my bra. Apparently, this is a very complicated act for boys, particularly to do one-handed, because it seemed to be taking him longer than I'd expected. But he'd almost managed it when —

Crunch!

The snowball smacked into the windshield, followed by a burst of retreating laughter from outside the car.

Ryder and I both groaned.

"Assholes," I said.

"Why are we here again?" he asked.

"Lyndway Hill is the cool place to make out. At least, so I've been told."

"Right, well, I would argue that my house is cooler." He eased off me, allowing me to sit up. He smirked at me as I attempted to smooth down my hair. "Might I suggest that we continue this there?"

I just grinned.

Unfortunately, Ryder's house was not as empty as we'd thought.

We burst through the door, laughing at the fresh snow that had fallen on us as we'd run up the front steps. He flicked snow from my hair, and I laughed, pushing him away. He caught my arms and moved me backward, so I was pressed against the front door as he leaned in to kiss me.

But our lips had barely met when we heard the loud "Ahem" and jumped apart.

"Mom," Ryder said, spinning around to face the woman that neither of us had noticed standing in the living room. "I didn't think you were home."

"And I thought you were," she said, her voice devoid of any humor. "Your car is in the garage."

"Right. I was with Sonny."

I raised a hand and gave a small wave. "Hi, Mrs. Cross." Yeah. This was not how I'd planned on meeting his mom for the first time.

"It's Ms. Tanner," she corrected. "I no longer use my married name."

"Right. Sorry."

I'm not going to lie. I was already pretty scared of Ryder's mother. She was so strict about how clean her house and even Ryder's car were kept. And Ryder, despite seeming to think she was perfect, had described her as pretty strict and cold, things that had only gotten worse since the separation. Not traits that particularly meshed with my personality.

As if that wasn't enough, in person, she was entirely intimidating. I'd known she was pretty from the photo I'd seen of Ryder and his family, with her smooth dark brown skin and dark eyes. But she was also quite tall. And had broad shoulders. And then there was the way she was dressed, in a crisp, neat, expensive navy-blue suit.

"Is that your car outside?" she asked, glancing out the window.

"Uh, yes, ma'am. It is." And then I tried, perhaps foolishly, to make her laugh. "I named her Gert."

But she didn't laugh. "Hmm. Charming. I'm sure the neighbors will be very curious about what a car like that is doing in the driveway."

Ouch.

I wanted to say something, to defend Gert, as silly as it sounds, but luckily Ryder spoke up first.

"It's vintage," he said, laughing. And the fact that he was obviously quoting me made me soften a bit.

"Indeed," Ms. Tanner said. "I'm sorry. I missed your name. What was it again?"

"Oh. Sonny," I said. But, because I thought it might be more impressive to her, I added, "Short for Sonya."

"Sonny," she repeated. "I must be behind on my son's love life. Here I was thinking he was interested in a girl named . . . Amy?"

"Not anymore," Ryder said. "Sonny and I have actually been seeing each other for about three weeks now."

"Wow," Ms. Tanner said. "You sure moved on fast. Must be that Cross DNA."

Ryder flinched.

"If you'll excuse me," she said, "I brought some work home with me that needs to get done. Nice to meet you, Sonny."

The feeling was not mutual.

When she'd left the room, I turned to Ryder. "That was . . . interesting."

He was staring at his feet, his hands shoved deep into his coat pockets. Clearly, the interaction had been just as unpleasant for him. But I knew not to say anything else.

"Should I go?" I asked.

"You don't have to," he said.

But something told me that there would be no getting to second base today after all.

"It's okay. I probably should. I have a lot of homework."

Ryder was quiet as he walked me out. When we reached my car, I turned to him. "Hey," I said, grabbing his hand. "Is everything okay?" I worried that maybe his mother's obvious disapproval of me and my poor-person vehicle might be enough to scare him off.

"Yeah," he said. "Everything's fine."

And even though there was no hesitation when he leaned in to kiss me good-bye, I knew something had changed. Something his mother had said was bothering Ryder, even if he wasn't telling me what just yet.

25

"What are you thinking about?" I asked Ryder.

It was another day when his mother wouldn't be home until the evening (we'd checked this time), which meant we were at his house, in his room, on his bed. Only Ryder didn't seem entirely there. Like he was preoccupied with something besides feeling me up.

"Amy," he said.

I frowned down at him. "Okay. Not the answer I was hoping for."

He shook his head. "Not like that," he said. "Obviously. I just feel like I should apologize to her."

"For . . . ?"

"This." He gestured between us. "I'm not exactly her biggest fan anymore, but we did have something going on between us for a while. It must be weird that I'm now dating her best friend."

"It's not," I assured him. "She's totally fine with it."

Which was mostly true. Amy knew that Ryder and I had been seeing each other for the past month, and she was totally supportive. Happy for me, even. She just thought Ryder was more informed than he really was. And of course, she had no idea that he now considered her to be one of the rudest, flakiest people on the planet. You know. Small details.

So far, I hadn't had to do much work to keep the truth from coming out. It wasn't as if Ryder and Amy hung out ever. And with the way Ryder felt about Amy now, I didn't think it would be too hard to keep them separated until graduation in May.

But Ryder and his damn conscience were going to ruin everything.

"I'm glad to hear that," he said. "I just . . . I don't want to be like my dad, you know?"

"How can you even say that?" I asked.

"You heard my mom the other day. Cross DNA."

"Are you serious? Ryder, you didn't cheat on Amy. You two never even kissed. I know you guys had a virtual connection . . ." Believe me, I knew all too well. "But, like you told me, there wasn't really anything there. She knows that. You're not like your dad."

"I hope not," he said, burying his hands in my curls as he leaned up to kiss me.

"But . . . speaking of your dad . . ."

He flopped back onto the bed with a groan. "Okay. Definitely not what I want to talk, or think, about when there's a girl in my bedroom."

"Sorry, but you started it," I said. "I was just curious if you'd heard from him lately."

Ryder sighed. "He called yesterday. Left a voice mail. The same old thing. He apologized and pretty much begged me to call him. He says he wants to see me. Thinks I should come to DC for spring break."

"Maybe you should."

He raised an eyebrow. "Wouldn't you miss me?"

"Of course," I said. "But I'm sure I can find someone else to make out with while you're away."

He gave me an exaggerated, playful frown, and I laughed as I leaned down to kiss the tip of his nose.

"Seriously, though. You should call him," I said. "I know he screwed up pretty terribly. But my dad has done some bad things, too. Prison-worthy bad things, in fact. But he's still my dad. And I'm glad to have him back in my life. And that's because of you." I smiled as I found his hand and twined our fingers together. "I owe you for that, so let me return the favor here. Give him a chance."

He sighed. "I'll think about it."

"Okay," I said, knowing that even that was serious progress.

"In the meantime . . ."

I squealed with laughter as he flipped me onto my back and placed a long kiss on my lips.

"No more talking about Amy," he whispered, his mouth a fraction of an inch from mine. "Or my dad."

I nodded, the kiss having left me breathless. "Deal."

But Ryder had barely gotten his hand up my shirt when his cell phone began to ring from the dresser.

"That's my mom's ringtone," he said, rolling off me.

"Of course it is," I said. "The universe is determined to keep me clothed."

"The universe is awful," he said. Then he picked up the phone. "Hello, Mom."

With the mood sufficiently killed, I climbed off the bed and began walking around Ryder's room, investigating areas I hadn't yet. Like his car, it was immaculately clean. Serial-killer clean. Even the DVDs and Blu-rays on his shelf were in alphabetical order.

"Yes. I'll be sure to do that. . . . See you tonight, Mom. I love you." He hung up the phone and turned to look at me. "Did you want to watch a movie?" he asked.

"Maybe. But only if we can watch . . ." I grabbed the DVD off the shelf and spun to face him, grinning. "*Clueless*?"

Ryder's eyes went wide. "I . . . um . . ."

"Or *Cruel Intentions*? Or maybe *10 Things I Hate About You*?"

"Okay, I get it."

"*She's All That*? *American Pie*? *Can't Hardly Wait*? That one wasn't even very good."

"It's not bad."

"I thought you didn't like mainstream Hollywood films?" I teased.

"Yes. All right. You caught me," he said. "I have a soft spot for nineties teen movies. It's a guilty pleasure. I'm not proud of it. Happy?"

"Ecstatic," I said, waving the *Clueless* DVD. "This proves to me that you are, indeed, human. And if we're being honest, it makes me like you so much more."

"Really?"

"Really." I walked over to where he sat on the bed and kissed him. He smiled against my lips, then tugged on my hand, pulling me closer, but I took a step back. "Oh, no," I said, holding the DVD up again. "Now I actually want to watch this."

And, at least for the moment, the subject of Amy was dropped.

But it didn't stay that way for long.

Everything fell apart on Valentine's Day.

Ryder hadn't dropped the whole apology thing. No matter how many times I assured him that Amy was cool with us dating, he kept bringing it up. I could have killed his mother for planting the seed in his head and making him think he was anything like his dad.

Keeping them away from each other was becoming increasingly difficult. I felt like a character in a sitcom, constantly juggling the two and keeping my stories straight.

So when I saw him walking toward us in the hallway at school, I knew shit was about to hit the fan — a metaphor that never failed to gross me out a little.

"We should go ice skating this weekend," Amy said as we walked to lunch. "The rink in Oak Hill will close soon, and we haven't gone all winter."

"That sounds fun," I said. "But I think I already have plans with Ryder. Valentine's Day weekend and all."

"Valentine's Day is a day, not a weekend."

"It can be a weekend if you do it right," I said, grinning.

"Oh." Amy looked down at her feet. "Yeah. I should've guessed you'd be busy."

I was about to suggest we watch a movie or something Sunday night instead, when Ryder walked up.

"Ryder," I said, forcing a smile. "What are you doing here?"

"I go to school here?"

"Right. I just mean you're usually not in this hallway." I cleared my throat. "Anyway, we're just heading to lunch, so —"

"This will only take a second," he said, kissing me on the cheek. There was a good chance that was the last kiss I'd ever get from him. "I just need to talk to Amy."

"Me?" she asked, surprised.

"You really don't," I said, shaking my head. "Everything's fine. Hey, let's go get some bad cafeteria lasagna."

"Amy," Ryder said, completely ignoring me. "I know these past few months have been strange, but I wanted to apologize and make sure there were no hard feelings about me seeing Sonny."

She frowned. "Of course there aren't. Why would there be?"

"See?" I said, trying to shove Ryder down the hall. "She's fine. Let's go."

He didn't budge. Instead, he scoffed. "I guess I shouldn't be too surprised by that reaction. It's fairly in keeping with the way you've been treating me."

"Excuse me?"

I wanted to hide. To run and lock myself in a bathroom stall. Or, better yet, to vanish completely. Because the cracks were beginning to show, and the lies I'd built between Amy and Ryder were about to come crashing down on top of me.

"Just that, despite a connection that seemed very real online, you've always acted as if nothing happened between us. So it's not exactly surprising that you'd continue the trend now, even though I've started dating your best friend. Something that would bother most people."

Amy gawked at him. "Wh-What?" She froze, and then, slowly, she turned to look at me. I shrank beneath her gaze, and the words she spoke next were so quiet, so cold, that they made me shiver. "You didn't tell him?"

"Tell me what?" Ryder asked.

They were both looking at me now, waiting for me to answer.

I was an excellent liar. But I had no lie for this. Nothing I could think to say or do that would fix it. Nothing that would let me keep them both.

Amy's eyes flashed, and I saw the fury there that I'd only seen once before, and I shrank away from her, flinching as if she'd struck me.

"Fine," she said, voice still low. "If you won't tell him, I will." She turned to face Ryder. "I never talked to you online, Ryder. I never instant messaged or texted you or any of that. It was all Sonny."

Ryder took a stumbling step backward. Like he'd just been shoved. "What? Sonny, is that . . . is that true?"

"I . . . um . . ." I swallowed. "Sort of."

Horror bloomed across his face and suddenly there was so much hurt in his eyes. "You were catfishing me?" he asked. I felt myself shrink away from him as the shame swelled inside of me. "Was it some sort of joke? Were you screwing with me?"

"No!" I cried. "Of course not."

"What the hell is wrong with you?" he demanded. "How could you let me think . . . Jesus Christ. This is so fucked up."

"Ryder, please, just let me explain."

"Explain what? That you pretended to be someone else? And lied to me? We've been dating for over a month and . . . were you just not going to tell me?"

"I . . ." *I hoped I wouldn't have to.* I cleared my throat. "Ryder, just give me a second."

He shook his head. "No. I should go."

"I'm sorry," Amy said. "She told me you knew."

"Well, then, looks like she lied to both of us."

"Ryder."

The disgust when he looked at me shattered any composure I might have had. I felt my lip begin to tremble. I'd had everything I wanted, and in a matter of seconds, it had all come tumbling down.

"I'm going to lunch," he said. He turned and began to walk away.

"Ryder!" I called out again. "Please. Just . . . listen."

But he didn't stop walking.

I spun to face Amy, anger and guilt and heartbreak at war inside me. "How could you do that to me?" I demanded, my hands balled into fists.

She leveled a steady, dark gaze at me. Then she shook her head. "How could *you* do that to *me*?" she asked.

I looked down at my feet, shame winning the fight. She was right. As much as I wanted to blame her for telling Ryder, it was all on me. I'd had the chance to tell him so many times, but I'd chickened out. And I'd kept lying to both of them. How stupid was I to think that they'd never find out the truth? That I wouldn't end up hurting them both?

"I'm sorry," I said.

But when I looked up, Amy was gone.

And I was completely alone.

26

Lonely was not a new feeling for me.

In fact, it was a feeling I knew better than most.

But normally, when I was feeling alone or abandoned, I knew I could go to Amy. I knew she'd be there for me. And recently I'd had Ryder, too.

But not anymore.

It had been a week since the Valentine's Day Massacre, and neither of them had spoken a word to me since.

I had tried to apologize to Ryder every day since the incident in the hall, but he wouldn't even look at me. I'd called, I'd texted, I'd e-mailed, and I'd gotten no response. In class, he wore his giant headphones, freezing me out until Mr. Buckley started teaching. So, one day, I tried a different tactic. One that had worked in the past.

I wrote a note.

Please. Give me a chance to explain. I know I screwed up, but it wasn't all a lie. Hear me out, okay? — S

I tossed it over Ryder's shoulder and held my breath as he read it, hoping he'd write something back. Instead, he put the note away and raised his hand.

"Yes, Mr. Cross?" Mr. Buckley said, already sounding exasperated.

"May I switch seats?"

I felt myself deflate.

"Why would you want to switch seats?" Mr. Buckley asked.

I thought he would out me. Play the tattletale and let Mr. Buckley know I was passing notes. It wasn't as if I didn't deserve it. But Ryder had more integrity than that. Which was one of the reasons I'd fallen for him, I guess.

"I'm having trouble seeing the board," Ryder said. "Could I sit closer?"

I felt like I'd just been kicked in the chest. I sank back into my seat, trying not to let my feelings show.

Mr. Buckley sighed. "Sure. Come on up. And maybe think about getting some real lenses for those glasses of yours."

He hadn't sat near me since.

Amy couldn't avoid me quite as easily, but damn if she didn't try.

We may have lived under the same roof, but Amy did her best to never be in the same room as me. When I walked downstairs, she went back up them. When I came into the kitchen, she moved to the living room. When I entered the rec room, she ran out.

"You've got to talk to me eventually," I said one Saturday as she brushed past me, heading out of the kitchen. I'd had enough of the silent treatment.

When Amy didn't look back, I followed her.

"Come on, Amy," I said. "I know you're pissed, and I'm sorry. I shouldn't have lied. How many times do I have to apologize?"

She stopped at the foot of the stairs and turned to face me. That same dark glint I'd seen the day she outed me to Ryder was there. That rare spark of anger.

"How many times?" Amy asked. "I don't know, Sonny. You've apologized a lot in the past. But I'm starting to think that words don't mean anything to you, because you always just go and do something worse."

She wasn't wrong. I'd apologized for making her flirt with that guy on Black Friday. I'd apologized for the texts to Ryder. I'd apologized for how long my plan had taken before swearing I'd be honest. But I'd just kept going, making it worse and worse.

"I'm sorry," I said again, because I had no clue what else I could say. "I mean it. I just got so caught up in everything with Ryder and me. . . . Amy, we have to work this out. We're best friends. We're Sonny and Amy. You mean more to me than anyone."

"Do I?"

"Of course," I said.

"Then why do you do this?" she demanded. It was the first time she'd ever raised her voice to me, that calm coolness totally gone. "If I'm so important to you, how can you keep walking all over me?"

"I —"

She shook her head. "Let me talk now. You always do the talking, Sonny. That's the problem. You never let me speak. I might be a quiet person, but that doesn't mean you have to speak for me or speak over me."

"I speak for you because you don't speak up!" I argued. "That's what I do. I defend you. I protect you."

"I never asked you to," she said. "And that's definitely not what you've been doing lately. None of this had anything to do with helping me. It was to help *you*. Because when I did speak up, when I told you how I felt in Tennessee, you just walked all over me. Completely disregarded everything I said. How is that defending me?"

"Amy —"

"I'm going to talk over you this time!" she shouted. It was so startling, so un-Amy-like, that I took a step back. "You are so selfish," she continued. "You say that I'm your best friend, but you used me. You pretended to *be* me. I can't understand that."

"Because everything's easy for you!" I yelled back. "Amy Rush: beautiful, rich, sweet. A good family. A good future ahead of you. Everything just falls into your fucking lap!"

"That's not true."

"Oh, right," I said. "You're shy. What a freaking challenge. How hard that must be," I scoffed. "You don't even realize how good you have it. Or how hard it is for the rest of us. Guess what, Amy? We're not going to be roommates in college. Because I never applied anywhere."

Amy blinked, startled. "What?"

"I'm not going to college," I said. "If you stopped and thought about it for two seconds, you'd know there's no way I'm going to Dartmouth or Brown or whatever. I don't have money. Your parents are paying for my gas right now! I don't even have a family to sign the damn financial aid forms. You're going to college, and I have no fucking clue what I'm doing after you leave."

249

"So you lied to me about that, too."

"Yeah," I said. "I did."

She shook her head, then turned and walked up the stairs. I followed her.

"That's it?" I asked. I was riled up now. Amy and I had never been in a fight before. Usually she just got quiet and I waited for her to come around. We'd never yelled at each other. It used to be a point of pride, actually, but now I wanted to yell. I knew I'd regret it later, but at the moment, I wanted to make her hurt as much as I did.

"Yeah," she said, stopping in her bedroom doorway. "That's it. I'm done, Sonny. I'm done letting you push me around and use me and . . ." She let out a long breath. She was calm now. Quiet. "I always knew you were a liar," she said. "I just never thought you'd lie to me. Guess I was wrong."

My instinct was to get the last word. That the person who spoke last won the fight. Logical, I know.

But her words hit me harder than anything else she'd said. As it turned out, I didn't need to make Amy hurt now. I already had.

And before I could come up with anything to say, anything that would make me feel even momentarily victorious, Amy slammed the door in my face.

Our fight went on for another week. Cold shoulders, angry glares, slamming doors. I spent most of my time in the guest room, wallowing in my misery.

More than once, I found myself dialing Ryder's number, wanting to hear his voice, to get his advice on what to do, to have him make me laugh. Then I'd remember that he hated me, too, and I'd be left even more crushed than I'd been a moment before.

I'd hoped Amy's parents hadn't picked up on the tension in the house, but of course they had.

"Sonny," Mrs. Rush said from outside the bedroom door. "Can we come in a second?"

"Yes," I said, sitting up. I'd been lying on my back, staring at the ceiling, contemplating how awful my life was. You know, productive stuff. "Come on in."

Mr. and Mrs. Rush stepped inside, and Mr. Rush shut the door behind him. I knew by the looks on their faces that nothing good was going to come of this.

"We wanted to come in and check on you," Mrs. Rush said, sitting on the edge of the bed.

"We know that things between you and Amy have been . . . off," Mr. Rush said.

Understatement of the century.

"Yeah . . . Um. I'm okay."

"That's good," Mrs. Rush said. "You know we love both you and Amy, and we're sure you two will work this out eventually."

I was glad she was, because I wasn't so sure.

"We don't know what's going on between you two," Mr. Rush said. "You've been very quiet on the topic. And that's your prerogative. We just want you to know that we're here for you both."

I could sense the "but" coming.

"We've been thinking, though," Mrs. Rush said. "This has been going on for two weeks, and . . . maybe the best thing for both of you is to take some time apart. To get some space from each other."

"Oh."

I felt the panic beginning to rise. Because I knew what came next. I knew what they were going to say.

And it was the last thing I wanted to hear.

"We've been happy to have you here," Mr. Rush said. "But living together is hard. Even for best friends. So perhaps it's time for you to go home."

27

They insisted on driving me.

I told them I had Gert. I told them I could go alone. I told them not to worry.

But they wouldn't hear it.

We pulled into the driveway around noon, and even though it was surprisingly sunny for the beginning of March, everything about my house seemed dark and gray. Like it was haunted. Like there was a permanent shadow hanging over it, clinging to the tree branches in the front yard.

"You don't have to come in," I said, forcing myself to sound confident. "I can talk to Mom on my own."

"Is she even here?" Mrs. Rush asked. "There's no car in the driveway."

"She's . . . she's probably at work," I said. "She'll be home soon. I have my key, so . . ."

"Why don't we wait with you," Mr. Rush said. It wasn't a question, though. He and Mrs. Rush wasted no time unbuckling their seat belts and getting out of the car.

But I stayed, frozen in the backseat.

No.

No, it couldn't happen like this.

"Come on, Sonny," Mrs. Rush said, opening the door next to me. "It'll be okay. I know it's probably scary to confront your mom, but that's why we're here."

But that wasn't what was scaring me.

I climbed out of the car, trying to keep my composure as panic bubbled in my stomach. I fumbled for my key, which had spent months at the bottom of my purse, unused, unwanted. I hesitated before sliding it into the lock.

"I appreciate you coming with me," I said. "But really, you don't have to stay. It . . . it'll probably be better if I talk to her alone. I can call you after —"

"I think we should be here," Mr. Rush said. "Based on what you told us before, your mom has a tendency to overreact. If we're here, maybe she'll keep a cooler head."

"We just want to make sure everything's okay," Mrs. Rush said, ruffling my hair a little. "Let's go on inside, Sonny. It's cold out here."

My hands were shaking so hard. "You really don't have to —"

"We know," Mr. Rush said. "But we want to."

With both of their eyes on me, I had no other choice but to unlock the front door and let them inside.

The living room was dark, the blinds drawn, and the stale odor of it nearly suffocated me. I shivered in my jacket. It wasn't much warmer inside. Out of the corner of my eye, I noticed Mr. and Mrs. Rush glance at each other, and the panic rose up into my throat.

"My mom might be a while," I said. "She works weird hours."

"We can wait," Mr. Rush said, but there was a skeptical tone to his voice. He sat down on the couch, a puff of dust rising around him. He had the grace to pretend he didn't notice. "Come sit with me. We'll wait together."

"Um . . ." I looked over at Mrs. Rush, who seemed to be scoping out the place, her eyes investigating every corner of the living room. "You know, my mom might not be okay with coming home to find so many people in the house. You don't know this about her, but she's really an introvert. This might be too overwhelming and —"

"Sonny," Mr. Rush said, "is there something wrong?"

"No." But my voice cracked. "No, I'm just worried my mom won't be okay with this when she gets home. I really should just talk to her myself."

"It's so dark in here," Mrs. Rush said. "Let me get the light."

"No!"

But it was too late. She'd flipped the switch on the wall.

And nothing had happened.

"Sonny," Mrs. Rush said quietly, "is there no electricity here?"

"No . . . the bulb's just burnt out."

"The heat's not on either."

"Mom likes it cold."

"Sonny," Mr. Rush said.

"It's fine. Everything's fine. You two need to go."

"No one's been here in months, have they?" Mrs. Rush asked. Her voice was so soft, so gentle, that it hurt.

I tried to laugh, but it came out maniacal and cold. "Don't be ridiculous. Mom's here every day. She'll be home soon."

Mr. Rush stood up and walked over to me, putting a hand on my shoulder. "You don't have to lie to us. Just tell us what's going on, okay?"

And that's when it broke, every ounce of cool I'd kept over the past few months. Maybe it was this house. Maybe it was the unwavering kindness in Mr. Rush's voice. Maybe it was being told not to lie for the thousandth time. But it just snapped and fell away.

And there was no way to pull together the pieces now.

"Nothing's going on!" I screamed. It left a sharp ache in my throat, and tears spilled from my eyes. "It's fine. Just go!"

"Sonny —"

"Go!" I pushed Mr. Rush's hand off my shoulder. "Get out!"

"Sonny!" Mrs. Rush gasped.

"Get out!" I screamed again, stomping my foot and clenching my fists, like a child throwing a tantrum. "Get out! Get out! Get the fuck out!"

"Sonya!" Mrs. Rush grabbed my arm, but I yanked it away.

"Just leave! Mom will be here soon — just GO!"

The tears were hot as they rolled down my face. My whole body shook as I pleaded with both of them to leave.

Leave so they wouldn't have to know.

Wouldn't find out.

But it was too late.

They knew.

The secret I'd kept from everyone. The most painful truth I'd locked away. It was about to come out, and I couldn't bear it.

"Stop, Sonny." Mr. Rush caught my wrists and pulled me to him, holding me in a hug so tight I couldn't resist anymore.

I thrashed for a minute to no avail. I was too tired. Too hurt.

"She's coming back," I cried. "She'll be here soon."

"Shhh," Mr. Rush said. "It's okay, Sonny."

He pulled me to the couch and we sank down together as I sobbed into his shoulder. He stroked my hair, the way my dad had when I was little and had nightmares. No one had held me like this in almost a decade. I should've been too old for it. Too old to be comforted this way.

But just then, I felt like a little kid again.

Like the little kid who had been left behind all those years ago.

I could hear Mrs. Rush walking around the house, but I never looked up. I never stopped crying.

"She's on her way," I mumbled every few minutes or so. "She's coming back."

But no one believed me anymore.

I didn't believe me anymore.

I don't know how much time passed like that, but eventually Mrs. Rush came to sit down on the couch with me and her husband. She rested a hand on my back, and the show of kindness just made me cry harder.

When the tears finally slowed and I was able to catch my breath, Mrs. Rush asked the question I'd been dreading.

"Where's your mother, Sonny?"

I shook my head, but I couldn't lie anymore. I didn't have the energy or the strength.

"I . . . I don't know."

"How long has she been gone?"

"A while." I swallowed and rubbed my eyes with the back of

my hand. "She leaves sometimes. But . . . but she always comes back. But this time . . ."

"Oh, Sonny," Mr. Rush murmured. "You were never kicked out."

I shook my head no.

They didn't ask why I'd lied, and for that I was eternally grateful. I didn't want to talk about it. I didn't want to talk about anything. I wanted to go back in time. Before the Rushes saw this empty, dusty, lonely house. Before I fucked up everything with Amy and Ryder.

Before I was alone.

"Come on," Mr. Rush said. "Let's go."

"No," I said, clutching at his arm. I hated myself. I hated the pathetic sound of my voice when I said, "Don't leave me. Please."

"Oh, sweetheart." Mrs. Rush wrapped her arms around me. "No. Sonny, we're not leaving you here. You're coming back with us, okay?"

"But Amy —"

"Loves you," Mr. Rush said. "And so do we."

"Whatever is going on with you two, you'll work it out," Mrs. Rush said. "And she'd want you to come back with us, too."

I wasn't so sure about that, though. Not after everything I'd done. This was just another lie I'd told her. Just another reason for her to hate me.

Mr. Rush walked me out to the car while Mrs. Rush gathered some more clothes from my bedroom. None of us said a word on the drive back to their house. I stared out the window, my eyes wet and burning.

It was over. The cat was out of the bag. I felt naked, humiliated. Raw.

When we got back to the Rushes' house, Amy was sitting in the living room, watching TV. She looked stunned to see me walk through the door.

I turned my face away from her, hiding. I didn't say a word to anyone, just ran up the stairs to the guest room where I'd been staying.

I didn't mean to slam the door behind me, but I did.

I fell onto the bed, my face in the pillow. But I didn't cry. I couldn't.

There weren't any tears left.

28

I didn't leave the guest room for two days.

Partly because I was sad and miserable and didn't want to inflict my pain on anyone else. But mostly because I was ashamed. Ashamed of my meltdown in front of Amy's parents. Ashamed of the truth.

Mr. and Mrs. Rush knocked on the door a few times, but I didn't answer.

I wanted to go to Amy, to find safety and comfort with her the way I always had. I wanted to call Ryder, or better yet, to have him here with me. To have him put an arm around me and tell me it would be okay. To say something pretentious and ridiculous so I could make fun of him and stop thinking about everything else.

I missed them.

But, more than anything, I wanted to barricade myself in this room, to be alone forever, punishing myself for every awful thing I'd done.

Eventually, however, my need for food outweighed my desire to lock myself away Rapunzel-style. I waited until everyone else was asleep before sneaking down to the kitchen.

At least, I thought everyone was asleep.

"Why didn't you tell me?"

I looked up from the bowl of cereal I'd just poured. Amy was standing in the kitchen doorway, dressed in pink-and-black-striped pajamas and fuzzy green slippers. I ducked my head and focused my attention on the Cocoa Puffs I was about to consume.

"I thought you'd be asleep," I said.

"I haven't slept well lately." She walked past me and opened a cabinet, grabbing a bowl for herself. Once she'd filled it with cereal, she came over to the island and stood across from me. "My parents told me what happened at your house. . . . I get why you didn't want them to know, but why didn't you tell me she was gone? I would've kept it secret for you. I would've tried to help." There was a note of hurt in her voice.

"I know you would have," I said, swirling my spoon in my bowl. My appetite was waning all of a sudden. "But . . . it wasn't about admitting it to you. It was about admitting it to myself."

"What do you mean?"

I shrugged. "I don't know. It was easier to say she'd kicked me out for doing something wrong. Then I could pretend it was true. It hurt less than acknowledging that she'd . . . she'd left me. Just left me."

"Do you have any idea where she went?"

I shook my head. "No. She was seeing a guy. She probably took off with him somewhere. Who knows? It's not like it's the first time."

I'd called my mother "flaky" for years, but that was an understatement. From the time I was eleven, I never knew if she'd be home when I got off the bus after school. Sometimes she'd stick around for months, and things would be almost normal. She might

261

forget my birthday or accidentally lock me out of the house, but she was around.

And then, sometimes, she wasn't.

I was in sixth grade the first time she pulled her disappearing act. She'd been seeing this guy, Dave. He was younger than her, and even then I knew he was kind of a loser. One day, I came home and the house was empty. Luckily, by then, I knew how to take care of myself. I lived off cereal and microwavable meals, even when she was home.

She'd come back three days later, tanned and happy. Dave had suggested an impromptu road trip to Florida, and she could've sworn she'd left a note. As if that made it better.

After Dave it was Carl.

After Carl it was Trevor.

And then I stopped keeping up with their names. It wasn't like I saw them much, anyway. Sometimes Mom would be gone for days, and I'd find out later she'd just been across town, crashing at her boyfriend's house. Sometimes she'd vanish for a week — a shopping trip in Atlanta, a romantic getaway in St. Louis, a week in Chicago. She lost several jobs because of those random trips.

So when I came home one afternoon last September, I wasn't surprised to find her gone.

But a week turned to two.

To three.

To four.

She'd never been gone that long. And the house was too quiet. The nightmares happened almost every night.

So I'd called Amy, told her I needed a place to stay. Told her

I'd been kicked out, because I didn't know how to say the truth: that my mom was gone for real this time. That she'd left, and I didn't think she'd be coming back.

"I'm sorry," Amy said. "But maybe things will get better. My parents used to be gone all the time, too, and —"

"It's different," I said. "Your parents were gone, but they paid the bills. They made sure you had a place to stay. You could call them, and you knew they'd be back eventually. I haven't heard from my mom in . . . five months?" I pushed my bowl away, barely touched. "Her phone doesn't even work anymore. For all I know she could be dead."

"Don't say that."

"Even if I don't say it, I can't not think it. And — this is terrible, but — sometimes I wonder if that would make me feel better. If I knew she hadn't come back because she *couldn't*. Not because she doesn't care." I shook my head. "Sorry. That's morbid. You already think I'm a bad person and I just told you I wish my mother was dead. Nice job, Sonny."

"I don't think you're a bad person," Amy said.

"No. Just a bad friend." I picked up my bowl and took it to the sink, dumping my food into the garbage disposal. Once it stopped running and I turned around, I found Amy staring at me.

"Can I tell you something?" she asked. "Since we're being honest with each other?"

"Sure. What is it?"

Amy chewed on her bottom lip and looked down at her own bowl. "I meant everything I said the other day. About you pushing me around. But that's not the only reason I was mad."

"What do you mean?"

"It's always been just us, you know?" she said. "Sonny and Amy. Amy and Sonny. We were a team. And then everything started happening with Ryder, and it felt like you only wanted me around to help you win him over."

Ryder. Just the mention of him caused a painful ache in my chest.

Amy continued, "And it wasn't just that you were pushing me around — I'm kind of used to that."

I grimaced. That wasn't something I wanted my best friend to be "used to."

"It's that you were doing it for him. You were doing *everything* for him. You talked about him all the time. And I started to realize you weren't opening up to me the way you used to. You were telling him things instead. I didn't even know you'd written to your dad until he called on Christmas. That's the kind of thing you used to talk to me about. And then when you started dating Ryder, you hardly spent time with me. I was jealous. So when I'd found out you'd lied about telling him the truth . . . It really hurt, Sonny. I didn't feel like we were a team anymore. It . . . it felt like you didn't care about me."

She looked up at me, eyes wide and a little wet.

And seeing her on the brink of tears brought me there, too.

"I'm sorry. For all of it. Of course I care about you, Amy. More than anybody. You're my best friend. I never meant to hurt you." I took a deep breath. "Part of the reason I spent less time with you after I started dating Ryder was the whole college thing."

Amy looked down at her feet.

"I shouldn't have said all that the other day, about you having it so easy."

"You weren't wrong," she said.

"I still shouldn't have said it. And I shouldn't have lied to you about college," I said. "But every time you talked about it, I just felt . . . scared. Because I knew you'd be leaving me. And I knew that if you knew I wasn't going, you'd be upset, too, and . . . I don't know. I didn't want to think about it. And I didn't have to when I was with Ryder."

"I'm sorry that I just assumed you were going," she said. "I guess I do take the good things in my life for granted sometimes."

"I think we're both probably guilty of that."

She hesitated. "Why did you lie to me about telling Ryder the truth?"

"Because I didn't want you to be mad at me?" I said. "That sounds ridiculous in hindsight. But I guess I just thought . . . I thought that if I lied, I might be able to keep you both. Instead, I lost you both."

"You didn't lose me," she said. "But you will if you keep doing this."

"I know," I said, wrapping my arms around myself. "But it's scary to tell the truth sometimes. I've always been able to hide behind lies. To shield myself."

"What are you shielding yourself from?" she asked.

"Judgment? Scorn? I don't know." I wanted to lie right then. To get out of this conversation before it got too honest. But Amy was right. I couldn't keep lying. "The funny thing is, I hid behind lies because I was scared that . . . that if people knew everything, saw all of me, they'd take off running. Like my mom did. So I'd only let bits and pieces show. Instead, the lies ended up driving everyone away."

"Not everyone," she said. "You've got the Rushes in your corner. But you've got to start letting us in. Letting us help. You know . . . you mentioned college."

"I don't want to talk about that anymore."

"Just hear me out," she said. "That's another thing. No more talking over me or pushing me around. That's got to change."

I nodded. "Sorry."

"That's on me, too," she said. "I've got to start speaking up. I've got to stop being quiet, weak Amy and start being . . . Fierce Amy."

"Fierce Amy?" I couldn't help but laugh. "Someone's been watching *America's Next Top Model*."

She ignored me. "Back to the college thing. It might be too late for next semester, but that doesn't mean it can never happen. There are scholarships — I'll help you find them. And my parents aren't just going to kick you out on the street after you graduate."

"I can't let them keep taking care of me."

"Then you can pay some rent when you find a job," she said. "But let us help. You're part of the family, Sonny. Whether you like it or not. You're stuck with us."

"I guess I can think of worse people to be stuck with," I said. "But what about us? Are we back to normal? Sonny and Amy?"

"Not quite," she said. "That's probably going to take a while. I love you, Sonny, but you're going to have to prove that I can trust you again. That you're not going to lie to me anymore."

"I can do that," I assured her. "It'll be a hard habit to break, but . . . but I can take an oath. A vow of honesty."

"That sounds a little more dramatic than what I was hoping for, but okay." She put her bowl in the sink. She hadn't eaten much of her midnight snack either. "Now come on. I know it's silly, but I have a hard time sleeping when you're in the other room."

We headed toward the stairs together. "You know," I said. "While we're trying to build a healthier friendship, we *might* want to deal with our whole codependency thing."

"Probably," she agreed. "But maybe another night."

29

"Okay. Here goes. Ahem. I, Sonny Elizabeth Ardmore —"

"Shouldn't it be Sonya?" Amy asked.

"No."

"I'm just saying, if you're going to be all official about it, it should probably say your full name."

"Ugh. Fine." I picked up a pen and scratched out *Sonny* before scribbling *Sonya* above it. "There. Sonya. Happy?"

Amy shrugged. "Personally, I still think the whole thing is a little on the ridiculous side. But I guess that's not really a surprise coming from you."

"Forgive me for liking a little bit of formality when it comes to taking my oaths." I picked up my paper again and cleared my throat. "I, *Sonya* Elizabeth Ardmore, hereafter swear to tell the whole truth, nothing but the truth, so help me —"

"Isn't that plagiarism?"

I looked up. "Huh?"

"Aren't you plagiarizing the oath people take on the stand?" Amy asked.

"I don't know if that's plagiarism."

"It might be."

"What if I change the last bit? From 'so help me God' to 'so help me' . . . Gert?"

"I'm not sure if it has quite the same power? Gert can't smite you."

"No, but she can stop running while I'm in the middle of a busy highway and get me killed."

"Fair point."

I scratched out *God* and replaced it with *Gert* to avoid any possible plagiarism allegations.

"Okay. Last try. I, Sonya Elizabeth Ardmore, hereafter —"

"Should it be 'hereafter' or 'hereby'?"

I dropped the paper back onto the desk. "I give up. I'm never reading anything out loud to you again."

Amy giggled. "Sorry. It's just hard to take this seriously! I'm glad you're determined to stop lying, but is this really necessary?"

"Yes. This makes it official. And it gives you license to punish me if I break the oath."

"Well, in that case . . ." She stood up from the bed and walked over to where I was sitting. "I know I'm teasing you, but I really am glad you're doing this, Sonny. Not the oath — that doesn't matter to me — but just trying to tell the truth."

"It's terrifying," I admitted. "It shouldn't be. I know it shouldn't be. But I've been able to hide behind made-up stories for so long, being honest feels like being vulnerable." I picked up the pen. "But clearly the lying didn't do me any favors, so . . ." I leaned forward and scribbled my signature beneath the typed-out oath. "So, there. It's official. No more lies for me. Not even tiny white ones."

"Hey, Sonny, what did you think of the chicken Dad made last night?"

"I can still plead the fifth."

Amy chuckled.

I picked up the signed oath. "Can I frame this? Do we have a frame?"

"I'm sure we can find one." She smiled at the piece of paper. "I think telling the truth will earn you some serious karma points, too. Have you talked to Ryder?"

"Karma doesn't like me that much. And neither does Ryder. He still won't speak to me." There was a squeezing feeling in my chest and the threat of tears whenever I mentioned him. I took a deep breath and tried to shake it off before standing up and stretching my arms over my head. "I think I have a long way to go before the universe starts doing me any favors."

Just then, my cell phone began to ring. I glanced down at the screen and was surprised to see a number I recognized. It belonged to Daphne's, one of the clothing stores in the Oak Hill Mall, where I'd applied back in December.

Amy must have noticed the startled smile on my face, because she laughed and said, "Or maybe not," before prancing out of the room.

I had made a vow to be honest about everything and with everyone, no matter how difficult it was.

And that meant I had to talk to my dad. In person.

It was a two-hour drive to the correctional facility, but Mr. Rush assured me that he didn't mind taking me.

When we arrived, a guard patted us both down, checking that we weren't bringing in anything illegal, then we were free to enter the room where the inmates waited. The room was lined with long, rectangular tables. The wearers of the orange jumpsuits were on one side, and the rest of us were on the other.

I may not have seen my dad in years, but I knew him the minute I saw him. Mostly because he looked so much like me. His hair was blond and curly, his nose had a slight upturn, and his ears stuck out just a little more than was fashionable. Yep. I was his spitting image, as the old folks say.

"Sonny." His face split into a wide, boyish grin when he saw me. "Wow. You're a grown-up. In my head, you're still this tall." He held his hand just a bit higher than the edge of the table.

"Well, you're not too far off," I said. I smiled, but the nerves were eating me alive. This man might look and sound like me — I definitely got my charm from him, not Mom — but I still didn't know him.

He could have been a liar like me, too.

He had been in the past.

Dad looked up and spotted Mr. Rush standing behind me. "Hello," he said.

"Dad, this is Mr. Rush," I said. "He's my friend Amy's dad."

"Oh, yeah. I remember little Amy. And that's where I called you on Christmas, right? At the Rushes' house?"

I nodded.

"Hi. I'm Collin," Mr. Rush said. "It's nice to meet you."

"You, too." Dad hesitated. "Thanks for bringing Sonny Bunny here to see me. I take it her mother refused? She's always been a little on the difficult side, if you know what I mean."

I sat down in the folding chair across from Dad and took a deep breath. Behind me, Mr. Rush cleared his throat.

"I'm going to step outside for a minute," he said. "Give you two a chance to talk."

When he was gone, Dad turned to me, confused. "What's going on, Sonny Bunny?"

"Dad, I . . . I need to talk to you about Mom."

I let it all spill out then. From her short disappearances when I was younger to her complete abandonment now. I told him about staying at Amy's and how kind the Rushes had been to me. I told him every little detail, even when it hurt like hell to say aloud. By the time I was done, his confident, smiling, all-charm demeanor had fallen away.

His head was in his hands, his shoulders slumped forward. And he looked like a different person. Older. Haggard. Like someone who'd been in prison for years.

"Fuck," he said. "Goddamn it."

"Dad?"

"I'm so, so sorry, Sonny." And I thought he might have been on the verge of tears. "I had no idea. Your mother was always unreliable, but I didn't think she'd ever . . . ." He took a deep breath and looked up, our eyes meeting. "I'm sorry."

"It's not your fault," I said.

"Yes, it is. I'm your father. I should've been there. Instead of

272

here." There was a note of anger in his voice now. This gruff tone that I hadn't expected. It was so startling that I scooted back in my seat a little. "I should've stayed in touch with you."

"You said you tried to write and call."

"I didn't try hard enough," he admitted. "I told myself I'd done everything I could. I'm a good liar that way."

"Yeah. Me, too."

"I figured you'd be fine with your mother. She didn't want me involved anyway, so . . . But damn it, if I had known she'd do this, I would've . . . God, I could kill her for leaving you."

"Maybe don't say that with so many guards around?" I suggested. "Look, the important part is that you're here now."

"Yeah." He reached across the table and took my hand in his, the anger in his voice fading. "I'm here now. And I'm not going anywhere."

"Literally," I joked. "Prison and all." I paused. "Sorry. Was that rude? I've been told I have a bad habit of undercutting serious moments with jokes."

But Dad was smiling. "You get that from me."

"I do?"

"Oh, yeah," he said. "It's gotten me into trouble a few times. As for being stuck here, though . . . Well, not for much longer. I should be getting out in a couple of months."

"Really?"

He nodded. "And . . . I know you don't really know me, and I don't even know where I'll be living yet, and you'll be graduating soon, but . . ." He cleared his throat. "But I hope we can spend more time together then."

273

"I'd like that," I said.

But I wasn't getting my hopes up just yet. Dad had been out of jail before. The question was, how long would he stay out?

I wasn't ready to trust him completely, but I was ready to try. To give him a chance and to let him surprise me. Now that he knew the truth about Mom, about everything, we at least had a place to start.

We talked for a while longer about the boring stuff: school, hobbies, et cetera. He asked about Amy, whom he vaguely remembered from my childhood, and he even inquired about my romantic status.

"I actually just went through a breakup," I admitted as the familiar ache of missing Ryder throbbed in my chest again.

"Oh, I'm sorry," he said, squeezing my hand. "Boys are the worst and you can't trust any of them. I should know."

"Well, not in this case. In this case, I'm the one who shouldn't have been trusted."

I was glad that Mr. Rush walked in before my dad could ask any more about that subject. Because — vow of honesty and all — I would have had to tell him the truth.

"Sonny," Mr. Rush said, putting a hand on my shoulder. "It's about time to go."

Dad stood up. "Thank you," he said to Mr. Rush. "For taking care of my daughter."

"There's no need to thank me," Mr. Rush said. "We love Sonny. We're glad to have her."

The guard signaled that it was time for us to go. I stood up and hugged Dad over the table. His scent overwhelmed me. The smell of generic soap and . . . him. I remembered being three or four years old, crying after I'd slammed my finger in the door as he held me to his chest, rocking me, telling me it would be okay.

Fast-forward fourteen years, and I was crying in his arms again.

"I love you, Sonny," he murmured into my hair.

He let me go slowly, and I wiped my eyes, not sure what had brought on the sudden tears this time. "Bye, Dad."

He waved as Mr. Rush led me out past the guards. It was hard to walk away from him. But we'd give this whole father-daughter thing a real try. And even if it didn't work out, as hard as that would be, I knew I wouldn't be alone this time.

"Thank you," I said to Mr. Rush once we were in the car.

"Of course," he said. "I don't mind driving you to visit your dad."

I shook my head.

Because that wasn't what I'd been thanking him for.

30

Meet me in the art room at lunch.

I frowned down at the message from Amy. It wasn't like her to text during school hours. Why, that was breaking the rules. Something Amy never did . . . unless I made her.

Nonetheless, I made my way toward the art room instead of the cafeteria. I figured Amy wanted to show me something she'd been working on — I knew her art class had been in the middle of some big project. And I was eager to tell her my good news. I'd gotten an e-mail from Daphne's that morning, letting me know that they'd like to hire me. Apparently, I had wowed them in my interview, and they wanted me to start immediately.

Hopefully I could hold on to this job for a while. I was tired of being poor.

But when I walked into the art room, Amy wasn't the only one waiting for me.

"Ryder," I said, startled. My stomach was already twisting itself into knots. "What are you doing in here?"

"He got the same text you did," Amy explained. "I figured that was a good way to communicate with you two. Considering the recent past."

Minor ouch there.

"But why?" I asked.

"I'm going," Ryder said, moving to the door. My heart sank. But Amy — to my surprise — blocked him.

"You're not," she said. "You're staying in here until you two talk."

I blinked at her. "You're . . . trapping us in a classroom?"

"It was the only way I could think of to get you two in the same room," she said. Her boldness was completely unexpected. She was really taking this whole Fierce Amy thing seriously. "No one will be in this room until after lunch, so you have half an hour. And you have a lot of talking to do. So I'll be outside." She turned and stepped into the hallway, her hand on the knob. "And don't even try to come out," she added. "I won't let you."

I was still staring, my jaw on the ground, as she closed the classroom door.

"Seems like you're not the only manipulative one in this friendship," Ryder muttered as he slid into a seat.

Okay. Major ouch.

"She's trying to help," I said.

He shrugged, his gaze deliberately pointed away from me.

"We should talk," I said. "She's right about that. Even if her methods are a little . . . extreme."

"I have nothing to say, Sonny."

I felt helpless but pressed on. "That's fine, because I have plenty to say." I walked across the room and sat down at the desk across from his. He didn't have to look at me, he just needed to listen. "I know you hate me, Ryder. And you have every reason to. But I made a promise to Amy — and to myself — that I'd be honest from now on. And that means telling you the truth, too."

I took a deep breath and clasped my hands in my lap, clutching my fingers so hard that it hurt.

"So I guess I'll start at the beginning. Um . . . It wasn't . . . I never meant for any of this to happen. That first night, when you IMed me — well, IMed Amy — I didn't realize I was on her account. We'd sent you that mean e-mail, and we both felt bad about it. So when I got that message, I thought it was for me. That's why I responded. And then we talked all night, and I didn't know that you thought I was Amy until you logged off. I was going to tell you immediately, but you wouldn't let me. I tried, and you just cut me off —"

"So you're blaming this on me?" Ryder asked, finally looking at me.

"No," I said quickly. "No, I'm not. Because what happened after that is still my fault."

I went through the whole story, every last detail. From the instant message conversations to the stupid, convoluted plan I'd dragged Amy into, to the texts and the kissing. I spilled my guts and laid them out on the table like an art project. And all the while, Ryder stayed painfully silent.

"So that's it. That's how all of this happened," I said. "And I know it's screwed up and I know I did a lot of bad things, but . . . you should know the truth."

"Fine," he said. "Now I know."

There was a long pause.

"Is that all you're going to say?" I asked.

"What else do you want me to say, Sonny?"

"I don't know," I said. "Something. Anything. I mean, this can't just be it. A couple of weeks ago, you thought we had a future together. You said I was incredible."

"You weren't who I thought you were," he said.

"But I was!"

I was on my feet, but I didn't remember standing up. Somehow I'd begun pacing back and forth between the desks, my hands twisting in my hair. I spun to face him, feeling desperate, determined to make him understand.

"I was exactly the girl you thought I was, Ryder. I was more honest with you than I ever have been with anyone. Even in the texts and the IMs, I was telling you more about myself than anyone knew. You just didn't know it was me. But everything I told you, about my mom . . . Ryder, you're the reason I called my dad. The reason we might have a relationship now. I've never even opened up to Amy about that. Maybe none of that means anything to you, but it matters to me."

"So you want me to forgive you?" he demanded. And then he was on his feet, too. "You want me to just forget all of this happened?"

"I never said that."

"Amy might be able to get over everything you did, but I'm not that forgiving."

"Oh, believe me, I know."

"What's that supposed to mean?"

I threw my hands in the air. "You know what? I'm being honest here, so I might as well be honest about this, too. I'm not the only one with problems."

"*I* have problems?"

"Have you called your dad yet, Ryder?"

"How does that have anything to do with —?"

"It has everything to do with it," I said. "When I first met you, you worshipped the ground he walked on. You hated your mom for dragging you away from him. But the minute you found out he wasn't perfect, you flipped. You thought your mom was a saint and your dad was the worst human who ever lived."

"My parents have nothing to do with this," he said.

"You put people on pedestals, Ryder. You tell yourself that they're perfect. You ignore all of their flaws, until one day they disappoint you just a little too much, and then you're done. You cut them out and think they're worthless."

Ryder and I were so close, staring each other down. My heart was beating so fast, and my breath was a little ragged.

"Your dad screwed up," I said, my voice lowered. "What he did was awful. But he's your dad and he wants to be a part of your life. You're lucky. And your mom —"

"Stop, Sonny."

"She's not perfect either," I insisted. "Maybe she's not as selfish as you thought she was when you first moved here, but she made some mistakes, too. She's cold and judgmental. And it's okay to see that. You can love people and still realize they're screwed up."

Ryder was silent again, and stiff as a board.

I swallowed, knowing I'd crossed a few lines. I hadn't meant to say any of this. I'd been holding it back, knowing it wasn't my place to get involved with his family. But it wasn't just his family anymore. Now, I was the one who'd fallen off that pedestal.

"You did it with Amy, too, you know. You acted like she was some sort of goddess, even when she was rude to you. You ignored it. You were in total denial. Until one day you realized you liked me more and . . . and then you acted like she was the worst person imaginable." I shook my head. "And now me. The same thing."

I looked down at my feet. Staring up at him was too much. Those green eyes were killing me, especially when I couldn't read them at all. A voice in my head was screaming at me to stop. To shut the hell up. But I couldn't put the brakes on now. I'd come too far.

"You act like people are either perfect or terrible," I said. "Like there's nothing in between. But there is. You might think I'm terrible right now — maybe I am. But there were things about me you liked. Things about me that . . ." I forced myself to look back up. "Things about me that you thought were incredible. Those things don't go away just because I messed up."

We stood there, staring at each other, our bodies less than a foot apart, for a long, long time. My hands were shaking, and I balled them into fists at my sides. This was the longest, most painful silence of my life.

Finally, quietly, he asked, "Are you done?"

"No," I murmured. "I have one more *honest* thing to tell you." I took a deep breath.

The classroom door opened and Amy stuck her head inside. "Sorry to interrupt," she said. "But lunch is almost over, so . . ."

The bell rang, right on cue.

We followed Amy out into the hallway, just as a huge crowd of students stampeded toward us. I turned to Ryder, hoping to finish what I'd been about to say, but he was swallowed up by the crowd.

I had the sudden urge to cry, and I forced it away. For a brief, foolish second, I'd thought I might be able to win him back. But instead, I'd lost him again.

Amy grabbed my wrist and pulled me into a little alcove, out of the path of our recently fed peers.

"How'd it go?" she asked.

"Could've gone better," I said.

"What did he say?"

"Not much of anything." I sighed and shook my head. "I didn't even finish everything I wanted to say."

"Well, then we've got to make him listen to you. Let you finish."

"How?" I asked. "It's not like you can lock us in a room again. I don't think he'll fall for that twice."

"You're probably right, but there's got to be some way."

"I don't know what it would be . . . unless . . ." I paused, an idea dawning on me.

"Uh-oh," Amy said. "That's your scheming face. Now I'm scared."

"Don't worry," I said. "You don't have to be part of it this time. It doesn't even involve any lies. All I need is . . . Remember that boom box Wesley had when we were little? He wouldn't still happen to have that, would he?"

31

I may not have been an overly romantic person, but I did have a soft spot for romantic comedies. Which meant I also had a soft spot for the cliché of the Grand Gesture. And I was hoping Ryder Cross did, too.

The problem with grand gestures, however, is that they can be really embarrassing for the gesturer. But then, maybe that's the real gesture: showing that you're willing to make a fool of yourself for another person.

These were the things I found myself musing over as I stood on Ryder's front lawn on a Friday afternoon, my hands trembling as I held a (surprisingly heavy) boom box over my head. It was blasting "Of Lions and Robots," the Goats Vote for Melons love song that I'd begun to associate with Ryder.

If his mother was worried about what the neighbors would think of my car, this was giving her a heart attack. I could see her face in the living room window, staring out at me with intense disapproval.

I tried to ignore that and focus only on Ryder's bedroom window, which — since he lived in a one-story house — was only a few feet away from my face.

I knew he was inside. I'd seen the curtains shift, so now I stood there, holding my breath, anxious and a little terrified as I waited for him to open the window.

But he did me one better.

He came outside.

"Sonny? What are you doing?"

I turned and saw him heading down the front steps. "Gesturing," I said, my heart racing. I smiled and lowered the boom box a little. My arms were killing me.

Slowly, he began to walk toward me. "You know, I like *nineties* teen movies," he said. "John Cusack holding a boom box over his head is from *Say Anything*, which is an eighties movie."

"Yeah, well, you try finding an iconic, grand romantic gesture that isn't lame in a nineties teen movie. At least I got the soundtrack right."

"Goats Vote for Melons grew on you?"

"You wish. I just happen to like this one song. And luckily, in dorky hipster fashion, they released this album on cassette. Weirdos."

He started to smile, but then he caught himself. "What are you doing here?" he asked again.

"At school the other day, in the art room, I didn't say everything I needed to."

"You sure?" he asked. "You said quite a bit."

I cringed. "I may have gone overboard."

"Well, you weren't entirely wrong." But he didn't elaborate beyond that. "Is that the flannel I gave Amy?"

I looked down at the red shirt. "Oh, yeah. It is. She's not really into grunge — that was all me — so she gave to me."

"It looks nice on you," he said.

"Thank you." The song on the boom box faded away, so I set the archaic machine down in the grass. "Listen, Ryder, there's one more thing I needed to —"

The garage door slid open and Ms. Tanner's car backed out, stopping in the middle of the driveway. She honked the horn once, then stared at us from the driver's-side window.

"Are you going somewhere?" I asked Ryder, surprised.

"The airport," he said.

"Oh. Where are you headed?"

"DC."

My face split into a smile I couldn't hold back. "You're visiting your dad?"

"Yeah. Mom's not too thrilled about it, but . . . So you had something you wanted to say, Sonny?"

"Right. Yeah." I took a deep breath. "I know I said a lot of things the other day, about your flaws. And I meant it. You're pretentious and stubborn and you drive me insane sometimes, but . . . I love you. And I just needed you to know that."

There, I'd said it. I now wanted to throw up. But I'd said it.

I hadn't expected him to say it back. I really hadn't. But for just a second, as we stood there in his front yard, I thought he might. I thought my grand gesture, my honesty, might have won him over.

He opened his mouth, but before any words could come out —

"Ryder!"

285

We both turned and saw his mother leaning out the open driver's-side window.

"We've got to go," she said.

"Yeah," he said, looking back at me. "I've got to go."

He started to walk away, but I panicked and grabbed his arm and nearly tripped over the boom box. "Wait," I said. "Just wait. Can . . . can you catch a later flight?"

"No," he said. "That only works in the movies."

I let go of his arm, feeling defeated all over again.

"Sonny, I . . ." He stopped himself, then shook his head. "I've got to go," he repeated.

"Okay," I said.

I stayed where I was, watching as he walked away.

He climbed into the passenger's side, and his mom rolled up her window. She acted as if I wasn't there now, a heartbroken teenage girl with an old boom box in the middle of her front lawn.

I felt my bottom lip begin to tremble, and I choked back the lump in my throat. I didn't want anyone, but especially her, to see me cry. I stood there, telling myself that this was exactly what I'd expected. That I'd had no preconceived notions of changing his mind or convincing him to forgive me. That I'd only come here to tell him how I felt, to finish off my confession.

But that vow of honesty meant I had to be honest with myself, too, and the truth was, part of me had held on to hope. Some small part of me had thought that this big romantic gesture and declaring my love for him eighties-movie-style would be enough. That maybe it would make him see that, no matter how I'd screwed up, I was still the girl he'd fallen for. Twice.

But his mom was pulling out of the driveway now, delicately maneuvering past Gert, and turning onto the street. Chauffeuring him off to a plane that would take him even farther from me.

It's over, I thought.

But then —

Maybe it was just my imagination or wishful thinking, but I thought I saw Ryder look back at me as they drove away.

32

I didn't hear from him.

I didn't expect to, but Amy did.

"I thought he would call," she said. "I was sure he would."

"See, this is why you need someone like me in your life," I said. "You are too optimistic for your own good, Amy Rush."

She sat down next to me on the bed. "Maybe after spring break . . . Maybe he's just busy with his dad in DC."

That was possible. The news coverage did make it seem like they were pretty busy. Ryder and Senator Cross had posed for photos with some foreign diplomats, and Greg Johnson had done a whole story about it.

Senator Cross might not have represented our region, but that hadn't stopped Ryder from becoming a bit of a local celebrity.

As much as seeing him on the screen had made me ache, it had also made me happy. In the photos, Ryder looked genuinely pleased to be there with his dad. I hoped that meant they were working things out.

Amy wrapped her arms around my shoulders and rested her head on top of mine. "If he can forgive his dad, maybe he'll —"

"Don't," I said. "Don't give me a reason to hope. I screwed up, Amy. He has no reason to forgive me. . . . I told him I loved him, Amy. And he didn't say it back."

"He's an idiot," she said.

"He's not, but thank you."

As much as it had sucked to lose Ryder, I knew I was lucky to have Amy back. Knowing how much I'd hurt her over the past few months still made me sick. She was, without question, the most important person in my life. And the most selfless friend I could have asked for.

I knew she didn't fully trust me yet, but we'd find our way back eventually. And no matter what, I would never, ever let anything — a boy, a lie, or my own insecurities — get between us again.

"Thank you, by the way," I said as she untangled herself from me. "For locking us in a room together and helping me find the boom box. I'm not sure I ever would have gotten him to listen to me if you hadn't done that."

"You're welcome," she said. "I wish it had made more of a difference. I just really thought if he heard you out . . ."

"It did help, though," I assured her. "It wasn't just about getting him to forgive me. It's about being honest. It's something I'm still working on."

"I like Honest Sonny."

"Good, because she's here to stay." I frowned. "And honestly? Honest Sonny is not a fan of that purple lipstick on you."

"Honest Sonny can get over it."

I grinned. "Oh. Fierce Amy is fun, too."

She blushed, but she smiled.

I was proud of Amy. She was still shy, still sweet, but she'd stopped letting people push her around. Even me.

Especially me.

Amy looked down at my phone again. "He'll call," she said.

"What makes you so sure?" I asked.

"I don't know. I just am. You two had something special, you know?"

"Yeah, I know," I said. I shook my head. "You're being too nice even for you. Bring Fierce Amy back. Hurry."

She tossed her brown curls over her shoulder and grinned. "This is Fierce Amy. And I am fierce in my assertion that he'll call."

I laughed and got to my feet and extended a hand to her. "Come on, Fierce Amy," I said, pulling her up, too. "Honest Sonny is honestly starving."

"Pizza?" Amy asked, heading for the bedroom door.

"Hell yes."

"Who are you writing to?" Wesley asked, looking at the pieces of pale blue stationery I had spread across a section of the dining room table. He'd arrived at the Rush house on the first night of spring break with a suitcase full of dirty laundry and a big grin on his face. As any college student would. But the week was nearly over, and he'd be flying back to New York the next day.

And I'd already handed him the last of my payments to cover

Gert's repairs, thanks to my new job at Daphne's. I was no longer in debt to him. At least not financially.

The truth was, I owed a lot to Wesley and his family. I'd never be able to pay them back for everything they'd done for me over these past few months. And I knew they'd never let me even if I could.

"My dad," I said, shaking out my aching wrist. "We've started writing letters to each other."

Wesley sat down across from me with his bowl of cereal. His gray eyes flicked over the table, counting the pages I'd already filled. I blushed. I'd only meant to write two or three, but this letter was beginning to resemble a novel.

"Why not type it?" he asked. "It would probably be faster."

"I think I've had my fill of technology for a while," I admitted. I put down my pen, deciding to give my wrist a break. This was the most I'd handwritten in years. "Besides. This feels more personal. And I think that's what my dad and I need right now."

Wesley smiled. "I am rather fond of handwritten letters."

"You write letters?"

"I wrote a couple in the past. You're right. They are more personal." He stared off for a minute, something wistful in his smile. Then he shook his head and focused on me again. "So everything's going all right with you and your dad?"

"Yeah. It's nice to have him back in my life. Even if it has to be like this. And hopefully he'll be out in a few months and . . . we can go from there."

"What about your mom? Have you heard from her?"

I shook my head, and Wesley knew better than to push. Talking about Mom was still too hard. Half the time I was angry at her for leaving me, bitter and almost glad I didn't have to live with her anymore. The other half, I was heartbroken, rejected. She was my mom, and I had no clue where she was or why she couldn't just stay home, stay with me. Sometimes I blamed myself. Sometimes I woke up, panicked from a nightmare, sure she was hurt or dead. Maybe she was. I had no way of knowing.

But I wasn't alone. I had the Rushes, people who knew me, who had seen every ugly part of me, and who loved me anyway. Maybe it wasn't blood, but it was family nonetheless.

And even though it scared me to hope too much, it was starting to look like I might have my dad, too.

"So," Wesley said after swallowing another bite of cereal. "You've got to catch me up. What's been going on with you and Amy since January?"

I raised an eyebrow. "We talk to you on the phone every week."

"Yes, but neither of you tell me anything interesting," he said, pointing an accusatory spoon at me. "And while I'm sure your grades and your new job are fascinating, I wouldn't mind something juicier."

I laughed. "What did you have in mind?"

"I don't know." He shrugged and chewed another bite. "What happened with that guy you were telling me about?"

I didn't need a mirror to know the color had just drained from my face. Leave it to Wesley to leave one uncomfortable subject only to land on another.

"Nothing," I mumbled, picking up my pen again and hoping he'd take the hint.

He didn't.

"That's obviously a lie," he said. "I thought you were taking a vow of honesty?"

I groaned. "It's . . . not exactly a lie. Nothing is happening with us now."

"Why not?"

I put the pen back down with great reluctance. "Fine, but you're only getting the short version." I took a deep breath, all too aware of the heavy ache in my chest. It made itself known every time I so much as thought of Ryder. "It turns out he did like me, but I ruined it. I messed things up too much, and there's no way Ryder is going to forgive me now."

Wesley watched me for a minute, looking like he was trying to come up with something to say. Before he could, though, there was a buzzing noise and my phone, sitting on his side of the table, began to play "Konstantine" by Something Corporate. What can I say? I'd been feeling rather emo lately.

Wesley glanced down at the screen and grinned. "You never know," he said, sliding the phone across the table to me. "He might surprise you."

I looked down at the display, and I almost didn't believe the words.

Ryder Cross was calling me.

"You'd better get that," Wesley said, still grinning. He stood up and left me alone in the dining room as, with shaking hands, I clicked the button to answer.

"H-Hello?" I choked out.

"Hey, Sonny." It was his voice. It was soft and nervous, but it was his voice.

The weight in my chest eased a little. I didn't know what he was going to say. He might still be mad, but if he was calling me, it was because he wanted to talk. And I had been so scared I'd never talk to him again. It felt like I'd finally gasped for air after holding my breath for too long.

"Sonny?" he said again when I didn't answer. "This . . . this is Sonny, right?"

"Yeah," I said. My voice cracked and I cleared my throat. "Yeah. It's really me this time."

Acknowledgments

It would be a lie to say I did this on my own. The truth is, there have been several amazing people helping to shepherd this book into existence, and I want to take a moment to thank them.

Thank you to my editor, Jody Corbett, who put so much time and energy into making this story the best it could be. Thank you to my agent, Joanna Volpe, who had faith in this story even when it was just a half-formed idea mentioned over coffee. And to the whole New Leaf Literary and Scholastic teams — there are no words for how happy and honored I am to work with all of you.

Special thanks to Phoebe North, who loved this story even when I didn't. To Amy Lukavics, who constantly makes me feel like a rock star. And to Lisa Desrochers, who made me laugh even when I was feeling pretty down. I'm so proud to know all three of you talented, smart, amazing women.

Thanks to everyone in my family for believing in me while also keeping me grounded. And special thanks to Mom, who is always there when I need her, and Dad, who never lets me doubt how proud he is. I'm lucky to have you all.

And since this is a book largely about friendship, I would be remiss not to thank my own best friends. Shana Hancock, it's hard to believe it's been almost nine years since that day we met in history class. We may be several states apart, but I adore you just as much now as I did then. Gaelyn Galbreath, you're the Ann to my Leslie, my soupsnake, and I can't imagine my life without you in it. Thank you both for always being there for me. I love you so much.

About the Author

Kody Keplinger was born and raised in a small Kentucky town. During her senior year of high school, she wrote her debut novel, *The DUFF*, which was a YALSA Top Ten Quick Pick for Reluctant Readers and a *Romantic Times* Top Pick. It has since been adapted into a major motion picture. Kody is also the author of *Shut Out* and *A Midsummer's Nightmare*, as well as the middle-grade novel *The Swift Boys & Me*. Currently, Kody lives in New York City, where she teaches writing workshops and continues to write books for kids and teens. You can find more about her and her books at www.kodykeplinger.com.